Sofie

BOOK 5 OF THE SELAH SERIES

Sofie

THE LETTERS

JONI D. HAYWORTH

XULON PRESS

Xulon Press
555 Winderley Pl, Suite 225
Maitland, FL 32751
407.339.4217
www.xulonpress.com

© 2024 by Joni D. Hayworth

All rights reserved solely by the author. The author guarantees all contents are original and do not infringe upon the legal rights of any other person or work. No part of this book may be reproduced in any form without the permission of the author.

Due to the changing nature of the Internet, if there are any web addresses, links, or URLs included in this manuscript, these may have been altered and may no longer be accessible. The views and opinions shared in this book belong solely to the author and do not necessarily reflect those of the publisher. The publisher therefore disclaims responsibility for the views or opinions expressed within the work.

Unless otherwise indicated, Scripture quotations taken from the Holy Bible, New International Version (NIV). Copyright © 1973, 1978, 1984, 2011 by Biblica, Inc.™. Used by permission. All rights reserved.

Paperback ISBN-13: 978-1-66289-734-4
Ebook ISBN-13: 978-1-66289-735-1

Dedication

—

Then we your people, the sheep of your pasture,
will praise you forever;
from generation to generation
we will proclaim your praise.
Psalm 79:13 (NIV)

Introduction

Faith. Trust. Love. Integrity. Hope. Perseverance. Joy. Strength. Trials. Courage. Justice. Grace. Prayer. Redemption. Forgiveness. Salvation. Honor. Covenant. Miracle. Worship. Messiah. Remnant. Peace. Mercy. Cost. Holy. Jesus. Spirit. God.

These are the words Sofie heard her entire life. They described her family. She dreamed of those she never met. Her great-grandmother Selah's legacy was in her bones, and she also carried the promises of Christ in her heart. She held onto her convictions hoping she would find someone who would write the words buried deep within the framework of her very being, waiting to spring forth and be recorded so the next generation could hold these same truths and carry them to the next one. This was her simple prayer. She wanted the words written down as a testimony to the lives that continued to speak to her through the stories that were told and retold over countless fires of fellowship. *Selah. Simon. Stone. Scout.* The people spoke these names with reverence. A common thread wove their lives together and she would rehearse the history of her legendary family in the quiet. The words she repeated painted the perfect picture of her family. She needed to write their letters.

Chapter One

Sofie was melancholy. She rocked in her favorite worn chair as the children ran by declaring she was old as the hills. Some days she thought they were right. She would look at her grandfather Simon's hill and be filled with memories that could last a lifetime, so she continued to rock and smile when the children laughed behind their hands. She never married. She would tell people she enjoyed the simple things of life, like listening to the stories of her family and the legacy they left. She was alone and had no one to carry her name, however, it didn't prevent her from living her life as best as she was able, and everyone came to Sofie's house for her words of wisdom and fresh honey cakes.

She kept her great-grandmother Selah's recipe for the small cakes close to her heart. She wondered who she would pass it down to and who would cherish it as she had. It was too personal to relinquish to someone who wouldn't take the time to listen to her instructions for the sweet treats so many of the family members enjoyed over the years. She thought of her oldest brother Scout. His granddaughter was named Hannah after their mother. Perhaps she would guard the secret of the cakes. *Oh, how she wished she could have met Selah!* She did indeed have a legacy, and she had gone over her story a hundred times hoping for the right person to continue proclaiming the truth of all her family had experienced. She was thirty-three. Most women her age paraded their grandchildren throughout the village afraid to smile, not wanting to offend the woman who sat alone in her chair.

Today, the letters would be read. She would make the short walk to the gathering place to hear the learned men speak about Jesus.

Sometimes she would close her eyes and try to imagine her great-grandmother standing in the women's court, straining her neck to see the One they called Messiah. Before her grandfather Simon's bones were placed in the cave of Elias, she sat at his feet asking him to tell her everything he remembered about his dear mother. These early memories are when she fell in love with words. They were powerful. Words could make her laugh and cry. Some words brought joy, others sorrow. The words of Jesus made her think and wonder, and now the words of those who knew Jesus were read each Sabbath, making her hunger for more.

She wanted to understand what these men had written. They had done so for her benefit. Today, they would read the letter from James. She sat mesmerized by the love she saw on the faces of those who came to listen. She didn't understand why they didn't meet daily to hear these wonderful words. Her heart continued to be stirred while she glanced around searching for who might help her put down all she had learned when her grandfather delighted her with stories of Elias, Benjamin, and her father Stone. She wouldn't let her eyes linger, but she couldn't help but notice one man she didn't recognize standing close to the only door of the small place they had come together that night. His head was covered in reverence, and like a ghost, he vanished from the room the next time she sought him, just like the phantom in her dreams.

Her brothers walked her to the home of their parents. She was given the house as no man had offered provisions. The family would share a meal with their baby sister as Samuel still referred to her, and Sofie would place bundles of honey cakes for each group to take home and enjoy. She prayed more words would be spoken around their tables so the children would never forget the sacrifices their past family members had made for them and the trials each one had endured. She preferred the quiet of the night in the only home she knew where she could rehearse her memories in private and enjoy the fond remembrances.

She watched the sun disappear behind Simon's hill and let her imagination run like the watchmen who scaled the rock each night. They remained faithful, and the people praised God for His protection. She hoped the days would pass quickly as she longed for more words. Today the letter of James told them to have joy when faced with trials, and that their faith would result in patience, yet she didn't have the

Chapter One

patience to wait until more words were spoken. She'd been waiting her entire life and she remained alone with the stories she hoped to remind her nieces and nephews so they would retell them to their children. She wanted them written down like the words of James and the other letters that were read each time the believers gathered.

She sat at the table of her father Stone. It also had its own story, and she ran her hands across the hewn wood closing her eyes to the past. These family accounts were the ones she desired someone to write for her. She shut her eyes even tighter and thought about the lone man who left the makeshift church and somehow, she knew he would be the one who would make all her memories come to life.

"My name is Aaron," he said.

Sofie studied his eyes. She saw wisdom and hoped he also had the coveted patience to listen to her request.

"You're always alone," she said.

"As you are also," he smiled.

"How is it we don't know each other?" she asked. "My family has been in this village for generations," she added.

"I know," he said.

"Where do you live?" She turned, wondering which direction he would point.

Aaron simply said, "Nearby."

Sofie grew nervous. Her brothers had already left, leaving others to escort her home. She had watched him for weeks, perhaps months when she finally dared to approach him.

"Do you understand the words that are spoken here?"

He smiled at her question, "Do you?"

She *was* trying to understand. She looked to see if anyone was paying attention to them. She had watched him walk alone and wondered if he ever married or had a family. She thought he must; there was too much warmth in his eyes.

"Please bear with me sir, I need…I would like help," she said.

Aaron raised an eyebrow. He knew who her family members were. He was curious about what kind of help she sought.

"Your family has resources," he began, "What do you need help with?"

"Can you write words?" She pointed to the closed cabinet where the special letters were kept. "Like the words in the box?"

Aaron had only stared a little confused at her question. She thought this was her only opportunity to speak freely, so she dared to come closer to him and whispered, "I wish to find someone who can write words. I want to leave letters like those in the box so the next generation will not forget," she said.

"I want the children to know the stories of my family and the sacrifices they made to keep this village safe, and I don't want them to forget we are Christians and follow the one true God who gave us Jesus."

She was whispering again, a1nd Aaron knew she struggled for several weeks to confront him to make such an inquiry.

"I can make the words," he said.

Sofie couldn't help smiling all the way home and told her personal watchman she was just happy at what was shared tonight. The reading was from the book of Isaiah when the people had asked God for a sign. It was the first scripture that had opened her heart long ago when told the Lord Himself would give them a sign and a virgin would bear a son, and that son was Jesus. Those first words thrilled her spirit, and her hunger grew for more, especially when her grandfather told her his mother Selah saw this Son, and the words of the prophet Isaiah were true! She would have to make arrangements for Aaron. She wanted him to sit at her father's table so he could also sense the truth and life the wood had supported, and he would have no doubt about what she desired him to record. Secretly, she also hoped given time, that he may teach her to read so she could be at peace the letters would be accurate.

Aaron left the darkness of the morning and walked the familiar path to the village of Stone. That's how he knew the small community. Everyone before him spoke of Simon, but he remembered Stone, the

Chapter One

boy who had run off to Tiberias and returned a man. It was the talk of the village for months, especially when so many had traveled back with the prodigal. There were too many people for his family, and they retreated to the hills. They found solace in the quiet rock and lived in privacy. A few families that happened upon the cluster of caves had been welcomed to stay. He met his wife, and then the children came. After the last one was born, he had to say goodbye to her, his son took her very breath, and he never left the hills until he heard about the letters. His love for words matched Sofie's and he came down once a week to listen to their promises and hope. He knew the law and the prophets, but now those who knew Jesus had penned His words, and somehow knowing they had been written brought a comfort than only hearing the oral traditions. This is why he agreed to write for Sofie. He wanted her to experience the same assurance.

He prayed now that he would see the caravans that traveled up and down the coast so he could procure the supplies he would need. This would be his gift to her. He was anxious to hear the stories that had brought her the deep love she had for God's truth. He said another prayer now that his own passion would be stirred for everything his father had taught him so Sofie would find him worthy of the task she presented.

"Her eyes were the color of the sea on a clear day," Sofie told Aaron.

"I asked my grandfather to describe her when he allowed me to ask every question I had in my heart. Someone once said it wasn't polite to speak of the dead, but Selah was alive, she was only living in another place!" Sofie looked directly at Aaron to see if he would accept her words and hurry to write them on his parchment. She watched every stroke and symbol he carefully placed on the heavy paper and continued.

"My grandfather said no one else in the family had her eye color and as I grew older, they hoped I might inherit the turquoise hue." She scooted the lamp closer to him and sat in the shadows. "I think

Selah was so special that God didn't want anyone else to have her unusual color."

"Did you just write that down?" she asked him.

"Yes," Aaron said. "It's a wonderful statement. God indeed made your great-grandmother very special."

"She lived in Jerusalem!" Sofie exclaimed.

"Can you imagine living in the Holy City? Oh, the things she must have seen! She had a donkey my grandfather told me, and named him Balaam," Sofie laughed.

Aaron laid down his writing instrument. "Balaam? Are you certain?"

"Yes. Grandfather said she had her stories confused. She was young and like me, she had no one to teach her."

Aaron thought she looked ashamed now in the dim light. "It is our custom for the men to learn," he said.

"I think she may have been scared to leave this village, but she left when her husband came for her. I can't imagine leaving my home," she barely whispered.

"Do you wish for me to write that down?"

"Yes, Aaron. Selah was brave. I want the children to know sometimes you must step out in faith and trust God that all will be well." She noticed he didn't seem to want to disturb the peacefulness that now filled the room, so she kept talking.

"She met an old merchant named Simon who my grandfather is named after. You can put that down," she said.

Aaron smiled to himself as she rose halfway out of her chair, leaning over the table to make sure he made his marks.

"Perhaps that's enough for tonight," he said. "If you like, I could come two times next week."

"I would be grateful. There is much to say." She handed him a bundle as he reached the door.

"No payment is necessary Sofie. I'm enjoying the stories," he told her.

"These are honey cakes for your family," she smiled.

Aaron took them from her hands, "I'll see you next week."

She bolted her door and sat at the rough table once more before retiring. As she brought the lamp close to extinguish its flame, she noticed a small, dark spot she hadn't seen before. When she went to wipe it, Aaron's ink stained her finger. It made her smile. She liked to

Chapter One

think he left a drop for her to discover. She wouldn't try to remove it from where it smeared on her thumb. She prayed he would make it safely back to his home, and she couldn't remember the last time she felt so much joy.

"*Sofie is missing!*" Hannah was frantic calling out to her oldest son Scout.

"Missing?" Scout grabbed his mother by the shoulders to calm her down.

"She has wandered off again! This daughter of mine! Call your brothers! Go find her Scout! The sun will go down within the hour!" Hannah pleaded.

"Joshua! Samuel!" Scout yelled for his younger brothers.

"Hurry! Mother can't find Sofie!" he shouted.

The two boys scrambled after Scout as he headed toward the hills away from the village. This wasn't the first time their baby sister lost track of time and simply walked and played until she realized she had gone too far.

She was oblivious to the family's concern when enjoying the freedom of the landscape and the stillness of the afternoon. She stood at the base of the small hill. This is where secrets lived. This is where Selah found her honey for the sweet cakes she had made since her grandfather was a small boy. Sofie wanted to see for herself. She believed her grandfather. She only wanted to try and locate exactly where her great-grandmother first discovered the bee's hiding place.

She heard them before she saw them. The hum of the hive tickled her ears. She was careful. She didn't dare look down, the climb up the small incline had been in blind faith. It wasn't a hill; it was more of a mound, and she had watched her brothers jumping from it for as long as she could remember. It was eerily quiet except for the buzzing bees. They seemed to be alerting her that she was now on sacred ground. She got goosebumps thinking of her great-grandmother inching closer to the coveted honeycomb. *Wouldn't her grandfather be surprised when she brought him a nice big piece?* He could teach her how to make the special cakes. The sun was barely visible peeking over the clouds. She sucked in her breath determined to retrieve the sweet substance. She wiped her hands on her tunic now covered in dirt. The desert sand and dirt stuck to her skin. Her mother had been diligent in massaging olive oil on her hands and feet and then would run her hands through her hair to smooth it down. Sofie liked it when she finished. She would leave the last little dab of oil on her lips, kissing her, and telling her how special she was. Her mother would be both angry and glad when she brought the honey home this late afternoon. The buzzing was becoming louder as she approached, and one little bee landed on her arm. She swatted it away not expecting it to land. This seemed to anger it and soon there were bees everywhere! She tried to remain calm, but the buzzing grew louder, and she felt one crawling in her ear!

"*Ouch!*" she cried out.

She felt another sting on her arm. And another. And another one on her leg. And then three more. She was swatting and running, and she began to cry. The bees were unhappy. She didn't understand why. She had only just stood there. She shouted at them now that she was related to Selah. She only wanted a little honey to impress her grandfather. She felt more stings on her neck and the pain was becoming unbearable. She fell to the ground and tried to cover her head. She blacked out.

"Are you alright?"

"Little girl, can you hear me?" The boy didn't know what to do. He heard her screaming and ran to find her on the ground. No one else was in the area and he bent low to try and wake her up.

"Please, tell me you're okay. Hello. Can you hear me?" He could see the welts all over her little body. *She was breathing.* He turned her gently to wipe the dirt from her face.

Sofie tried to open her eyes. They were almost swollen shut! The bees had their vengeance today. She had never been in so much pain in her life! She heard a boy's voice, but it wasn't any of her brothers, and she tried to force her eyes to open wider to see who had come to her aid. The sky was blurry. All she saw were shadows. At least she didn't hear any buzzing.

"What can I do?" he asked her.

Chapter One

"Where are you from?" He looked around hoping she wasn't alone.

"Shall I carry you home?" *She looked so frail.* "Can you speak?" He held his breath.

Sofie shut her eyes. She wanted to go to sleep. She wanted her mother. She would know what to do. *Oh, what a mess she got into!*

"Sofie! Sofie!" Scout called out. His brothers were behind him also yelling out her name.

The boy looked down. Her name must be Sofie. He leaned down one last time as their voices were close.

"Help is coming. You'll be fine. Be careful little girl," and he hurried down the other side of the hill. He watched the three who came to the girl's rescue. One could be her father and he became afraid. *Who knows what they might think finding him with her in this distress?* He knew what happened. She was stung by bees. Several times. *Poor little thing.* She would be alright. He waited until the older of the three lifted her gently and carried her back down the hill.

Sofie woke up with a start! She hadn't had that dream for several years. She was still sitting at her father's table with her ink-stained thumb. *What in the world?* She didn't realize how late it was and how tired she must have been to fall asleep at the table. She also hadn't done that for years! *Why tonight did she have that dream?* She touched the back of her neck where one little scar remained, the only one from the first day she went to find the bees. Her mother told her she scratched it until it became infected. She remembered being bathed in vinegar head to foot! It was awful! Someone from the village said bees didn't like olive oil. She was soaked in it when she visited the bees. Her mother had felt guilty, but she had no idea her daughter was on a treasure hunt, and it wasn't long after that day when she returned and grabbed the largest piece of honeycomb her hands could hold.

She made friends with the bees and made sure she didn't put any scents or oils on her skin when she journeyed to the special place for Selah's honey. She had made several trips, too many to count. No one was ever there. She asked Scout if he saw the boy who waited with her until he arrived that day. He had only looked at her like the venom of the bees made her delirious.

"There was no one there waiting with you Sofie." He had held her hand concerned for his little sister.

"I saw him," she said. "I know I was in pain and my eyes were swollen shut, but I heard him."

The family had whispered into the night wondering if perhaps an angel had ministered to her. She didn't think so. It was too real. She looked up just then to the heavens.

"I'm sorry Lord, maybe it was an angel. Whether he came from You or just happened by, thank You."

"So, you would like to continue with Selah?" Aaron asked.

It had been three days since he came to her house, and he noticed the faded ink spot on her thumb which made him smile inwardly.

"Yes, Aaron, I wish for you to write all I can remember. I have forgotten already where we left off." She watched him carefully take out his parchments and saw his eyes move right to left reading the words she had instructed him to pen.

Aaron observed her under hooded eyes. It overjoyed him at her desire to learn. He continued to watch her as he scanned the place where they stopped for the evening.

"You told me about a man named Simon, a merchant Selah met," he replied.

"I was told everyone who met him loved him! My grandfather grew up with his stories. My great-grandmother was *spirited*," Sofie laughed.

"Is that a word? Do you not know how to spell it?"

Aaron laid down his pen and folded his arms. "I see the love you have for your family and the wonder of each life, and I prefer to listen first, and we'll write later."

She sat back in her chair, relaxed at his friendship. She poured him a cup of wine and pushed the plate of bread and dates closer to his reach.

"It was Simon who took Selah one night and followed a man named Nicodemus," she said.

"Nicodemus!" Aaron repeated. Now he sat up intrigued.

"Yes. That was the first time Selah saw Jesus!" Sofie answered.

Aaron filled his cup, "Please Sofie, tell me more!"

Chapter One

She took her time. She loved having this one-on-one conversation. She had been alone for over half her life and was pleased in Aaron's interest.

"That night began my great-grandmother's journey of learning who this man Jesus was." She looked at Aaron to determine how much personal information she would reveal.

"As you know, women, well, it wasn't easy for her to discover these things. Her husband was a servant at the Temple."

Aaron took the liberty and poured more oil into the solitary lamp resting between them, his pen begging for his attention, however, this information took precedence over his ink and parchment.

"She didn't know or understand what he did, Malchus, that was his name," Sofie said.

"Wait! Selah's husband was Malchus? He worked at the Temple? This is the same Malchus? The one whose ear was cut off when our Lord was arrested?" Aaron was halfway standing now when Sofie saw his eyes dance at her words.

"Aaron! How do you know this?" Her eyes were as big as his in amazement.

"It is written," he said. "In your books," he told her as he nodded towards the meeting place where she first approached him.

"I can't believe it," he whispered to himself.

Sofie heard him, "You think I'm telling you an untruth?"

"No, of course not! I'm only surprised. I want to know everything!" he assured her.

"Are you hungry?" she asked him. "I have lentil soup. It was Selah's favorite, Malchus' too!"

Sofie filled Aaron's bowl three times. She didn't know if he was that hungry or was just being polite, but he proclaimed her soup was the best he ever tasted. She thought his enjoyment came from the seasoning of Selah's story. Either way, she began to treasure his company and looked forward to him writing her recollections.

"I always wondered what happened to this man," Aaron said, as he sopped up the last of his lentils.

"What did he think when Jesus restored his ear? Did his heart cry out in agony at this love that reached down to him, especially when he came to take this same love back to the High Priest? Oh, Sofie, this is amazing!"

He didn't want to leave. But he had to; the night was growing late again, and his home was a good hour's journey. She hadn't pressed him anymore about his family or home. He sensed she knew they both were content speaking about hers.

"What time shall I arrive tomorrow?" he asked.

"You will come back so soon?" Sofie couldn't hide her pleasure.

"We have only just begun, yes?" Aaron answered.

"Your supplies," Sofie looked where his parchments remained waiting for life to spring upon them.

"May I leave them?" he asked. "I would feel better if they stayed within the walls that have heard these stories over the years."

She couldn't look at his eyes after he exposed his heart in this farewell. He seemed to understand. She thought she was the only one who sensed the honor and sacrifice that had filled this space. It was home, but it was so much more, and this man of the hills seemed to be stirred by the same passion she held onto since understanding the price that was paid by Jesus for all of them.

Aaron stood at her door waiting until she could look at him to say goodnight. "Tomorrow then," he said.

Sofie watched him disappear into the night walking towards her grandfather's hill.

"Where have you been Father?"

Aaron pretended he didn't hear his youngest son who always waited for him to arrive home.

"Father, did you not hear me?" Finn was getting concerned. His father had traveled to the small village three times this week. He brought no supplies back or shared any reason with his family why he made these unexpected trips.

"Son, I heard you. You know where I've been," he chuckled.

"What are you doing down there?" Finn asked.

Chapter One

"Helping a friend," Aaron responded. "Now, I need rest as I plan to go back down tomorrow."

Finn could see his father was tired. It would be pointless to ask him any more questions as his father moved quickly to retire for the evening. Finn waited until he released his nightly prayers and made his way to the space in the large rock they called home. This is where the family lived, and this cave could hold many. His father had lived here most of his life, first out of necessity, later from preference. He stepped outside to scan the valley below. Most in the village knew his father and there would be no reason for anyone to follow him, but he checked for any movement under the moonlight one last time. This was a practice learned from his youth. His father slept soundly and Finn loaded more wood on the fire. His father would tell him about the friend he was helping when he needed to if at all. The patriarch of this family was greatly loved and respected, much like the legend of the small village that also lay sleeping on the tranquil valley floor.

Sofie rose early to prepare for another day of storytelling. She didn't think too much about what she wanted to relay to Aaron; she wanted her heart to speak to this man who would put her love onto his parchments. The spilled ink remained, and she ran her finger over it hoping to feel its power once more. She would serve Aaron lentils again unless she sought her brothers to see if they had fish or perhaps a chicken. It was the least she could do. She hurried through the community to reach her brother Samuel's door.

"Brother, greetings!" she called out.

"What brings you so early?" he asked. "Is all well with you?"

"Yes, I only came to see if you might have some fish," she said.

"Fish?" Samuel repeated. "We'll have dinner later. You'll join us, I'm not sure what my wife is preparing."

Sofie began to shuffle her feet trying to decide what she would tell him. "I'm having a guest. I wanted to cook myself this evening," she finally said.

Samuel stopped what he was doing. "Bring them with you, we always have plenty."

"No Samuel, I want to prepare the meal so I can eat when I want."

"Who is this guest?" he asked.

She wouldn't be able to hide Aaron's visits, so she looked at her brother closely, "The man from the hills, Aaron, he is my guest," she smiled.

She noticed Samuel raise an eyebrow and before he could say anything, she pointed to one of his chickens, "May I have a chicken?"

She knew her brother wouldn't deny her anything and as she began to collect her dinner, she heard him laughing as he called out that he would check on her later.

"No reason to come over Samuel. I have all I need. Thank you, brother," and she quickly walked back to her house.

Aaron's arrival was perfect. She had her door propped open and she saw his surprised look when he inhaled the fresh roasted chicken. She had bread and wine on the table, a safe distance from his writing supplies. She told him to make himself comfortable.

"Sofie, I don't expect you to cook for me," he said. "But I'm glad you did. It smells wonderful!"

"Of course, I cooked," she said. "It's our custom, yes?"

"Yes," Aaron agreed. "We are a hospitable people."

He prayed. They both had their heads bowed in thankfulness. Sofie was glad; she didn't want him to notice her joy in a man's voice in her home. It had been missed. The last time she heard this prayer was from her brother Samuel right before he was joined in marriage, and she had convinced all her brothers she would be fine living in their father's house by herself. She never felt lonely but hearing the deep tones of Aaron's voice and smelling the aromas of a meal prepared in kindness, brought a flood of emotion she couldn't hide.

Aaron studied the woman across the table. She had a strong face, yet the softness of years of peace and acceptance had graced her eyes and smile. He wondered about her at this moment with his roasted chicken in his hands, flavored with herbs and love. He could easily taste the time and preparation in all that was set before him. He could imagine her grandfather sitting at this very table and he released his breath.

Sofie looked up, "May I offer you more bread?"

Chapter One

"I was thinking of you and your family sharing meals around this table, and now we are doing the same," he said.

He wasn't sure what he saw in her eyes just now, so he quickly added, "What I meant is we are sharing a meal at the same table writing your family's legacy and I almost feel as if I'm sharing a meal with them myself."

Sofie nodded. She missed her grandfather the most. She was young when he drew his last breath, perhaps seven or eight.

"Grandfather smelled like the weather," she said.

"The weather?" he repeated.

"What?" She didn't realize she was speaking out loud. She laughed, "Yes, it's the only word I know to describe his hugs."

"Some days when he came down from his roof, he would pick me up to say a blessing over me," she began.

"I could smell the sun on his skin and the heat of the day in his clothes. When he and my father went hunting, I would come close and guess the way they traveled by the wind that remained with them. The wind smells different, do you agree?" she asked.

"Yes," Aaron said.

"But my favorite memory was when they returned from the sea. My grandfather seemed so happy, and I think I could even smell that. They would bring so many fish and my mother would tell stories of my father fishing in Tiberias and much laughter would be shared around the fire. Grandfather insisted we all sit outside under the stars." She hoped he wasn't bored or would tire of her thoughts this evening.

"Simon's stars," she smiled. "That's a whole other story."

"Tell me," Aaron said, and he grabbed his pen.

"Selah met Simon when she first came to Jerusalem. They became very dear friends and even traveled back here. They wanted to see Jesus. I was told the people gathered by the thousands to hear Him, and the day they arrived here, the village was empty, except for one older woman who told Simon she wanted to look at her stars. That's when he began to spend more time on his roof. I think they were all beginning to realize who Jesus was and Simon took the time to admire all of God's creation. We go through life not thanking Him for His goodness as we should. Life gets in the way."

"Does that make sense?" She watched him write her words and he stopped to answer.

"Yes, it makes sense," he said. "Please, go on."

"My great-grandfather Malchus had many questions on that journey. This man Simon was also searching for the truth. It was Malchus who made them question their hearts," she said.

"How so?" Aaron asked.

"The Pharisees and those at the Temple didn't like Jesus and they reminded my great-grandfather each day that Jesus wasn't who He claimed to be. Of course, they were wrong," Sofie laughed. "But all of them were seeking to know what the Scriptures meant. I think God brought Simon wisdom when He saw he took the time to thank Him and gaze at the stars each night."

"Would you like to take a break and step outside?" he asked. "We could also look at the stars."

He saw her surprise at this invitation and thought maybe this was too forward and personal, but she jumped up and grabbed her outer garment, and headed for the door.

She leaned against the doorpost like she had all her life seeing her parents and grandparents do the same. They stood for hours it seemed some nights, and she wondered how long Aaron would stand.

Aaron looked up thinking of the old merchant Simon and breathed in the air of the village. He grew up without doors, the natural shape of the cave's opening providing privacy between each chamber. He moved to allow Sofie more room and chose the sturdy wall of the house to support his star gazing. He cast a glance at her. Her eyes were closed now, and he wondered if she resembled Selah. He imagined both women spent countless hours embraced by the familiar wood praying it would support family members for generations to come. Yet Sofie never married. He heard the children refer to her as *"the old maiden"* or that she was as *"old as the hills"*. He didn't feel sorry for her. He figured there were reasons she didn't marry and wondered if these words would be a part of her letters. He didn't think so. It was too personal. He was a stranger in many regards. Tonight, with the moonlight shining upon the ancient hill of the village, he couldn't wait to hear about her grandfather and the trouble he found himself in, but they had just started and he suspected she would never get tired of talking about

Chapter One

her great-grandmother, a woman she never met and yet looking at her again, her head lifted high with peace resting across her eyes, he suspected she was just like Selah.

Sofie remained at her door longer than she planned after Aaron left. The night was clear, and she let her imagination have its way. She thought of the old village woman who was left alone when everyone traveled to see Jesus, telling Simon she wanted to look at her stars. Sofie thought it was her way to worship, and the travel was too much for her. Jesus was moving through the region like wildfire she was told, and who knew how many days the people would be gone. She looked up at her grandfather's roof and sighed. She missed him terribly. She wondered if someone would tell stories about her on their rooftop like her ancestors watching for falling stars, calling her the *old woman*. She quickly came inside latching her door and brought the lamp from the table closer to her cookfire. She hoped Aaron liked leftovers. She would make him stew tomorrow.

Finn surprised his father at the base of the hill. Aaron knew his boy worried about him climbing in darkness, but both had done so their entire lives and he laughed to himself knowing Finn was probably trying to determine what kind of help his father was providing for a friend.

"Son, do you think I need assistance?"

"I only thought to keep you company," Finn replied. "Can you not tell me what you're doing?"

"I did tell you," Aaron replied. "I'm helping a friend."

They began their climb. Aaron stopped halfway and took a deep breath.

"I'm helping the granddaughter of Simon write her memories," he told his son. He saw Finn didn't seem surprised, so he turned and began climbing again.

Finn wouldn't tell his brothers; if his father wanted them to know, he would tell them. They had been careful with words, and their father had no tolerance for idle gossip and chatter. Finn hoped his father knew he wouldn't speak of his village visits. Now, he wondered how old the granddaughter of Simon was and if her family were as close-mouthed as his. The only thing he did know was his father looked robust, he obviously had shared a meal as he was never hungry, and he slept soundly through the night. There were years when he didn't. Watching his father now puttering around getting ready for his slumber, he hoped Simon's granddaughter had a lot to say.

Chapter Two

Samuel and Joshua knocked on their sister's door early this morning. They saw the hill man leave under the moon. They had been sitting at the gate when the young boy was seen in the distance. They were familiar with the family. Aaron was around the same age as them and they recalled when they first realized he and his family lived in the caves and decided not to live among the community. Most in the village never saw the family; they stayed away and were almost forgotten.

"Brothers! Good morning, come in," Sofie was expecting them. She assumed they saw Aaron both coming and leaving yesterday.

"Do you want to tell us about this man?" Joshua didn't waste time.

Just then Samuel saw the pile of parchments. "What are these?"

Sofie quickly gathered Aaron's writings bringing them close so her brothers couldn't see her words.

"Sofie, what are you hiding? Let us see these papers!" Samuel sounded angry.

"Sister, please, sit and tell us what these papers are," Joshua said with more love.

Sofie did as they instructed and turned the parchments over so they could see them. "I have asked the man they call Aaron to write letters for me," she began.

"Letters? Who are you writing?" Samuel laughed a little. He looked at Joshua questioning who their sister knew could read a letter.

Sofie became uneasy. Her brothers may have objections to her disclosing personal stories of their family to a stranger.

"I only hoped to have someone write my memories," she said.

"Memories?" Samuel repeated.

"I want those who come after us to know about our great-grandmother Selah and our grandfather and even our father," she spoke slowly letting her words sink in.

"I have no children, but you both do, and Scout has Hannah. I want your families to never forget the sacrifices our ancestors made to live in this land. I have wonderful memories of what Grandfather told us and I thought…well, I only wanted to have someone write the stories so they could be passed down."

"Why did you not ask us?" Joshua looked at Samuel to agree.

"I don't know," she said. "You both are busy and when I saw the man, Aaron, I thought he would help me and perhaps…."

"Perhaps?" Samuel asked.

"Teach me also to read and write." She held her breath. Her brothers only looked at each other, and she thought they were trying to determine who would speak first.

"Is this man Aaron willing to teach you?" Joshua asked.

"Yes," Sofie answered.

"His family has no problem with him being here so often?" Samuel asked.

She didn't know. He never spoke about his own family. "He's only here a few hours, not every day."

"What have you told him?" Joshua wanted to know.

"I have only told him about Selah and the merchant Simon, her friend." She stood hoping her brothers would also. She wanted to start preparing her stew.

"Was the chicken for Aaron?" Samuel laughed again now winking at his brother. "Shall I bring over another?"

Her brothers stood and hugged her. "He sounds like a kind man," Joshua said. "He's been alone for some time. I imagine he likes your company and your cooking!"

"Alone?" Sofie repeated.

The brothers once again exchanged looks. They didn't know how much Aaron had shared with their sister.

"Let us know if you have any needs. Our family will be honored by your memories. Perhaps we may join you." Joshua stopped speaking.

Chapter Two

His little sister seemed nervous by his words. "I only meant if you need us to also remember," he said.

Samuel tugged on his brother's tunic, "They're Sofie's memories, but should you want our input, we'd be more than happy to tell this man about our grandfather."

"Thank you, brothers. I will tell Aaron."

She almost pushed them out the door anxious to start cooking. Her stew tasted best when it was simmered on a low flame all day. Her brother's words swirled around in her head. *His family.* She was so caught up and focused on telling him about hers, she didn't inquire about his. She only knew he had come to the village alone. He was private in his intentions, and she was hesitant to intrude. Now her curiosity worked overtime. She knew her brothers would continue with their questions. She saw Samuel notice the ink stain on the table. Like her, he had run his finger over it finding it had now taken permanent residence and had been settled there for days.

Joshua didn't see his brother's actions, but Sofie swore Samuel smiled like he knew this was only the beginning of something special. And her imagination continued while cutting the onions and leeks. She needed more honey. The bees would move, however, they always returned to allow her to glean their offering as if they too knew they would be a part of the letters. She would use the last of it today for Aaron to take fresh honey cakes to his family and maybe he would tell her on his next visit how much they liked them. She assumed he had no wife, otherwise, he would have told her when she first approached him that he would bring her also. She found herself blushing now for the first time in years and she stepped outside, away from the heat of her open flame. After several minutes, she convinced herself it was the fire that made her face flush and she sat at the table staring at Aaron's parchments.

Aaron brought a skin of wine. He knew Sofie would have a meal prepared and he wanted to contribute. He also knew her brothers provided all her needs, and he imagined it was difficult for her to sometimes ask.

"Shalom Aaron, please come in," Sofie said as she opened the door wide.

The table was ready for fellowship and words. His parchments were in a small, neat stack. "I brought wine," he said.

"Thank you. Shall I pour us a cup now?" She didn't wait for him to answer and busied herself bringing cups to the table.

"So, I've been thinking about Selah," he started.

"She saw Jesus at the Temple. My family went to Jerusalem, but unfortunately, as you know the Temple was destroyed," Sofie said.

"Yes," Aaron replied, "I can't imagine the splendor."

"Do you think heaven will look like the Temple?" she asked him.

Aaron laid down his cup. He never thought about this. "I can't imagine this either. I know it will be glorious! Our Messiah will be there, and we'll worship our King and our God forever. It is enough, yes?"

"Yes," Sofie answered. "I wonder what Selah thought the first time she saw the Temple. She was young. She traveled with her family for the annual feasts."

"As did mine," he said.

This was Sofie's opportunity to ask about his family, but he began speaking again.

"Was your grandfather Selah's only child?" Aaron was ready to write.

"Yes, as I told you he was named after Simon the merchant. He was very kind to Selah and Malchus and all their friends. They were on this journey together," Sofie replied.

"The journey back to this village you told me about?" he asked.

"Yes, well no, their journey lasted a lifetime. It was a man named Benjamin who remembered the time when our stories were retold. Oh Aaron, how I wish I could have been there when Jesus lived."

Aaron refilled his cup, "God knew the time we would be on this earth, and Jesus lives," he smiled.

"Of course," she nodded, happy he smiled at her remarks.

"Please, I didn't mean to interrupt," he said.

"We were told Selah and her friends kept their thoughts and questions in their hearts and were careful at first to share them," Sofie told him.

"Why?" Aaron asked.

"It was because of Malchus and his position at the Temple. He had difficulty. He was commissioned to find out all he could for the High Priest," she said.

Chapter Two

Aaron saw sadness for the first time in Sofie's eyes, so he changed the subject. "When did Selah return to this village?"

"Soon after the resurrection. Simon was born here. He grew up without his father as he constantly traveled, and then one day Malchus simply didn't return."

Aaron saw more sadness and didn't know what to do. "Besides the merchant, who was Selah close with?" he asked.

Now her face lit up! "Kezi!"

"By the look on your face, I think I'll need more paper," Aaron raised his cup. It was a salute to her fondness, and he was enjoying himself, and it wasn't the wine.

"Tell me about Kezi. If I forget anything, I'll just ask so we make sure all is written down," he encouraged her.

All Sofie heard was *"we"*. The imaginations began creeping slowly into her mind and she reached for the bowl closest to her. "Did you have enough to eat?"

"Yes, thank you, Sofie, you're a good cook," he said.

"I made more honey cakes for you to take to your family."

"They will enjoy them, thank you again," Aaron said. He knew she was curious, but he was here to learn about her family.

"Is it enough for today? Are you tired Sofie?"

"No, but you, I mean you still need to walk home. I think I could talk all night," she laughed.

Aaron knew his youngest son would be waiting, but he hadn't been here too long, so he poured another cup of wine.

"Tell me more," he said.

"Jerusalem was new and big, and it was loud, unlike this village. Selah didn't like to stay home all day. She met a woman at the market who sold scarves and pillows and beautiful things. This was Kezi who was from Magdala. They became like sisters and were seldom apart. It was Selah, Kezi, and the old merchant Simon who began meeting secretly in the early mornings to talk about Jesus and what they knew of the Holy Scriptures. This is the personal journey they were on. I think Selah and Kezi believed in Jesus when no one else did. It was their faith that sustained them through the years. Their hearts had been touched and they had no doubt who Jesus was even when…. perhaps it is enough for the evening Aaron. I'm certain your family waits even now for your return, and the moon is hidden tonight," she reminded him.

Aaron smiled inwardly at her mention of his family. "You're right, I should go," he said.

"Tomorrow Sabbath begins," she said.

"I will see you then at the church," he said.

"Goodnight Aaron, safe travels home."

He left his papers and the honey cakes! She grabbed them and ran out the door calling his name. He turned when he heard her shout. "The honey cakes," she said as she handed him the tied-up bundle.

"Hurry back inside. I will wait until you latch your door," he told her.

She wasn't used to this. Her brothers knew the whole village kept their eyes on the house of Stone, but this was different. She wondered if Joshua and Samuel sat on their roofs watching. She didn't look up and hurried to her door as Aaron instructed her.

Sofie couldn't wait until sundown. That's when she would see Aaron and they would both be under the same roof listening and learning. Of course, her brothers and their families would be in attendance, and she practiced a polite smile so that when she saw Aaron, her brothers couldn't see her imagination of late. She whispered a prayer before she put on her outer garment asking the Lord to help with her thoughts of the man of the hills especially when she was under her brother's scrutiny. It didn't surprise her one bit when she opened her door to their smiling faces.

"Shabbat Shalom," they said together. "We'll escort you today," Samuel said.

She never grew tired of their amusement on her behalf, so she simply looped her arms through theirs and greeted them with a kiss.

"I thought I smelled honey cakes yesterday as I passed by," Samuel said. "I hope you have some for me."

"No, I don't," Sofie answered. "In fact, I was going to ask you to get me more honey."

Chapter Two

Samuel didn't like collecting the honey. He had been stung often through the years and he wished he had a large honeycomb that he could break her off a piece. He hadn't forgotten the time they rescued their sister from their great-grandmother's discovery.

"I will go," Joshua said. He enjoyed the short trip to the secret place and would indulge in the sweetness all the way home.

"I'll come too," Sofie laughed.

"We will need to wait until after Sabbath," Joshua reminded her.

Sofie swallowed. *Sabbath. She wouldn't see Aaron tomorrow or perhaps the next day if she went with Joshua.*

"Of course," she finally said. "It will be like old times. I remember when grandfather took us," she smiled.

"Will you tell Aaron to put that in your letters?" Samuel asked her. He was teasing her and even at their age, he noticed Sofie still treasured their affection.

"Yes, why not," she answered.

Joshua stopped walking. "But you can't tell him where!" he protested.

"I won't," Sofie said, "But someone will need to know to carry on the tradition."

Her brothers knew this was part of the reason their sister wanted the letters written. She didn't want anyone to forget the former things, especially when it was all she had. They both grieved for their baby sister. They thought she sacrificed the most by taking care of their parents while they were starting their families. She had no time for love. That's how she phrased it. Her heart was full, she told them, looking after their mother and father. As their final days ended, Sofie's appetite for the past grew and she requested their father to repeat everything he remembered of his father and the stories he was told around countless fires. Their uncle Caleb was gone now too, and their oldest brother Scout had been in Magdala for almost a year preparing to celebrate his granddaughter's wedding. The brothers picked up their pace knowing their sister was probably anxious to see her letter writer.

Aaron was in his usual corner. He seemed content to stand in the shadows drawing no attention to himself. That's exactly what Sofie was attracted to. A young man stood by him this night and had a strong resemblance. She was separated however and wouldn't call out her inquiry. Her brothers had reserved seats. They also didn't like attention, but the community of believers said they wouldn't even have this place to worship had it not been for their family, so they sat in honor of Simon, their grandfather.

Aaron only looked at Sofie once. He didn't want Finn to stare at her, and he didn't want his son to think about his father having a possible attraction to another woman besides the boy's mother. It had been a long time, and he wasn't convinced what he was feeling was an attraction. He instead directed his focus to Sofie's brothers, the sons of Stone. He wondered how much information Sofie would share with him about their father and his firstborn Scout. He remembered him standing watch as his family traversed the smaller hills surrounding Simon's. He was young and noticed two smaller boys who stood alongside him. It was Joshua and Samuel. They had grown up together yet knew nothing of each other. Now he wondered after all these years if that would change. Surely they knew what he was doing helping Sofie record the family's legacy. He saw them escorting her tonight.

He felt ashamed now. He had no idea what words were shared during his daydreaming. They were ready for communion and Finn gave him a little jab to take the bread. He *was* distracted. He never thought another woman would cause the yearning he was now experiencing. He'd rather be at Sofie's table eating warm bread and listening to her heart as she poured out her memories. He knew his son studied him while they prayed. They would leave immediately, mindful of the time. He imagined his son would be full of questions on the walk back home, but Finn remained quiet. The families of Aaron would be gathered in the largest space anxious to hear about the words spoken this evening. They relied on their father's understanding of scripture and were comfortable remaining home. He greeted his family, Sofie's honey cakes sat on the end of the table, the small children waiting for the sweet treats.

Finn turned to his father, "Was the woman who made these the same you couldn't look away from?" he smiled.

Aaron didn't answer, only telling him to take his seat so they could eat. Afterward, the women cleared plates and bowls while the children sat with Sofie's honey cakes and Finn left the shelter to find his father

Chapter Two

outside. They looked down upon the village, low fires burning in each home. Finn wondered which one belonged to the cake woman.

"It's late Father, are you not tired?" Finn asked.

"Yes, I only wanted some fresh air," he said turning to his son. "We will have plenty of rest tomorrow," he added.

"The family will enjoy you being here," Finn said.

"What? I'm always here," Aaron said.

"No Father, lately you've been spending the better part of your day in the village." Finn directed his attention down, watching the fading light of the fires.

Aaron looked at the infamous hill of Simon. He couldn't see the watchmen, but he had no doubt they saw him. He thought about waving to them, but Finn would only ask why he did so this night. He asked himself. *They were family. Sofie's family.* He wondered if she was ever brought to the summit and allowed to sit around the men's circle of influence. He would ask her. He hoped she had several stories of what took place on the high hill. *Enough stories to last a lifetime.*

Finn heard his father suck in his breath at whatever he was thinking about and looked down again at the sleepy village disappearing into the night. *The cake woman*, he thought, and he wasn't sure how he felt about this.

Sofie sat at Joshua's table enjoying the banter between her brothers and their family's excited voices. They were all traveling for the wedding of Scout's granddaughter. They would leave soon, and Scout and Pella would return with them. She declined to go, stating she wasn't comfortable with the journey. The brothers, including Scout, knew their mother kept Sofie close. She was the baby and the only girl, and their mother Hannah protested each time their father wanted to take the children up the coast. Sofie had never left the village and the family members gave up on trying to convince her to travel.

"I'm fine here," she told everyone. "The whole village knows us and will look after me if that's your concern," she added.

She could take care of herself, she reminded them. She made a few coins and bartered her honey cakes for other supplies she didn't want to ask her brothers for, and she didn't want to be away from Aaron and her letters. Samuel sat across from her with the biggest grin she had ever seen from him.

"What is it?" she asked.

He only looked at her knowing she knew exactly what he was thinking. She tried not to smile. She took a bite of her bread and casually addressed him.

"Did you get my honey?" She knew he hated the bees, and the big grin he wore turned into a sheepish one.

"I got your honey," Joshua said.

"Thank you, brother," Sofie laughed. "I'm sorry I didn't go with you."

They would be gone for over a month. Samuel couldn't remember if his sister had ever been alone for this amount of time. Of course, his thoughts turned to Aaron. He hoped Sofie would use wisdom while they were away, and the community would squelch any busybody's chatter about her having a man in the house. It would be different without her family there. He would speak to Joshua to see what he thought. He saw his brother hand Sofie the honey and a small purse of money. She accepted it but Samuel knew she wouldn't spend one coin. His sister was resourceful and proud. He wondered if this man Aaron was attracted to her independence. Most men had difficulty with the sister of the sons of Stone. They simply couldn't measure up. It wasn't their fault; it was just the blessings of God had been poured out on the family.

No man had ever been able to capture his baby sister's interest. Until Aaron. Samuel saw her looking at him earlier. He turned to see where she was staring halfway through the service. The man Aaron wasn't much older than him and Joshua. Samuel knew he had lost his wife. What he didn't know was if he had found another. He didn't think so and this is what made him anxious and pleased at the same time. They walked Sofie home, Joshua surveying her cooking space, calculating how long her supplies might last. Sofie knew what they were thinking. They had exchanged looks all through dinner and now examined her house. Both let their eyes settle on Aaron's papers a little longer than they meant to and Sofie tried not to smile.

"I'm not a young girl," she reminded them. "I'll be fine. I have money and plenty of oil."

She was quite capable of taking care of herself. She practically pushed them out the door, hugging and kissing them, telling them over and over how much she would miss them, and couldn't wait for Scout to return. At the mention of their older brother's name, they left, anxious for the Sabbath to end so they could begin their preparations. It would take a few weeks to get ready for the journey.

The night was quiet. Sofie brought the lamp close to Aaron's parchments. She studied the letters trying to see patterns or the same symbols used. She wondered how many times he had written Selah. She would ask him to show her the name when he came the next time. Her mind desired to learn, and she knew he would be patient to teach her. She closed her eyes and could see him concentrating while he made his marks. His eyes were light brown with a hint of gold like the color of her honey. As she extinguished the lamp, she hoped she was the only one who was thinking about his golden-brown eyes.

"Selah and Kezi were good friends with Mary of Magdala," Sofie said quite candidly. She loved seeing Aaron's eyebrows raise when she revealed more information for him to record.

"Did Kezi know Mary when they both lived in Magdala?" Aaron asked.

"No, I don't think so, but it was the change in her that Selah couldn't get out of her mind. She was like a brand-new person. It finally made sense to them my grandfather told us after they heard Jesus telling Nicodemus that he must be born again. Mary had been born again. They all struggled with this term at first, especially Malchus," she took a breath while Aaron wrote her words.

"May I watch how you make your marks?" she asked him.

Aaron stopped. She would have to come closer. She smelled like wildflowers in the spring, and he wasn't sure he could concentrate with the scent of lilac and lavender.

"Of course," he said, and he reached for a new parchment.

"I can write both Hebrew and Greek," he said. "Which one do you want to learn?"

Sofie looked down at the papers. She had no idea.

"I can teach you both," Aaron smiled, "But this will take a long time I fear."

Sofie smiled, "I would like to learn both."

The next week Sofie practiced speaking the letters. She asked Aaron if he would write the name Selah on a parchment she could keep. She pulled it out now, running her fingers over the letters carefully. She requested Selah's name be written in both languages and now looking at them, she became frustrated because she couldn't remember which symbols represented each language. Aaron had been so kind, telling her perhaps she could learn the alphabet, but when he started reciting the letters, she became uneasy at the thought of memorizing both the markings and how to pronounce each one. He saw her confusion and rolled up his parchment saying there was no hurry and maybe she should concentrate on one letter at a time.

"Speak it, and then write it," he told her.

She didn't want to take up his time so she told him she would practice on her own. Besides she couldn't resist how his face would light up with her stories. He had made his private notes writing the names of all the people she had mentioned so far. He told her on his walks home he would try and imagine Selah or Kezi at the market in Jerusalem selling all things women coveted and Simon peddling his fruit and vegetables. Sofie had made him laugh with tales of her great-grandmother's donkey. All Aaron knew was they loved Jesus and He had changed their lives. Once again, this had been difficult for Malchus. During the turmoil this time brought, a small orphan boy had come into their lives. His name was Benjamin.

Aaron had to tell Sofie to stop often as she blurted out everything she knew about him. It was remarkable! The boy had become like a son to Kezi. Later he discovered his own father who then married Selah! He thought he saw hope in Sofie's eyes when she told him Selah had found love again, and she had grabbed his arm that evening also saying it was truly a miracle after what she and Kezi had gone through.

Aaron stopped writing to listen, but Sofie wasn't ready to speak about this. Instead, she told him about Benjamin's dream and how he

Chapter Two

and the old merchant Simon saw their resurrected Lord. Aaron's eyes watered, and their closeness at the table became uncomfortable. He left earlier than normal telling her he was a little tired this evening. They were learning about each other. She was genuine with a passion for the things of the Lord and how they influenced her family. Aaron had the same love for God's Word and the stories he had heard growing up were coming to life as her family had been an eyewitness to this pivotal time in history.

Her grandfather Simon grew up without his father. He thought of Finn now never knowing his mother. He looked over at Simon's hill. He knew something had happened, and this was part of the story Sofie wasn't ready to share. He wouldn't glance back down at the village tonight. He knew it was standing in the shadows. He suspected Finn thought his father was spending an awful lot of time with his new friend. Aaron wasn't sure how he felt about this himself. Sofie only requested he write for her and perhaps teach her to write herself. Once she learned, she would no longer need him. His thoughts were leading him to a foreign place. He determined his thinking was due to her stories. The people were real. He knew she spoke the truth. He felt a deep connection with them. It was their faith. Some days he wondered if his parents lacked an understanding of this faith, so they retreated to the caves hidden above Simon's village.

The Temple was gone, and all the records were burned. The Romans couldn't tax people who didn't exist, so they lived simply, and Aaron watched the tiny village from above. Now he was learning that life had gone on in the community and when Stone returned, it gave the people great joy that he also recognized the faith of his father and there would be no more running or hiding. He was too young to understand sheltered with his family, living in darkness, but Sofie had renewed his mind with hope. There was a remnant of believers and they had settled in Simon's village and now generations later, God's Word was spoken freely, and he rejoiced!

He found himself smiling at Simon's stars. Sofie had stirred his passion with her account of the time her family members walked the earth alongside their Savior. It was wonderful! They weren't just stories. He thanked the Lord for this opportunity to help her write her memories, and he prayed she had many more.

Chapter Three

"Where did Benjamin come from?" Aaron asked Sofie. "I want to make sure I have everything correct."

Today, they sat in the courtyard for all the village to witness. Sofie's brothers would be pleased to silence the old gossips who liked to spread their own stories when Sofie remained behind closed doors. They sat with no parchments. Aaron would only listen today and write later.

"Benjamin didn't know where he came from or how old he might be. Nothing mattered to Kezi. She told everyone she fell in love with his big brown eyes the first night Simon brought him to her house. He found out much later in life that he was from Syria," Sofie said.

"Syria!" Aaron couldn't believe it. "And you said his father married Selah?" He wanted to make sure he heard her right.

"Yes! Only God could have brought these two lives together. Benjamin and his wife traveled after…." Sofie stopped again, she still wasn't ready to tell him about Selah and Kezi's trouble.

"Benjamin traveled and lived in Antioch before returning here. He met a merchant who reminded him of Simon. He was also a believer. They sold in the market and that's where Benjamin's grandmother recognized him. The older woman had seen him the first day he arrived in the city, and Aaron, I believe her heart could feel his presence. After some time, she found him alone one day and told him who she was." She sat up a little straighter as she was about to tell Aaron more amazement.

"She recognized a scar Benjamin had on his hand. She told him his mother was her daughter and she gave him hope to learn about his family. Nathan, the merchant, and Benjamin were part of the first church, and it was there Benjamin's father revealed himself. This was Nassar who Selah found love with so unexpectantly," Sofie smiled.

"I was told he was a very kind man, and my grandfather came to love him as his own father. Kezi was shocked when Benjamin brought Nassar to the village. Father and son were identical in looks and there could be no doubt Nassar was Benjamin's father. Of course, everyone was thrilled when he and Selah entered their marriage covenant. We were also told all our lives it was God," she said.

"My family believes God ordains everything. All our steps are ordered and there is reason and purpose. I believe this also."

She stopped talking and Aaron thought she was waiting for him to comment. "I also believe," he simply said.

She wouldn't ask him, but she wondered if he thought God ordained them to meet in the gathering place so she could make her requests known and now share these stories in the sundrenched courtyard of her home. She didn't dare look at him now thinking he would be able to discern her thoughts, and she was certain the sun would tell his honey-colored eyes her deepest feelings. She was troubled by them. She had been preoccupied with her family's needs for so long that she couldn't remember the last time she welcomed her thoughts.

"Do you need to rest?" Aaron asked. "The sun is growing warmer."

Oh, she hoped her face wasn't flushed with her emotion. Now she felt bad not offering for them to sit in the cooler house. She didn't care what people thought. Aaron was a friend, and he was helping her. The village had talked behind their hands about her since she realized they did. They said, *"Poor Sofie, she never married"*, or *"She only sits rocking in her courtyard waiting for her last breath".*

"Her great-grandmother's honey cakes are her only legacy". "Oh, what a tragedy!" They weren't quiet with their whispering, and she heard everything.

She rose to go inside and Aaron wondered what their next remarks would sound like. He didn't think he would hear *"Poor Sofie."* He was also familiar with the women of the village. They needed more to occupy their time. Sofie wasn't poor, she was rich! Rich in spirit, wealthy with a past filled with love, and family who all had a tremendous personal relationship with the living Christ. Not many in this

Chapter Three

community could boast of this heritage and yet Sofie nor her family made special requests. They were humble. She had also inherited their strength and boldness. No, there was nothing poor about her. Her eyes sparkled even in the low light of her home, and she took no notice of her beauty. At least he thought she was one of the most striking women who lived in Simon's village. He remembered when she was known to try and keep up with her brothers as they raced to greet their father after a long day of traveling. That's about the same time his parents decided to leave and live with their own people, excluding all others.

Sofie was waiting for him to turn and follow her inside to ensure the old women would have no doubt they were in the house alone and could make their statements without falsehood. This made her laugh and Aaron knew what brought this temporary delight. He saw the busybodies shuffling by like their bones ached and they couldn't move any faster.

He looked at Sofie squarely, the sunlight trying to cast its shadow and simply said, "Shall we?"

They both heard the collective gasps which only made Sofie leave the door open a little longer so the village women could also hear their rich laughter. People would always make their assumptions and both Sofie and Aaron knew there was simply nothing they could do about the actions of others. She hated to close the door wanting to see how long the women would walk back and forth, but Aaron wanted to write while she prepared their meal. It was becoming very comfortable to share space and they were truly becoming friends. Aaron knew his son Finn was making his assumptions like the old women still lingering outside and Sofie wondered what her brothers would think if they were subject to the latest gossip about their baby sister. Especially Scout.

The summer desert sky was breathtaking, and Aaron wished he was still in Sofie's courtyard enjoying her company. He had more names to meditate on and remember, Maya, and Sarah, the woman who married Benjamin. Their story took his breath away just as the colors of scarlet and lavender were doing now. Sarah had come to this village after losing her brother Stephen, the very first martyr for his witness of Jesus. Aaron had put his head in his hands not believing the words poured out over Stone's table today. He had yelled out when the same man who held the garments of those who stoned Stephen showed up in Antioch, now a believer with his name changed to Paul, and this brave, young woman Sarah had the strength and love to forgive and accept him as her brother in the Lord. What work the Lord did in this family and both Benjamin and Sarah lived a long, beautiful life. It made his heart ache for his wife, gone almost fifteen years now.

His family wouldn't give him the solitude he craved. Instead, they surrounded him all day and into the late evening reminding him that life remained in the large cave. He wouldn't find love again unless he went down into the village, and now it seemed he was here more than he was home, and his family wondered if love had blossomed again in his heart. They didn't inquire as he told them often that he was only helping a friend. They saw the permanent ink on his hand, yet some hoped he might marry again. He was a family man, and they knew it grieved him that his entire family didn't join him for Shabbat service, but they had heard too many stories themselves of those taken from the hills and Rome hadn't gone away entirely.

Aaron didn't push them by his convictions; each person had to make their own decision when determining their worship of God. He counted his blessings. They did worship, but they chose to do it by themselves with only their family as a witness, except for Finn. It was hard to look at him on some days. He was the last person his sweet wife saw before releasing her final breath and Aaron couldn't help but see her in the boy's features. He had her high cheekbones, but he was his father's son. Aaron saw him now waiting to climb home, smiling as he approached.

"What, no honey cakes today?" he asked.

Aaron tried to hide his amusement, "Is that truly what you wish to ask me?"

"No, it isn't Father," he answered. "You like this woman."

"We are becoming friends, that is all," Aaron replied.

Finn didn't think so. Something changed in his father's appearance. He couldn't put his finger on it, but it was obvious. If he had to make

— *Chapter Three* —

a statement, he guessed he would say his father didn't seem as sad and was smiling more. It wasn't the honey cakes and the sweetened flavor that rested in his mouth, he hadn't even seen his father eat one! It was the woman. Finn had practically run from the base of the hill on the days his father went down to the village, the woman waiting for him. He wondered how long the cake lady would prolong her storytelling. He wasn't sure how he felt about his father spending so much time with her. Things happened and they were not children, however, if the old village women were honest, poor Sofie had no idea what it meant to be joined to someone in an intimate way. If he was honest with himself, he had heard enough information about the family of Simon he could quite possibly write his own stories. *What if the cake woman fell for his father? Would he have to call her mother?* This was too much to think about with the sky demanding his attention.

"So, just friends," Finn repeated.

"There could be nothing else," Aaron told his son.

"Why?" Finn asked.

"Because," Aaron said.

"Because?" Finn tried to encourage his father to have a conversation by dragging out his one-word inquiry.

"As I said, because we're only getting acquainted while I'm helping her."

His father seemed nervous, and Finn couldn't remember the last time he stumbled over his words.

"Let's hurry home and we can watch the sunset over your friend's grandfather's hill," Finn laughed.

"When did you get so old?" Aaron gave his son a little push.

Father and son sat on the top of the ridge and said goodnight to the sun. Finn jumped down and Aaron stayed.

"I want to wait for the stars," he told Finn.

Finn looked up; he didn't think the stars would dot the sky for some time. "You wish to sit out here by yourself until they appear?"

"Yes, I'm looking forward to it. Go in son, I will see you in the morning."

Finn couldn't help but look down upon the community resting from its day and he wondered if his father would go back down to tell his *"friend"* goodnight. He still couldn't make up his mind if he was glad about the possibility.

"My great-grandmother had a circle of love that encouraged her through the years," Sofie told Aaron this morning.

"Kezi was her rock, but there was also a younger woman named Avi who worked in the house of Pilate when she lived in Jerusalem."

Aaron held up his hands, "Who are you, Sofie?"

"I don't know what you mean," she saw confusion on his face for the first time.

"Your family and friends were involved with key people while in Jerusalem and I find it fascinating!" he said.

"It just astounds me sitting at this table knowing your family members also shared bread around it while they spoke of their lives and what they witnessed and lived through. I feel honored."

"My grandfather used to say we earn respect, it is not given, and my family has been honored through the years, but it was nothing they did Aaron," she said.

"I believe God blessed us because of their faithfulness and when times were very difficult and they were faced with personal trials, they didn't waiver. We have already spoken about God ordaining our steps. Who can know His ways?" Sofie took a breath.

"Selah never thought she would live in the Holy City. She longed to return to the sea and live a quiet life and she did. Her friends came with her. It was here the true test of their faith was given and had they not experienced what they did in Jerusalem, I'm not sure they would have survived. Avi not only served Pilate's wife Claudia, but she also served in the house of Herod." Sofie saw the confusion on Aaron's face turn to shock and disbelief, but as she continued, she realized it was awesome wonder. She had grown up with these names and events that had taken place. They were in her blood. Selah, Kezi, Avi, Sarah, and even her mother had been the covering she found safety. Each life had been surrendered to Jesus. They overcame by the words of their testimony.

She ran her hands over the worn wood of the table recounting many tears shed over it, both in sorrow and joy. This is where she sat at her grandfather's feet and begged for one more story before her mother made her lie down to sleep. She didn't know what Aaron wore now on his face and it made her uncomfortable.

Chapter Three

"I'm jealous," he said. "My family knew the Lord, but they didn't trust Him as yours. We made our home deep in the hills and my family is still reluctant to be a part of this daily communion with the village. Your ancestors seem to have challenged anything the enemy could throw at them."

"I think because of what my family experienced, it taught them to be strong." Sofie hoped her words would bring comfort, Aaron seemed troubled.

"Perhaps your parents had no one to encourage them. As I said, if it were not for Kezi constantly telling Selah who she was in Christ, I'm not certain she would have survived when the...."

"Sofie, what happened? Did Selah suffer hardship in Jerusalem? Was it her husband? Forgive me please, we can change the subject," he said. He smoothed out his parchments and secured the top corner with his ink. He waited for her to speak.

"There is a special lookout Benjamin found and he took my grandfather there when he was able to make the climb. They could see a great distance. One day, a lone man was seen running across the valley as if he was being chased, and the dust of many horses followed," Sofie told him.

"Was it Romans?" Aaron asked excitedly.

"No, they thought so at first, but it was a fast-moving storm, a whirlwind that came off the sea that day. Kezi and Selah were directed to some local fishermen's boats thinking it was Roman soldiers and they would simply wait on the water until they left."

"But it was a storm," Aaron said dryly.

"That night my grandmother said she perished," Sofie whispered.

"Perished? I don't understand," he said.

"Kezi and Selah were taken from the banks of the sea by Roman soldiers who had deserted," Sofie spoke evenly and quietly.

Aaron only looked down at the table wondering how many fists had banged on it in anguish at this retelling.

"Somehow, after many months, they escaped and made it back to this house. The man who ran across the valley to warn them was the same man who discovered them lying on the floor in this very room. Everyone presumed they had died the night of the storm. Several boats had been found broken apart and the one Kezi and Selah climbed in was among them."

"What a shock to this man!" Aaron said.

"You want a bigger shock?" Sofie was smiling now, and Aaron was practically out of his seat.

"The man was Elias, and he and Kezi fell deeply in love and were married!" Sofie clapped her hands in delight at Aaron's expression.

Aaron sat with his mouth open shaking his head, "My family used to speak of the cave of Elias. Was it named after this man?"

"Yes! Elias found it!" Sofie said.

"This is unbelievable and wonderful, and I'm filled with praise!" Aaron shouted. "I have so many questions."

"Everyone loved Elias. My grandfather would weep every time his name was mentioned," she said.

"I feel like crying for joy now and I didn't even know him!" Aaron blurted out.

His eyes were all sparkly again Sofie thought, and her candles and lamps only made the golden honey color more pronounced. She couldn't tell him now of the trauma her great-grandmother suffered. The room wouldn't allow it.

"I have lentils prepared," she said. "Would you like some?"

After several cups of wine and bowls of soup, Aaron rose to leave. He wasn't dizzy, but he wasn't feeling any pain and he scolded himself under his breath for his liberty in enjoying Sofie's company and hospitality, and for the very good wine! When they stepped outside, he exhaled deeply and realized he didn't have the strength to travel home. He knew no one inside the village gates. He had a dilemma.

"Is everything alright Aaron?" Sofie also had perhaps too much wine as they truly enjoyed the day together.

"I'm afraid I may have overindulged in your delicious lentils and your good wine!" he answered.

She laughed along with him, "Are you saying you cannot make it home?"

Aaron just stood there not wanting to admit he didn't think he could make the climb.

"I have an idea," Sofie said, "If you're agreeable."

She was whispering behind her hand which made Aaron come closer to her. She thought he looked like a young boy in the moonlight, his cheeks a little flushed from the wine as if he was about to find out a secret from the girl he liked.

"You can sleep on the roof," she said.

Aaron looked up. Climbing stairs would be much more negotiable than the hill.

"What about the village women?" He burst out laughing, turning to see if they were watching.

Sofie was doubled over. She hadn't laughed like this in a very long time.

"*Shhh,*" she held her fingers to her mouth. "You may sleep on the roof next door," she indicated with a nod.

"Whose house is it?" Aaron asked.

"My brother Scout's. He's traveling. Come, let's see what you might need," she scurried around the corner before he could object.

They giggled all the way up the stairs and when Aaron reached the top, he felt like he was home. It was a man's space. Several rugs layered the floor under a beautiful covering with assorted pillows and a low table rested on the furthest side.

"This is perfect!" Aaron said. "Are you certain there will be no problems?"

"Why would there be any issues? Please, look around and tell me if you require anything," Sofie said.

Aaron looked at the sky instead. The night was warm with a slight breeze and now that he didn't have to walk home, he got his second wind.

"I don't need one thing," he said, "However, what I would like is for us to share one more cup of wine and enjoy these stars."

Sofie headed towards the low table where her brother would have a few wineskins under the covered place. Aaron thought it looked like she glided over the rugs. They sat and drank slowly without sharing unnecessary words.

"I must go now. Goodnight Aaron," she said.

"Thank you for a beautiful day, and I hardly think I'll be able to sleep thinking of Elias and the young Benjamin," he replied.

Sofie waited until she reached the top step before turning around to address him one last time, "I pray you have a good rest," she smiled. "Enjoy your stars as my grandfather Simon did. This was his roof."

Aaron couldn't move. He never wanted to leave. It scared him.

— *Sofie* —

Finn was beside himself. His father never came home. He wasn't concerned, he was perplexed. It was the cake woman. It was the only reasonable conclusion. It would be scandalous, the talk of the village for the rest of the year. *What was his father thinking?* He saw the village bathed in soft amber tones and he gazed at the steep hill leading down to the sleepy community while searching for his father. He had scanned it several times this morning and was certain his father hadn't fallen or was hurt. He had climbed the hill for over thirty years. They were friends and Finn also knew his father was convinced the Lord would never let his foot slip. So, it had to be the cake woman who kept him from returning. His father also taught his children to cast down their imaginations, so he decided to wait until his father came home. He would listen to his excuse as to why he stayed away from his home the first and only time Finn could remember.

He also knew he wouldn't question his father; he would only inquire about his health and tell him he was worried. Of course, his father would assume this, so he was anxious to see his expression when relaying his reasons for sleeping in the village. He paced back and forth until he saw movement from the corner of his eye. *Just a rabbit* he said out loud, and he continued his pacing.

Aaron had the best sleep on Simon's roof. The cave didn't offer the fresh air found under the stars. He sat resting on the many pillows scattered under the covering and inhaled the smells of the cookfires of the entire village. He peeked over the side once to see if Sofie was in her courtyard readying her fire, but he only saw the empty wineskin where he left it lying behind an overturned chair.

"Lord, what a night," he mouthed.

"Lord, what a night!" he repeated now smiling to himself.

How would the clan of village women not see him scramble down the adjoining house? And then he thought that's exactly what they needed to see. He took his time, each step also seemed to want to share a story with him and he climbed over the short courtyard wall to knock on Sofie's door.

Sofie had been awake for some time. She had fresh bread already made and an assortment of figs and dates on the table.

"Good morning, Shalom, come in Aaron," Sofie couldn't help but look over his shoulder to see if the women were gathered.

"Please, make yourself comfortable," she told him.

Aaron felt strange. He felt alive, but he also felt like an intruder. The family of Selah laid open for him to peer into their struggles, their hope, their joy, and he was an outsider. He was more than honored to sleep on Simon's roof. When Sofie told him before leaving that it was her grandfather's house, he almost followed her back down claiming he didn't feel worthy of this coveted space. His mind had raced. Simon, his son Stone and now Scout, Sofie's oldest brother walked the steps where these men of God would share their victory in overcoming life's challenges and shout to the wind when a new son was born. Here they enjoyed the heavens filled with God's glory and he could almost see each one last night standing at the ledge, gazing out over the valley, the watchmen signaling all was well, and he got a lump in his throat.

Sofie was exposing this legacy. She thought him worthy to divulge this information and that he would hold it in his heart as she did, and more importantly, he praised God for her family who had kept watch faithfully throughout the years so even his family could feel safe in the surrounding hills. He sat at the table not knowing what he wanted to say to her this morning.

She brought over the warm bread and told him to eat. "I enjoyed my grandfather's roof," she said. "It's been a while since I've been up there. My brother Scout likes his privacy. Besides, he tells me I have my own roof to enjoy. He's right, but it's not the same. There has been no one to share the memories."

Aaron thought she looked like she was sorry she just told him her thoughts. He didn't want her to feel uneasy.

"My son probably wonders why I didn't come home last night," he started. "I...we...I mean I had a nice evening."

"I enjoyed it also," Sofie said. "Do you need to go?"

Aaron didn't have anything else to do and picked up another piece of bread. "The village women didn't see me come down this morning, and now I fear they will wag their tongues if they see me leave from your front door."

"What shall we do?" Sofie had a smile on her face.

Aaron couldn't tell if she was truly concerned. "If it's alright with you, I'll stay inside until the usual time," he answered.

"That's fine with me," she said.

"I want to tell you more about the men who encouraged and taught my grandfather. Benjamin of course was like a big brother to him and later my grandfather called him uncle. It was after Selah and Kezi disappeared. Oh, I never finished their story."

"Tell me what you will Sofie. I have made many notes and have rehearsed their names often, so I don't forget who's who. We will write your letters, so they make sense," he said.

Sofie nodded. Aaron said *"we"* again. She had never been a *"we"* with a man, and her heart was stirred.

"You have memorized everyone's names?" she asked him.

"Yes," he answered, "I have."

She was impressed, this was deeper. She almost wanted him to recite the names and their associations only to hear them spoken by another. This is why she requested the letters be written. She wanted strangers to know the legacy of Selah.

Aaron was taking pleasure in this quiet morning with her. He shifted his position and made himself more comfortable. He could watch her all day. He could see the love she had for her family and realized she only wanted others to feel the warmth and connection she had known. They both knew many never sensed this love and he suspected that was another story she would tell. It was the time her father brought several people back with him from Tiberias.

"Shall I tell you?" Aaron smiled.

"Tell me?" Sofie asked.

"About your family," he answered.

The shine on her face was all he needed to indicate her pleasure. This woman understood the faithfulness of Christ had enabled her family to endure much, and she truly held on to the wisdom and passion they passed down and taught their children. God could be trusted. If any child learned anything in this family, it was God alone. He was all they needed. The words Sofie's great-grandmother heard whispered in the markets that Jesus had spoken had been lovingly stored in each family member's heart, and now Sofie craved to understand those same words kept in the house of the Lord for everyone to be reminded. *'Seek first the kingdom of God, and all will be added'!* Sofie's family had sought, and she understood the deep convictions of her grandfather Simon, her father Stone, and each person in this community who had sought the One called Jesus.

"Aaron, your family...won't they be looking for you?" she asked.

She wouldn't intrude, but she *was* curious. Like her, it seemed he had no one waiting to share each moment of the life they had been given. She had made peace with this fact in the past and wondered if Aaron had, or did he have a longing for the closeness he shared at one time. She stole a look at him also wondering if he thought she was a restless soul. She would agree she was during the early years of her life, but her heart was tethered to her roots. They were strong and anyone would be hard-pressed to sever the bonds of Simon's family. This was her comfort. She rested in love, hope, and faith. Love had covered her all her life, and it was the faith of her parents and grandfather that she held on to, but hope, on occasion, seemed unattainable.

Sometimes she would wait until the sun went down hoping for that last glimmer of light to expose the deep desires of her heart and then she could join hope with love and faith. This is what she didn't want Aaron to see as he sat across from her.

"Yes, I should leave," he said. "Shall I see you tomorrow?"

"I hope so," Sofie said.

"Father, why would you make us worry?"

Finn scolded his father all the way home. He came down to the village looking for him when he saw him leaving the cake lady's house. He waited until his father was on the main path to make himself known.

"I didn't mean to cause you to worry," Aaron answered.

"Is that all you're going to say?" Finn asked.

Aaron stopped walking. "What else would you like me to tell you, son?"

"Where have you been?" Finn asked.

"Why didn't you come home? Did you have trouble?" Finn couldn't be certain, but his father seemed to be holding back a smile at all his inquiries.

"I'm fine son," Aaron said. "I may have had one too many cups of wine and decided it was late in the night to journey home, so I stayed in the village."

"At the cake lady's?" Finn asked. He backed up now. What he saw on his father's face didn't resemble any kind of a smile.

"What did you say?" Aaron stood with his feet apart.

Finn swallowed, "The woman...the one who makes the honey cakes."

"That is not what you just said," Aaron replied.

"I called her the cake lady. You have never told me her name," Finn offered, hoping his father would accept this as an apology.

"Her name is Sofie. She is the daughter of Stone, son of Simon," Aaron told him.

Everyone knew of Simon and Aaron reasoned he wouldn't have to say anymore. Finn, however, wasn't satisfied and Aaron saw more questions in his son's eyes.

"I didn't stay with the cake lady," he laughed while throwing his arm around Finn's shoulders. "I was given the roof of Simon for my sleep. It was nice to rest under the sky."

"Yes Father, you look well rested," Finn said.

Perhaps the smile he saw was simply that his father had a good night's sleep. He hoped the roof of Simon wouldn't become a habit. He genuinely missed his father's presence, even his snoring which he had heard each night for as long as he could remember.

Aaron wasn't surprised to see his entire family gathered, waiting for his arrival. They wouldn't ask any questions as Finn would repeat to them all he told him. He knew they were concerned, but he was the head of this family, and he didn't think he needed to explain his actions to anyone. The women busied themselves preparing for their midday meal. Aaron was surrounded by his grandchildren, all of them hoping for one of his tall tales. He was grateful for the distraction. The sun

Chapter Three

was setting, and it would tell the sky to cover itself. All he could think about was Simon's rooftop.

Sofie waited until her courtyard saw its last onlooker. She was used to moving around in the dark and she hurried up the stairs to Scout's roof. She laughed when she saw Aaron had straightened up the place where they shared wine, and every pillow was lined up perfectly. She looked toward the direction she thought he lived. No fires dotted the hillside and her dreams once again of finding hope dissolved into the darkened blue sky. She chided herself for this feeling. Where was her faith? She knew her hope was in the Lord. What she struggled with was that she hadn't hoped for anything in years. She had all she needed. She was secure in her family home, her brothers made sure her needs were met and she had peace in her heart. Until Aaron.

Peace didn't leave, but now her heart ached for more. It was simply too late. Aaron had his family, and he was only helping her to complete a task that she wasn't able to do on her own. She sat and poured the last of the wineskin's contents into the lone cup. She adjusted the pillows and leaned back as her grandfather did to watch the night pass by. She never sat on her roof. Perhaps she should ready it as her grandfather had. Scout would be home in a few weeks and then where would she and Aaron watch the stars together and enjoy a cup of wine? *Sofie!* She couldn't bury the thoughts that continued to claim space in her mind. Aaron had been so kind and giving of his time. She was reading more into this arrangement. She needed to stop. She stood abruptly; her grandfather's pillows were left scattered on the floor.

"I would like to tell you more about the women," Sofie told Aaron, "That is before I tell you about the men in their lives." Aaron had showed up early this morning and said he was free the entire day and ready to write.

"The woman Kezi had trouble at a young age," Sofie lowered her eyes. "It made her strong and she found more trouble as I told you. She met many nobles but never forgot those who had left their homes because of the shame they felt they brought to their families. Would you like to see the slippers that Claudia, wife of Pilate gave her?" Sofie's eyes were now wide with excitement. Somehow, she thought if Aaron could see and touch things that connected people, his writing would come alive for the reader.

"Yes!" Aaron exclaimed.

Sofie brought a small chest to the table. She carefully removed the items covering the treasure that had been passed down. Wrapped in silk, she brought the beaded slippers out to rest on the table for Aaron's pleasure. The craftsmanship no one could deny, and he marveled at the blue and silver beads that still sparkled as the morning sun shone through the window.

"The wife of Pontius Pilate," he whispered. "May I?" he asked Sofie, extending his hand to examine them more closely.

"Of course," she replied.

"They're exquisite, yes? They have to be close to one hundred years old," she added.

"One hundred," Aaron repeated.

"Close," Sofie smiled.

Aaron placed them back on the table. "Amazing, thank you for showing me," he said.

He couldn't help himself and peered into the open chest to see what else might be clothed in her memories. Sofie pulled out a shimmering scarf that also cast joy through the room.

"What a magnificent color!" Aaron said.

"It was Selah's." Sofie held the turquoise material up to the window.

"My great-grandmother saw this the first time she went to the market. Kezi owned the shop, and she gave it to Selah as a gift telling her it matched her eyes. Their friendship began that day." Sofie folded and wrapped it back in its protective covering.

"Eyes the color of the sea," Aaron said.

"Yes, no one else in the family inherited her color as I told you. I think that's one of the things that made her so special. Oh, how I wish I could have known her!" Sofie exclaimed.

"But you do!" Aaron said.

Chapter Three

"These beautiful stories have been handed down so you could know her, and now you're making sure others will know her too." He saw the first tears begin to cascade down her cheeks and he stood to go to her.

"I'm fine," she said, "But I want to tell you Aaron that what you just said were the most loving words I have heard in a very long time."

"It is my prayer I write all the words you have carried in your heart."

Sofie could only stare at him. The thoughts were making her mind busy again. She distracted herself by taking the small wooden chest back for safekeeping and asked over her shoulder if he would like some soup.

"Is it your grandmother's lentils?" he asked.

"Come, grab some bowls," she laughed.

Chapter Four

For the next two weeks, Aaron came every day. He went home each night even though he would rather stay on the rooftop of Scout's house. Sofie told him she now had gone up there almost every night.

"I can almost hear my father and grandfather's voices carried by the breeze when I'm enjoying the space," she told Aaron.

"Also, with you here listening to all my stories has brought back so many memories. I hope you know how much I appreciate your time. You must tell me what I can do for you…to repay you. I have kept you from your family, and…."

"And?" Aaron asked.

"And I feel we have only just begun," she said.

Aaron hoped she couldn't see his pleasure at this statement. He knew she hadn't even started to say what she wanted her family members to hold onto and carry with them for generations to follow. She was providing him with information on each person so he would know how they interacted with each other, but she hadn't shared the message in boldness that he thought she couldn't wait to shout to her loved ones. He would be ready. He wanted to hear everything! They were her letters. She had given him a peek into the lives of men he only heard about, great men he never dreamed he would be privy to such personal insight. Sofie had given him a great gift. She owed him nothing. He didn't want to deceive her or hide his intent and asked her if she would mind if he made notes on each person she had spoken of for his own remembrance. It seemed several minutes passed before she smiled and told him how his words blessed her.

That was the last time they shared the evening on Simon's roof enjoying the stars. He was drawing close to her. He was becoming familiar with her scent. He was attracted to her. My Lord, he was falling in love with her, he thought. He felt like a foolish boy and that's when he decided he wouldn't climb the stairs anymore but would return to his dark cave each night so she wouldn't see his silly thoughts. Now, he sat wondering how long he could keep them hidden from her. She obviously hadn't noticed which he was grateful.

She was strong like her great-grandmother Selah. She had an unshakable faith like Simon, her grandfather. He couldn't wait until he started writing about her mother and father to determine what she inherited from each one. She had the kindest eyes, full of love and concern. One morning he saw her in her courtyard, a basket of fresh honey cakes tucked under her arm while the children of the village clamored around her waiting for her to hand them one of the sweet cakes. It brought her much joy and he waited until she went inside to finish walking to her house.

He wanted to give her time to bask in the happiness of the children's voices as they continued to call out their love to her. This was a woman who had peace. He was restless. He hoped to achieve the same restful spirit she walked with so easily. This is the message and the words his pen waited patiently for. He knew she was looking at him trying to discern his thoughts. It was almost time for him to journey home, the shadows of the room telling him to hurry. His son would be waiting. Finn now called Sofie by her name after he grew weary of hearing his son calling this precious woman his *"cake lady"*. He reprimanded Finn telling him Sofie had become a friend, and it was simply disrespectful to refer to her as such.

"You like her!" Finn had stopped walking to see his father's reaction.

Aaron told his son most people liked their friends, or they wouldn't be friends. Finn had given him a funny look. He hoped his boy didn't think his father was kind of mean to say that making him sound uncaring. But now Finn always asked how his friend Sofie was and he would answer she was well. That's all. He couldn't disclose to his youngest that Sofie was more than well. She was beautiful. She was kind and had a generous heart. She had a sense of humor and enjoyed a good riddle. She loved God. This was the most attractive thing about her.

Chapter Four

She had sought someone to help her make sure her nieces and nephews would know and understand who their parents and grandparents were, and the one who began her spiritual journey be known to them, and that this journey began in this tiny village by the sea. It had changed their lives. The Lord Jesus had changed Selah's life and Sofie prayed these letters would be passed down from generation to generation so the stories of her family's faith and perseverance would encourage them no matter what they might encounter in their own lives. There was One they could trust. His name was Jesus.

One night as Aaron gathered his papers, Sofie began to sing. He didn't think she even realized she was praising the God she loved so much, the name of Jesus she kept repeating over and over again, and her sweet voice brought tears to his eyes. He heard her commitment. The melody of faith and hope filled the house, and he didn't feel worthy to be in the presence of her pure heart. She might make delicious honey cakes, but her name was Sofie.

Scout and his family would be delayed in their travels. Samuel had received the message all was well and Scout asked if his brothers were looking after their sister's needs.

"Shall I send word the man Aaron is looking after you?" he asked his sister.

"Is that what everyone thinks?" Sofie grabbed his wrist.

"I'm teasing," Samuel said, but he saw panic in her eyes.

"Scout's house will remain empty I expect another month." He thought he saw the same alarm. "Perhaps your friend could stay there if the night grows late when you're visiting."

"Visiting?" Sofie repeated.

"What else would you call it?" he asked her.

"He's only helping me with my letters," Sofie replied.

"That must be one long letter!" Samuel laughed.

"We've only just started," Sofie told him which made her break out in laughter at her brother's expression.

"Well then, maybe you could offer this man a place to stay while you're writing this letter," Samuel watched her closely. He thought she was trying to hide her smile.

"Has he already stayed? Sister, has he?"

"Twice he slept on the roof," she answered. "You're right Samuel, the night grew late, and I didn't want him to have to journey home with no moon."

"His family didn't mind?" Samuel asked.

"He doesn't speak too much about his family and I don't ask. There's enough busybodies in the village."

Now Samuel let out a hearty laugh. Stories of his sister never marrying had been fodder for the older women for years. They had thought she was cursed, barren, or had a hidden illness unfamiliar to them. But when they saw the care she gave to her parents until they drew their last breath, and the time she spent making her special honey cakes for the children, they had relinquished their gossip for a season. Now, they lingered outside Sofie's courtyard hoping to overhear words between her and the man who came almost every day. Some thought it scandalous especially when Scout wasn't home, and her other brothers couldn't keep an eye on her as they were busy with their own families.

Samuel stood to leave, "Why don't you offer Aaron the house while Scout's away? I'm certain he would appreciate it, especially during Sabbath."

Sofie couldn't believe her brother's words. He wasn't concerned about the old women and their hushed conversations, and she knew Aaron enjoyed the rooftop of her grandfather.

"I will extend an invitation to him," she said.

Sofie sat thinking about Samuel's words, surprised he suggested Aaron stay. Except for sleep, she and Aaron would be together all the time. She wasn't sure how she felt about this. She scolded herself just then; she hadn't even extended the invitation. He may decline. He would be separated from his own family. *What were they thinking?* Perhaps it would be better not to mention the house would remain empty and should there be another evening when time got away from them, she would tell him that he was welcome to stay. He would be arriving soon. She smiled to herself thinking they were getting a late start today.

Chapter Four

"I would like to address this letter to the young boys," Sofie told Aaron as he laid out his supplies.

"Whose young boys?" he asked.

"All the boys of the village. I want them to know about the men who stood watch and made sure our homes were safe. They sacrificed time away from their families so everyone else could rest with peace in their hearts that they were protected. My grandfather Simon learned from Benjamin. There was Elias and my father Stone, his brother Caleb, and another man Jonathan."

Aaron was familiar with all the men, but he wrote their names down again for Sofie's enjoyment.

"Benjamin became a pillar of this village. All the men sought his wisdom and counsel. He was faithful," she said.

Aaron looked up from his parchment, "Yes, he was faithful in?"

"In everything," Sofie replied.

Aaron laid down his pen. "If he were here right now, what would you say to him?" He noticed her eyes grow wide at his question.

"Oh Aaron, what a wonderful thing to ask! You don't know how many times I've sat here imagining all these men sitting at this table where I could speak with each one, ask them everything I've thought about, and tell them...."

"Tell them?" Aaron pressed her.

"Tell them how much I admire them and how they continue to reach others and impact each life even though they no longer live," she answered.

"I would ask Benjamin if he was scared when he found himself alone as a small child, or did he think the caravans he traveled with were all his family members and they were on a great adventure! I would ask him what he thought when he first saw Jerusalem even though he had no idea he was in the Holy City. I wonder if his sweet little heart missed a beat when Kezi called him son." She stole a peek at Aaron just now and his expression told her he didn't want her to stop speaking.

"The old merchant Simon taught him to buy and sell and he became skilled in the markets. But Kezi was his rock! She was always there for him, and he saw strength and perseverance. He also wouldn't be moved," Sofie rearranged the cups and bowls set before her.

"And Aaron, there were plenty of times he could have run and considered a life away from Kezi, Simon, and Selah. I would ask him if he ever thought about leaving Jerusalem to find out where he came from, but Kezi held his heart. When they left to journey back here, he became the man of the house to all the women. He was very young, and it was Benjamin who discovered the lookout and the perfect place to keep watch over this village. I would ask him what he saw first on my grandfather's hill. Was it a goat? Smoke from a distant fire? Or did he simply enjoy the silence and behold God's creation spilling out below and around him? I would ask him if his heart grew faint waiting for loved ones to return. Did he ever for a moment lose hope?" Sofie smiled.

"Ah, Uncle Benjamin," Aaron laughed. He thought if he didn't laugh, he would cry. Who was he kidding? He was glad Sofie didn't see his tears. They were of joy, and she couldn't talk fast enough. He leaned in hoping she would talk into the night, so he had the excuse to stay.

"My grandfather loved him like a father. Benjamin taught him everything! And when the young girl named Sarah came to live here, Benjamin's heart was lost to her. If he were here right now, I would ask him how he felt the moment he laid eyes on her. They were kindred spirits and in a matter of days, he knew they would be together. Kezi knew. Love is funny."

"Funny?" Aaron repeated.

"Perhaps that's not the right word. Did you write that down?" she laughed.

"I would ask Uncle Benjamin did the love he felt for Sarah measure the same as he had for Kezi. I know they're different."

Aaron thought she sounded tired with this last comment, and he took the opportunity to stand and stretch.

Sofie stood also, "Do you need to leave?"

"No, but what about you? Am I keeping you from anything?"

"No, I only need to prepare for tomorrow and I may go up...." She wasn't sure if she should invite Aaron to join her on the roof tonight. She felt vulnerable this afternoon and didn't know why. She caught him wiping his eyes when telling him all the questions she would ask Benjamin and wondered if he thought she was too sensitive.

"Would you like to continue our conversation on the roof? The wind has shifted and it's not as hot," she told him.

Chapter Four

"I would like that very much," Aaron smiled. "Shall we bring our wine?"

They stopped and talked on each step. The narrow passage brought them closer than sitting across the table from each other. Aaron settled on the pillows of Simon and Sofie sat closer to him than she ever had. It wasn't awkward silence but a comfortable moment of just enjoying each other's company. She waited for him to speak first.

"You're right Sofie," he said, "The air is cooler tonight. It makes a man sleepy!"

"You are tired Aaron?"

"I'm relaxed," he held up his cup.

"I love this space. There's something to be said about sleeping under the stars. I'm certain there's a benefit to good wine, good company, and all this fresh air! It must be good for the soul!" he laughed.

"To Simon's stars!" Sofie joined him in his salutation.

They talked and laughed through two wineskins. The night air continued to drop in temperature and Sofie found herself leaning in towards Aaron's shoulder for warmth. Neither could say when he put his arm around her and drew her closer, but they remained that way for the rest of the evening.

The neighbor's rooster called its morning greeting and Sofie smiled remembering the wonderful evening. Then she opened her eyes to find herself still embraced in Aaron's hold on her grandfather's roof. He had pulled a blanket over them and slept soundly. *How did this happen? How could she allow this to happen? What would her neighbors think? Where would Aaron tell his family he'd been? What on earth would she say when he woke up?* She didn't move. She hoped the rooster would fly right up on the roof and announce again it was morning! As soon as she sensed him move, she would close her eyes and pretend she was still sleeping to leave it up to him to discover they slept together under the stars. *My God,* she thought, *those were words she never spoke! They slept together.* Truly, it was only sleep. She closed her eyes tightly. She had never felt so warm and content. It wasn't the pillows and certainly not the threadbare blanket, it was Aaron. She had never experienced this kind of closeness. His left hand draped her shoulder, and she smiled as it was ink free. His hands looked strong and sensitive at the same time. She felt safe in his embrace. She could feel her rapid heartbeat as her thoughts were unfamiliar to her. *Why now did she long for this closeness? She had been just fine alone all these years. She was simply too old to enter into a relationship. The older women of the village would talk about this for weeks!* Her head rested upon Aaron's breast. In the quiet of the morning, she thought she could also hear the steady beat of his heart. She closed her eyes again to listen to his soul.

Aaron was awake. He sensed Sofie's movement, snuggling closer to his chest and he tried to control the rush of emotion he felt. He was certain she could hear the throbbing of his heart and prayed she would think it normal. He heard the rooster and was shocked morning had been declared by the fowl. *Why didn't she wake him if he was dozing off? Did she fall asleep before him?* He had no recollection, but they had to have greeted the peaceful end of the night in unity. And this scared him too! Yet he didn't feel as anxious now with the scent of her hair filling the beginning of the day. He inhaled her presence one last time. He needed to leave.

"Good morning," he said.

Sofie didn't want the day to continue and waited for him to speak again.

"Sofie," he tried to shift his position.

She looked up, "Good morning," she said a little timidly. "I can't believe we fell asleep."

"I can," Aaron smiled.

They both sat up and Aaron stretched. "The air was cool, the wine was excellent, and the company...." He didn't want to make her uncomfortable. "We had an enjoyable evening, that is all."

"Yes, the night was so pleasant. I didn't realize I was so tired," Sofie replied.

The empty wineskins lay by Aaron's side and they both looked at them at the same time.

"Tired, was it?" he laughed.

Sofie put her hand over her mouth wondering if the busybody women were standing in her courtyard waiting to see when Aaron would arrive today. Boy, would they be surprised! Her thoughts were all over the place.

"You can stay here," she blurted out.

"What?"

Chapter Four

"My brother, he'll be gone for weeks. If you like, you can remain here," she looked at his face, especially his eyes.

"I know how much you enjoy sleeping up here," she quickly added, "And you're welcome to stay."

"Truly, your brother wouldn't mind?" Aaron asked.

"No, and it was my youngest brother who suggested it," she smiled. "I only thought it might be helpful and you wouldn't have to travel at night when the time gets away from us," she lowered her eyes.

"Like it did last night?"

"Yes," Sofie responded. "Of course, I understand your family may be disagreeable."

"My family would have no objection," he smiled. "I would have this whole house?"

"Yes," Sofie told him and then pointed downstairs. "Perhaps you can come through my brother's door today in case...."

"The old birds are fluttering around?" he laughed.

"How will I get down to my own house away from their prying eyes?" she laughed.

"You won't have to," Aaron suggested. "They don't know if I arrived this morning. Come, I have a plan."

They made their way down through Scout's house and it was Aaron who opened the door. The older women had begun to gather in their usual place where they stood and leaned on the wall of Sofie's courtyard. Aaron raised his voice to ensure they heard him and looked in their direction so they would see him leaving instead of entering the house.

"Thank you Sofie for showing me the house so early. Are you certain Scout will have no objection to me staying?"

"You're more than welcome Aaron," Sofie replied.

"Would you like to see the rooftop also?" she asked him while trying to keep her composure.

"Yes!" He clapped his hands in delight especially when he saw the old hens turn away. *They had fooled them!* He closed the door and he and Sofie laughed until they were both holding their sides. Aaron took the opportunity to examine Scout's house. It was a man's home, even though the large rugs and women's touches were evident throughout each space.

"I know the answer, but I'll ask again." He turned to her, "Are you sure it's alright for me to stay?"

"Yes, Aaron, I'm sure."

"I know your brothers have no concerns but do you?" he asked.

"Me?" Sofie wondered if he felt uncomfortable.

"Why would I care? I mean, no, Aaron, I had hoped you would stay."

The words had left her mouth before she realized what she said. They stood in the middle of her brother's house only staring at each other with the bond they both felt.

"I will stay," he simply said.

"I should go now and bring some of my belongings. I'll be back to share our midday meal. Can I bring you anything?" he asked.

Sofie couldn't speak. Aaron said *"our"*. Somehow, they were becoming *"our"*. She hadn't noticed he had moved closer to her and the door. He was waiting for her response.

"I could use more oil," she finally said. She supposed her brother had plenty, but she felt vulnerable now with his kindness.

"What about honey? Do you have enough?" he asked.

"Is that your way of requesting more cakes?" she laughed.

Aaron practically ran home. His son would be filled with questions while he gathered his supplies. The rest of the family members would be too busy with their children to stop and inquire. He knew they cared but he also knew they hoped his later years would be filled again with love. They didn't see this as an impossibility and now he was certain Finn had kept them updated with his visits to the cake lady. He smiled now thinking about Sofie's expression this morning when he announced to the circle of old hens he would be staying.

He knew what brought her anxiety. He suggested they were a couple. Our midday meal is what made her blush. He didn't know how else to say it. They were spending a lot of time together. They were sharing meals and the rooftop time at the end of the day had become more special than either of them realized. At least that's how he felt. He stopped just then and turned around to look back at the house of Simon. He knew they would have liked each other immediately, and the time he spent on his roof made him feel he was a part of the legacy he was now writing about. He didn't know he would sense such a strong connection to this family, but he felt it in his bones he was

Chapter Four

a part of Selah, and he knew it was because of a great-granddaughter she never met. *Sofie.* He wondered now if she stood on the roof of the legend watching him make his way home. She only knew of Finn. It seemed she didn't want to know anymore. She had been reluctant to inquire about his personal life, maybe becoming disappointed at no opportunity of a future, or she simply wasn't interested. But this morning before the rooster crowed, before the sun took its place, she had sought his warmth, and he drew her closer. And she reacted. They both couldn't deny the obvious and he was certain it scared her as much as it did him. Now, he was heading home to pack a few things so he could return quickly to Simon's roof. And Sofie.

Sofie saw Aaron stop. He just stood looking at her brother's house for what seemed an eternity. She was watching him until he turned suddenly, and she quickly ducked down out of his sight. *Did he change his mind? Had he forgotten something? Was he standing there trying to figure out how to tell her he couldn't stay after all?* She had straightened up the place where they slept. She could smell him on her grandfather's pillow, an earthy scent of land, firewood, and grapes. She brought the blanket close to her and inhaled his presence one last time before folding the old fabric. She didn't toss it by the awaiting pillows, but carefully laid it down hoping it would cover them again. This thought made her blush, and she was thankful she was hidden from the old hens and they couldn't see her unexpected desire.

How could she miss him already? He had only just left, and she hoped he wouldn't tarry in his hilltop dwelling. She thought of him now secure inside the dark, cool rock where no one could wait in his courtyard in the early morning, shuffling their feet hoping for some shocking tidbit to proclaim to their group of friends. She stood for any onlookers to wave their greetings but the place in front of her had been abandoned. She hurried down to exit her brother's house to find Samuel at the door.

"Brother, you startled me!" She was flushed.

Samuel looked beyond her lifting his head as if he expected Aaron to appear any moment.

Sofie followed his gaze, "Did you hear something?"

"Is he up there?" Samuel smiled.

He couldn't help but notice the color rise on her cheeks, so he pretended he didn't see the man called Aaron first thing this morning walking towards the low hills.

"No, he's not on grandfather's roof, but I did tell him he could stay at the house while Scout is away," she said.

"When is he coming back?" he asked his sister.

Sofie stepped back out of her brother's reach, "Samuel! You saw him leaving! Do you think anyone else did? Oh no! Maybe this wasn't a good idea!"

Samuel thought she was getting upset and he didn't mean to cause her to worry. He just enjoyed teasing her.

"Sofie, everyone knows Scout is gone and many have stayed in the house. They didn't see you," he laughed.

"Did you see me?"

Now Samuel felt the heat rise on his face. "What do you mean?"

"I was up there straightening up," she said. "That's all I meant."

"I just arrived," he told her.

"When you didn't answer your door, I figured you were here preparing for your friend. I've never seen you so nervous."

"Has this man made you uncomfortable? Do you not wish for him to stay here now?" Samuel noticed she was now biting her lip.

"Sister! You must tell me if this man has done or said something out of line!" He was growing concerned.

Sofie couldn't tell him how she was feeling. He might think her foolish, especially if her imagination was getting the better of her from smelling a blanket.

"No, of course not," she said. "He's a kind man and he would never speak words that were improper."

Samuel wasn't convinced. His little sister was hiding something.

"Sofie, you must tell me. "We're leaving and you'll be alone," he kept his eyes fixed on hers. He thought he saw a shimmer of light and joy now reside within her dark eyes.

"Sister," he barely said.

"Samuel, I'm fine. I don't feel alone in this village when my brothers travel. Everyone knows me and I'm sure you and Joshua have already made provisions for me."

Chapter Four

She came close to hug him. It afforded her time to hide her enjoyment of the morning as she could still somehow smell the man from the hills. Her brothers would journey this day and she wondered if the entire village would gather at her courtyard and shuffle back and forth with their whisperings about the man on the roof of Simon's house.

Aaron arrived sooner than Sofie expected, and she took a deep breath before opening the door to greet him. He had provisions. He stood with a big smile and wineskins crisscrossed on his chest with bundles in each hand.

"Come in, let me help you," she said.

"Why don't I go ahead and place my belongings next door," he said while indicating with a small nod the village women were watching.

"Of course," Sofie replied.

They moved slowly allowing the women to take inventory of Aaron's belongings. Anyone could determine he would be a guest in Scout's house more than a few evenings. It was still light, so Sofie didn't light a lamp but showed Aaron where the oil was kept.

"I brought fish," he said pulling a wrapped package from his bundle. "We should cook it today," he added.

Sofie could see the salt-encrusted parcel had been wrapped carefully and she took it from his hands.

"I'll prepare it now," she smiled, and she left so he could get settled and so she could wave at the older gatekeepers at her courtyard wall.

It wasn't hot, her fire hadn't been stoked, but she was sweating. It was Aaron. He had brushed her fingers while handing her the small fish. He would be close to her all night, and the next day, and the following day, and for perhaps a month! She took another deep breath and scolded herself for her imagination. He only gave her fish to cook.

Maybe she was the one that lingered hoping to feel the strength of his hands. *Lord in heaven!* She was becoming delirious! Now she had to prepare her fire and her room would be hotter which would make her appear to be sweating even more and Aaron might think her smitten by his presence. *Stop it, Sofie!* What on earth was she doing? Her mind was so dizzy with thoughts swirling around like bugs at an evening fire that she found herself placing her hands at each side of her head in an attempt to quiet it down. She had never reacted like this. Aaron was just a man. She grew up with three strong brothers and a father and grandfather that everyone admired and respected. She was used to men. *Why was this man causing her this conflict?* It seemed she had inhaled all the air in the room and Aaron would return to her door soon. She busied herself preparing their meal and tried to concentrate on the salted fish.

Aaron took his time exploring the space he would occupy. He wouldn't sleep in the private room of Scout preferring the roof. He hoped to spend most of his time under the stars. He took his new parchments and supplies and laid them on Scout's table. The coarse papers seemed to come alive dancing in the breeze of the open window waiting for Sofie's words to be written. He wasn't sure how long he would stay. He imagined if he took advantage of the entire month, all the letters would be completed and then Sofie would have no reason to seek his help. This thought troubled him, and he hurried up the stairs for some fresh air.

Sofie had straightened up the area which brought a smile. He hoped to mess it up again. With her. Perhaps tonight. Maybe every night. He would suggest they end each evening on the roof toasting their accomplishments and Simon's stars. *Who was he kidding?* He wanted her close to him, snuggled up in his arms so he could smell her hair and dream of her at his side. He was certain she never shared this space with any man. Only her family members had the pleasure of her joy, her innocence, her passion for the things of the Lord, and her brothers had protected her all these years from anyone who might take advantage of her naivety or who may hurt her heart. They didn't know him. He prayed now they would know he only wanted to bring her heart happiness. Writing these letters is where she could express her memories of those who lived and were instrumental in who she knew brought her this happiness.

He could easily see the watchmen on Simon's hill and one man waved his greeting. Surely, he didn't think he was Scout returning from his journey. He waved back. Maybe they knew exactly who stood on this roof. Sofie's brothers certainly made the elders of the village aware of the circumstances, and there was the troop of older women who also claimed themselves as the watchers of all the small community witnessed each day. Sofie was probably waiting for him. He could smell her cookfire. He turned to look back at his hilltop home wondering

— Chapter Four —

if Finn stood watch. His son had been quiet as he gathered the few items he brought down the hill. He couldn't tell if Finn was happy or sad. He had no doubt that his boy saw his excitement even though he tried his hardest to merely say he had an opportunity to finish helping Sofie with her project and it only made sense to stay in the village. Finn had only nodded his agreement, but Aaron saw the smile he tried to stop as his son turned to wait for him outside. He knew Finn watched him traverse the hill to the valley floor and he had to purpose to walk at a steady pace even though he was anxious to see Sofie and continue their day together. The fish had no smell, but the onions and spices Sofie added filled the room and he looked around one last time before leaving. His wineskins were draped over a chair. He started to grab one but changed his mind when thinking he would enjoy it later. On the roof. With Sofie.

Finn followed his father from a safe distance. He never saw his father practically run to the small village. *The cake woman.* There was no other reason for his father to have a spring in his step today. He wouldn't intrude but he was just so curious. He had studied his father closely for the past several weeks. He detected the twinkle in his eye when his father searched the room for the cake lady at Sabbath service and the smile he tried to prevent when his youngest son questioned him at the end of the day while he was hard-pressed to look away from the village snuggled up for its rest. He wasn't jealous of the woman Sofie. He wasn't angry at the attention his father was giving her. He was simply curious. He suspected his father knew he wouldn't let him out of his sight but that didn't stop Aaron from his fast pace to the house of the one they called Simon.

Finn stopped and leaned against the nearest wall. The cake woman was the granddaughter of the founder of this village. They were like royalty, but the family truly gave no notice of the position so many had given them through the years. This is why everyone admired them, and the legacy written on the surrounding hills. Now he thought his father was becoming a part of this and he was confused about how he felt about it. His thoughts made him begin to sweat. He was certain his father had reached the house and was most likely enjoying his midday meal while the cake woman kept him enthralled with the popular stories that had been retold for generations. His father was writing them down for her. He was also teaching her to read and write but Finn thought his father was probably taking his time with this task. The cake woman would no longer need his father if she was able to write her own letters.

He lifted his eyes to the hills that embraced Sofie's village. It *was* hers. She had never left its love and protective arms. He heard the rumors of the village women and the children who sang about the old woman and her honey cakes. He swallowed this thought until it reached his heart. Sofie was beautiful. She was indeed a mystery. He imagined her now on the occasions he had a good look at her. She wore peace. She was content. She looked as if she didn't have a care in the world. He watched her closely on Sabbath when the scrolls were read. He didn't think she even blinked the entire time the holy Scriptures came to life in the small room. She knew the truth. Like his father. They had this in common. This is the peace they both had discovered and brought the joy and contentment of their solitary lives. *But now they were together!* That's how he thought of them this sunny afternoon. He shook his head and pushed himself off the rocky wall. He wouldn't linger in the village today. His father deserved privacy. He needed this time with his new friend. He never saw him happier. He hoped the cake woman would take her time repeating the stories she had kept in her heart.

Chapter Five

Scout worried about his granddaughter Hannah. She seemed happy, but there was no joy in her eyes. She would be married within the week. His brothers would arrive in the next few days. As the patriarch of the family, he had committed to stay and oversee all the arrangements for the wedding celebration, and Hannah was like his own daughter. The party would last at least one full week. Hannah would stay in Tiberias, and the rest of the family would return to the village they called home. He wished his little sister would surprise him, but he didn't expect her. She simply didn't like traveling. Now looking at his granddaughter, he prayed Sofie would change her mind. Hannah and Sofie had always had a special bond and he thought Sofie could discover why Hannah's eyes held no light. At least he didn't detect the sparkle of excitement in most brides-to-be. The young man who had made his intentions known over a year ago was from a good family, a successful family and Hannah would be well taken care of. *So why did his heart stir when he thought about her living with the boy's family instead of her own?* The answer was easy for Scout. Family. He was selfish and protective of every member. *How could he protect his granddaughter from so far away?* He couldn't. And he didn't like it. His wife knew it. His brothers also, and he suspected Hannah thought she was causing this quiet grief in his spirit. Perhaps that is what chased the light from her eyes. He let out a heavy sigh.

"What's wrong?" Pella laid her hand on his forehead out of habit.

"Nothing," Scout said. "I'm tired. My brothers will be here soon and I'm ready to go home."

— Sofie —

"Our granddaughter will be sad to see us leave," she said.

Scout drew his wife close which still could make her blush. "What is it, Scout? Why are you troubled?" Pella asked.

"Your eyes," he answered.

"My eyes," Pella repeated.

"They are clear and bright. I remember how they used to turn dark gray, like a stormy sky," he laughed. "Our granddaughter's eyes are not clear or bright."

Pella turned to look at Hannah. She was sitting staring out the window, the sun resting in her lap. Pella had noticed, but she knew nerves could get the best of a person. Her parents were gone. She only had her grandparents and some things you just couldn't share. She needed her Aunt Sofie. All her life her aunt had singled her out, a young girl surrounded by boys and large men who frightened most. Sofie would make her honey cakes and go on special walks or to a place where they would sit among the flowers and enjoy the sweet cakes without the noise of all the brothers, fathers, uncles, and yes, even a grandfather. Pella had watched them through the years. Sofie was more like a mother to the girl. Hannah practically grew up in the house alongside Sofie until her great-grandparent's health began to fail. Sofie's attention was then focused on them with little time for her niece.

When Hannah returned from Tiberias last summer, Sofie was the first person she ran to inform her of her engagement. Sofie had wept over her, happy tears, but Pella thought a few sad tears were also shed that her mother's namesake would be leaving. The women would be on their own, separated by hills and valleys, those of which Hannah knew Sofie wouldn't cross, and she would be by the sea surrounded by strangers. This is the panic Pella thought her husband now saw in his granddaughter's eyes. Reality was setting in, and the young girl was doing her best to hide it from her loving grandfather. Everyone knew their story. She would be living in the very city where her grandparents met but it wasn't home for them either. Her great-grandfather Stone met Hannah there, and now she met James, her future husband. They would become one in a few short days and her heart had almost beat out of her chest, not from the excitement of the celebration, but that she would be separated from her family. Hannah knew her grandfather

Chapter Five

studied her even now while she sat in silence with her thoughts. She was grateful he had stayed all this time, but he would also go home. Soon.

It wasn't the sun streaming in that made her feel the sudden rush of heat on her face and neck. She was scared. For the first time in her life, her big protective family wouldn't be close watching over her as they had done her entire life. James and his family had their business. They were not going anywhere! She thought there were plenty of fishermen to take James' place and his family could spare one man, but James loved the sea and wouldn't be moved. She had cried one night when she built up enough courage to tell him her concern about being away from her family. He only reminded her that's the way it is, and this wasn't or shouldn't be a surprise to her, and that she had agreed to this arrangement. *Arrangement?* He didn't like her questioning his words and tried to calm her down by coming as close to her as he could, telling her they would have a good life.

She didn't think so. For the past year, she didn't even see him except for the Sabbath. He prepared his nets all morning, ate his meals with his family and the men who worked for them, and then checked his nets again for tears upon his return, and then sold his fish. She had waited on several occasions at the smelly dock, hoping to speak with him only for him to tell her he needed rest. This wasn't the life she dreamed about. This wasn't the life she wanted. She felt trapped!

Her giant family towered over everyone the past week directing them where to place tents and of course what food would be prepared, what musicians would be hired, and all she needed to do was rest and enjoy the process. But she wasn't enjoying anything. If it wasn't for her grandparents, she thought she would simply scream and find her way back home to her hills.

And her family. And Aunt Sofie who was alone. This thought made tears well up in her eyes. She wondered if there was a James in her life who wanted to take her away from the village. Perhaps that's why she never left. Maybe she was afraid she would never return. She understood. Especially now. Her grandfather stood. She didn't have to look; his large frame had its own distinct sound. She forced a smile so he wouldn't see her distress.

"Grandfather, are you hungry? Shall we go to a cafe today?" Hannah asked.

"What a great idea!" Scout replied. "We'll go for a walk."

"I'll stay here," Pella called over her shoulder.

"Your brothers may show up early," she said. "Besides, I have plenty to do. You two go and enjoy the afternoon."

Pella knew her husband. He would take his granddaughter to the hill where his father spent many days gazing out at the sea and talking to God. This was a special place and Scout hoped Hannah would sense the tranquility that rested there, and the safety of her words wouldn't leave the confines of the hill.

"Grandfather, are we going to your cave?" Hannah laughed as she pointed towards the hidden rock.

"We can if you would like to, but I thought we would sit in the open air today," he smiled.

"Do you and grandmother sneak up here and reminisce?"

Scout gave her a wink, "Sometimes."

"Grandfather! I was only kidding!" she laughed.

Scout stopped. "There's no kidding when it comes to love, and the one God has joined you with."

He saw the hint of panic again, so he grabbed her hand in comfort. "Yes, we come and reminisce. Often," he added which made Hannah laugh.

They were both glad the clouds decided to arrive early and the climb today more tolerable. They settled in the familiar place where dreams were realized, and the call of home breathed its greetings. Scout purposed to be still so Hannah could simply inhale the sea and clear her mind.

"Grandfather, you know how much I love you," she started.

"As I you my child," Scout answered.

"I miss father," and the tears began.

Scout groaned inside. Caleb was his only son named after his uncle. Hannah was only seven when he died from an infection. His wife drew her last breath the following year, most thought from a broken heart. Scout and Pella raised Hannah as their own. Sofie took the young girl under her wing while they both watched over the house of Stone and their aging family members. Hannah, like Sofie, never grew tired of the stories of her relatives and was only sad that her father departed the earth to not also be included in the legacy. Sofie had scolded her

— Chapter Five —

the day she said this reminding her she was a part of this heritage. And her children would be also. That day Hannah grew even closer to her aunt Sofie and mourned not only the loss of her parents but that her aunt didn't have children of her own. She felt a heavy responsibility to continue the legacy, and now sitting on the hill where her great-grandfather Stone had his *awakening*, she swallowed her anxiety hoping her grandfather wouldn't notice.

She sat perfectly still; another practice that had been passed down. Aunt Sofie told her it was written in the Holy Scriptures. *"Be still and know that I am God."* She heard it all her life and she tried to keep this tradition in her daily life as well. It was difficult. Especially now when she wanted to stand and burst out every thought she was thinking.

"Go ahead," Scout said out of nowhere.

"What did you say, Grandfather?"

"Go ahead," he smiled.

"Grandfather, how do you know so much?"

Hannah did stand and he watched her demeanor grow from calmness to animated while she talked with her hands for the next hour pouring out her doubts and conflicts on her great-grandfather's hill.

"I don't think I love James," she barely said. She looked at her grandfather to see if he was surprised, shocked, or angry.

"Speak your mind," he encouraged her.

"I don't like it here," she said. "His family...well...they're not *our* family. They seem to have no time for me. Everyone is so busy with this fishing business, and I feel alone most days. If it wasn't for you and grandmother, I think...."

"You think?" Scout wanted her to spill out everything in her heart.

"When James is finished with his work, he stops at the inn and drinks with his brothers and hired men. I think maybe he drinks too much." She stole another look at him. She would recognize the clenched jaw of disappointment.

"I hear when he gets home, his brothers are loud and they're usually laughing and joking around and...."

"And?" Scout prayed she would continue.

"I don't like it, Grandfather. They are filled with wine and then they fall asleep most days without even eating or they just shove down the food we prepared and practically fall asleep in their bowls! This is not the life I want to live! What shall I do Grandfather? You have spent so much money! James will never leave here! I may never see my hills again! I won't have any family members close by. I can't sit and stare out the window all day waiting for my husband to come home full of wine only to gulp down a cold dinner and fall asleep at the table! Oh, Grandfather, what have I done? What am I going to do? Uncle Joshua and Samuel are on the way with their families, and this is all happening too fast! I want to go home, Grandfather!" She collapsed in his arms and cried until the last of the sun ducked beneath the sea.

1Scout tossed and turned the entire night. There were laws. The family of James wouldn't accept Hannah simply saying she changed her mind. Pella lay awake listening to her husband mumble his frustration.

She spoke in the darkness, "There's a way Scout, but we need to hurry."

His wife never surprised him but in the quiet of the late evening, he began laughing. He pulled her closer. "Tell me."

"I will need to look up some old friends," Pella said.

"Some of the women who used to come to the cafe are now the ones who know all of the city's secrets," she continued. "We need to find out if James had a prior commitment. Truly, it's the only way unless...."

"Unless?" Scout asked.

"You know," she said.

"We can't follow him around so let me see what I can find out. Now, go to sleep. There's much to do in the next few days and I will not leave our granddaughter here if this isn't where she wants to be." Pella blew out the lamp finalizing her words and that the evening was over.

Scout dreamed of a young Pella darting through the people making her way down the docks, zigzagging around baskets and nets making everyone dizzy. She could still move as fast as when he first met her. People remembered her. They remembered Wolf. They also remembered she married one of the giant men and more would fill the streets soon as they traveled for the wedding of one of the most prominent families in the fishing business.

Pella hoped she could find some older women looking to release the things they saw when no one thought they took notice. The local men would be filled with wine while the older women whose bones ached from age sat at their windows with the curtains pulled for a

Chapter Five

glimpse of lives that were carefree, and without pain that kept them up half the night. She would go to the local part of the city where those same women gathered, observing the fishermen they had watched grow up to be skilled fishermen. The men would place small bundles of sardines in their baskets and even a few coins. The women were grateful, and the late mornings often turned into afternoons of storytelling.

Pella hurried to the first cafe where she saw three women sitting at the outside tables. It didn't take long for the older women to chatter on about all those who called Tiberias home and had lived there for ages. Pella smiled all the way home anxious to tell Scout what the women divulged.

"He was previously engaged and had a commitment! I'm certain Hannah has no idea, and the family has kept this from us," Pella said.

Scout thought about his father. He had brought a woman home years before, but his mother knew everything, and it was his past and she only thought about their future.

"I will speak to James' father," Scout said.

Hannah was found sitting at the window again when both Scout and Pella walked in. She looked at her grandfather who stood confident of the outcome both he and his granddaughter desired. She ran into his arms.

"Are we going home, Grandfather?" She didn't wait for him to answer. She grabbed Pella's hands and asked her to help her start packing.

"Child, wait," Scout said warmly. "I will speak with James also, but you cannot enter into this covenant with him."

"Has he been unfaithful to me?" Hannah wanted to know.

"Grandmother, what did you find out?" Hannah was young, but not naïve.

"Sit down Hannah," Pella said.

Hannah was impatient. She hoped and prayed her grandfather figured out a way to release her from this betrothal. Pella saw the girl tapping her feet, anxious for resolution. Pella needed to take her time. Scout needed to confirm the women's gossip. Hannah needed to tell her plainly she didn't love James and wanted to return home no matter the consequences. Pella set warm broth and bread on the table. Her granddaughter looked thin. She would need all her strength for the next few days.

"Your grandfather will come home once he's certain of what he wants to say to James," Pella told her. "We need to be careful."

"Careful? I don't understand," Hannah replied.

"The bride price has been paid," Pella said. "And we don't want to make a false accusation."

"Accusation? Grandmother! You must tell me what James has done!"

Hannah was restless and the foot tapping sounded more like a wild animal trying to escape a trap. Pella knew her husband trusted her. What they didn't know was how Hannah would react. They didn't want her to storm out and approach James with angry words and cause a scene with his family. They were well known and respected in the community.

"Grandmother, please, I need to know. Now." Hannah pleaded with her.

"James committed himself to another. Your grandfather is searching for the family of the girl to make sure this is true and how long ago this promise was given." She took Hannah's hand that now shook along with her feet.

"Did he ever speak of another? Someone from his past? A first love?" Pella hated to ask.

"No Grandmother," Hannah answered.

The tapping came to a stop and Hannah withdrew her hand from hers. "Do you believe this is true Grandmother?"

Pella did. James was a handsome man, probably used to getting his own way, and even though he worked hard all day, there were certain benefits that successful families seemed to rule over others with promises of a better life casually mentioned over cups of wine to gullible young girls. These promises might have become misinterpreted as an exaggerated tale for the town's mature women to repeat. Scout would find out. They just needed to wait.

"If it's true, how do you think James will react when confronted?" Pella asked her granddaughter.

Hannah didn't know. She wondered why he even sought her out. But he had during one of their trips to the coast. He was so sure of himself, his skin dark from the sea and his genuine smile. He traveled to their village several times and her grandparents brought her to Tiberias for an extended stay so the young couple could determine

Chapter Five

their fondness for one another. That had been several months ago, and Hannah felt like she didn't know James at all. She had no idea how he would react. He may shrug his shoulders, wish her well, and head off to the nearest inn to drink his sorrows away, or his pleasure that he wasn't obligated to marry her after all. She was biting her nails now trying to determine if there would be an outburst or indifference.

Oh, she wished Aunt Sofie were here! She would know what to do, and what to say, and make her feel special no matter what the outcome. She could tell her anything. Some things she wasn't comfortable speaking about to her grandparents. They had been so wonderful to her, so loving and caring. She didn't want to disappoint them. She didn't think they would understand the deep stirrings of her heart, the fears, and the unanswered questions. Aunt Sofie would. They were very much alike. Aunt Sofie had deep stirrings. Hannah didn't think her aunt feared leaving the village, she just had no desire to. But there were unanswered questions. Hannah was certain of that. She had only asked her aunt one time if she ever liked a boy. Sofie fought the smile that formed on its own. The boy wasn't real. He only showed up in her dreams, a faint memory that became blurrier and obscure the older she got. But that day, sitting in the flowers eating fresh honey cakes, Hannah saw pure sadness on her aunt's face, and that faraway look of a love that would never be realized. Hannah had dropped her cake and rushed into her aunt's arms apologizing for asking such a personal question. She never asked her again, but she caught her often staring in the same direction of where Hannah thought she found that love. Now she sat in the same chair day after day thinking of the love she thought she knew but was also lost. Lost at sea, lost on the docks, lost at the inns, and now perhaps lost with another.

"I hope Grandfather returns soon," Hannah finally said. "I truly don't know what to expect. I only know I'm terribly homesick and I miss Aunt Sofie."

Sofie and Aaron were on the roof. Aaron brought his parchment with him. The room had grown warm with her cooking fire and their emotions neither wanted to confess. He asked her to stop for a moment before suggesting they finish on Simon's rooftop. She had started the day telling him about Benjamin again and Kezi, and the special relationship they had. It was Sofie's retelling of the day Kezi had given the small boy a braided wristband to wear with two red beads. The boy had run to the old merchant Simon and presented his *promise* that he and Kezi would always be together. Both Aaron and Sofie had sniffled at the boy's innocence and words and Aaron knew the story was difficult. Sofie had no son of her own.

She talked about Hannah, her niece, but Aaron knew nothing could compare to one's own child. He wanted to embrace her at that moment but wouldn't. They didn't know each other well enough for this closeness. Falling asleep together was a different story. It wasn't intentional and they both understood the circumstances. Her grandfather Simon looked to his uncle Benjamin as any boy would look to his father and Aaron hoped his sons thought him as faithful. Finn pulled at his heartstrings. He knew his youngest followed him. He hadn't said much to him about Sofie, but Finn was old enough to understand friendship is where relationships started. And he did tell him Sofie was a friend. He figured that was all his son needed to know to make the likelihood of a more permanent involvement with the cake woman.

He walked to the edge and looked toward his home. He missed his family, but what he was experiencing with Sofie, reliving her family's past excited him like no other story he ever heard. She wove her words with love and wonder, and he knew all she told him was true. He wanted to climb to the young boy Benjamin's lookout, but he wanted Sofie to join him. She was waiting for him to continue to write. She seemed fascinated with the letters and symbols placed on his parchments. She began to recognize a few letters and he would write small words for her to study and then read to him each day. She was shy to do so at first, but now she was ready for longer words she told him this afternoon.

He walked back to Simon's pillows and made himself comfortable. He brought no wine with him. It was too vulnerable of a day. Sofie's skin was warm from her cooking, and she smelled of spices and freshly

Chapter Five

baked bread. He didn't dare try and smell her hair. He knew he would become undone. He sat opposite her so he could see every detail of her face in the sun, and he prayed his pen would capture every emotion of her expressions while thrilling him with faith and persecution, love and tragedy, babies and joy, sorrow, and loss, but mostly he wanted to please her in this request she made of him.

"My family is challenging. Wait! Don't write that down. Maybe that isn't the right word."

Aaron could see a frown start to appear and saw the first hint of lines on her forehead while she concentrated and searched for a different word.

"I guess challenging is the right word. I only meant they were faced with so many things in each of their lives. I think this village and the people they met found them challenging to know, or perhaps they felt they couldn't live up to their standards. Oh, I'm afraid I'm not making much sense. Maybe we should stop for the evening," she told him.

It was early. The moon wouldn't greet them for hours. Aaron thought he should try and help her say what she was struggling to convey to him.

"Shall I go downstairs and bring some wine?" he asked. He didn't want the day to end now. *What would he do all night?*

"Yes, Aaron, that would be nice." She waited until she heard him going through her brother's door. She smoothed her hair after she took off her covering. She wiped her hands on the end of the blanket and bit her lips for some color.

Aaron had a cup in her hand before she could make any other adjustments to their seating arrangements. She didn't have to; he sat right next to her.

"To your challenging family!" Aaron toasted.

Sofie laughed and the rest of the daylight was filled with the characteristics of each family member. It was personal and Aaron thought it too intimate for his parchment. He noticed Sofie had his papers neatly stacked with a beaded pillow propped on top to prevent her stories from reaching readers before they were finished. The rooftop spoke to him. It was a man's sanctuary he reckoned at the end of a full day. They were strong, faithful men who took pride in their tiny community of believers who trusted God first and trusted the men to follow His ways.

He could imagine Simon standing with his sons, Stone, and Caleb, looking down at the fires of the village, everyone living in peace, the watchmen signaling any trouble on the horizon. And there had been plenty of hardships. The men they trusted with their lives were just as faithful and he admired each one. Simon and Benjamin had been boys when left with such a tremendous responsibility watching over the women. Apart from the Romans, Aaron was certain no other foes would come near this village. He swore he had a dream about the man Elias. *Oh, how he wished he could have met this man!* He hoped Sofie would tell him more even though he wasn't a family member, they considered him as such, and Aaron thought rehearsing the attributes of the men in this family could be the reason why no one felt they lived up to the standards they set. Maybe this is why no man had ever approached Sofie.

He couldn't look at her right now. He was certain she would misread his eyes. It wasn't pity. Now he struggled for the right word. He hoped her oldest brother Scout might be delayed in his travels. He enjoyed the convenience of the village. Finn wouldn't understand. He had told his family their entire lives that living above the small community was more to his liking. He realized his selfishness in this statement. His family was just as challenging. He thought without a mother for his sons, he became more involved in ensuring their needs were met and there was no reason to venture into the village. The elders who sat at the gate were the same men he was now writing about. They *were* intimidating. He didn't need the scrutiny, he had enough from his own clan. His parents lived long enough to help him raise his children and explain why they retreated to the caves. It was simply the preferred living space. They didn't complicate the reason with idle words. He was happy others had decided to live among them so his sons would have wives and children of their own.

Finn was his concern. He didn't seem interested in any cave girls. He chuckled a little at this thought. Sofie came close to light a lamp and refill his cup. Now he got a whiff of her hair in the soft breeze. He wasn't sure what she rubbed in it, but he was thankful she removed her covering so he could watch it dance this evening.

"Shall I get us some olives and a little cheese?" she asked.

"Do you need help?" Aaron replied.

Chapter Five

"No, sit and relax. I won't be long."

She hoped the women were not gathered outside of her courtyard. She would have to leave her brother's door, go to her own house, and then return to Scout's. And it was dark now. She barely opened the door to peek outside. She had removed her shoes and hurried across the space. She fixed a small plate and raced around her room lighting lamps and running her fingers through her hair with a dab of cassia oil. She was running low on the pungent spice and wondered if Aaron would notice the fresh smell. She hoped he wouldn't think she did it for him. But she did. She dabbed a drop on both her wrists and practically ran up the stairs.

A few olives fell off the plate, but she didn't stop to retrieve them. She hoped she wasn't breathing hard, but she did seem winded. She was more concerned about the women seeing her barefoot, hair loose and flowing down her back with her cheeks flushed from wine and Aaron's company. It reminded her of another story, and she hurried up the last few steps.

Aaron was indeed relaxed, lounging on his left side, the solitary lamp casting its soft glow on his face. He looked so peaceful. He looked strong. He looked just as confident on this rooftop as her grandfather and father. She took a breath before joining him back on the pillows. Aaron started to sit up, but she shook her head and her hair moved with the wind again and he felt lightheaded. He could smell the cassia oil she had to have just reapplied. *What was happening?* This was too familiar. This was a man and a woman becoming close in their mature years. There was no chaperone. They did not need watchful eyes. His heart was racing. Sofie was beautiful! She didn't know how beautiful she was. He wondered if any man ever told her.

She set the plate in front of him and sat in the same place. He waited for her to settle before reaching for any food. The air had changed. The light of the moon seduced his thoughts. The atmosphere was charged with her cassia oil-scented hair and before he dwelled on more improper thoughts, he reached for a handful of olives. He then gobbled down a sizable piece of cheese. Both seemed salty and he gulped down his wine. Sofie only stared wondering if he was feeling ill, but she refilled his cup again at his prompting. It was uncomfortable and they both knew the reason why which only made Aaron eat more salty olives which made him drink more wine until Sofie asked if she should get another wineskin.

The moonlight made her hair shimmer, and everything was becoming cloudy with her scent making him dizzy. As much as he wanted to stay and enjoy the evening and taste the salt on Sofie's lips when he snuck a kiss, he wouldn't. It could change everything. He didn't trust himself on Simon's pillows, so he sat up and stretched as if he was tired and ready to retire for the evening. Sofie looked confused. He prayed she wasn't offended by his actions. He practically consumed the entire plate of cheese without giving her a second thought that she might want to linger and talk into the night. She should have never applied more oil to her hair and on her skin. It was intoxicating and she had no clue how taken he was with her.

He didn't understand why she never married. One day soon he would come right out and ask her. He felt foolish now trying to act as if she didn't matter or rather that her womanly charms had no bearing or influenced his behavior. All he knew was he had drunk too much. His hands were wet with sweat and cheese remnants and before he said something or did something out of character that would embarrass both of them, he needed to end the evening.

"I'm sorry Sofie. I didn't realize how much wine I've consumed. It has made me sleepy this evening. Please forgive me but I must end this day. Thank you for everything. We'll start again in the morning." He helped her rise and picked up the empty plate.

Sofie took it without looking at him and simply told him goodnight, that she had enjoyed the day also and hoped he rested well. He watched her head for the stairs. He couldn't even walk her down. The passageway was too narrow. He wanted to grab her and pull her into his arms and kiss her over and over again proclaiming his desire and admiration. He would tell her how beautiful she was inside and out. *Would she be shocked, or would she welcome his advance?* Tonight wasn't the night to find out.

Sofie couldn't stop her tears from falling. She prayed Aaron wouldn't hear her cries. She didn't understand what happened. They were simply ending the day on her grandfather's roof like they had before. What was different? She knew. She had expectations this time. *Why would she take the trouble of smoothing her hair?* She hoped for

Chapter Five

Aaron to be attracted to her. But he wasn't, and to not offend her he had drank cup after cup of wine and gobbled down a plate of cheese so he wouldn't have to pretend he liked her. She was the one who sat next to him. He hadn't moved. *Oh, what a fool I am!* If he wanted to be close, he would have watched his consumption and made small talk as before. She misread him. There was something in the way he looked tonight when she returned with the food that made her so calm, but that soon left when he did everything but shoo her away with a wave of his hand. She wiped the plate and sat at her father's table wondering how she could face him in the morning.

 Aaron couldn't breathe. He stood at the short wall of the roof and inhaled deeply for several minutes. All he could smell was Sofie. He was so mad at himself! He needed to get a grip. He ruined their evening. Especially after the earlier conversation about the two red beaded bracelet. A promise of two hearts that would always be together. *Aaaggghhh!* Maybe that's why Sofie was so intoxicating. The talk of closeness and bonding secured on the wrist of a young boy. Who was he kidding? It was the wine and food, the stories and rooftop of Simon, the night air, and the soft glow of lamps. It was the woman Sofie and her dancing hair and perfumed skin. It was her innocence and pure heart. He was ashamed of his actions and swore he would never allow himself to get so close to her again that he lost his mind. He would purpose to keep this friendship as friends, nothing more. He would not bring dishonor to Simon's roof. He would stand knowing he could face her brothers without any hesitation or remorse. Perhaps he should run down and apologize now. It had only been a few minutes and the night *was* young.

 Once again, he asked himself who he was kidding. He wanted to see her and run his fingers through her hair and hoped her scent remained until morning. He found himself pacing. He stopped suddenly. *The watchmen! Could they see him? Had they been observing Simon's roof the entire evening? Would they report to Scout the disaster of the night? He ducked down like a little child. He was an absolute mess! Sofie!*

 "Yes?"

 He turned so quickly he lost his balance. The moon waited to see what he would do. He stood to his full height and reached her within seconds. "Sofie."

Sofie

The stars were falling, the wind stopped and the last of the oil released its life. He was holding her close, mumbling into her hair, his embrace warm and strong and Sofie hoped he would never release her. He smelled like a vineyard ready for harvest and she found herself wrapping her arms around him to draw him closer. He responded with more mumbling, words that she couldn't hear clearly but there was no doubt they were soft and endearing. She was becoming familiar with everything about him. His voice was deep and vibrating her ears. His hands were as wide as her back, and she had never experienced this closeness. His beard brushed the side of her face, and it took her breath away. It seemed he drew even closer if it were possible. Never had she been in a situation like this. She found herself resting her head on his chest, her hands beginning to explore his shoulders and there were more unintelligible words uttered. She began to shiver at both the excited new feeling and the desert air that now made its presence known.

"Sofie," he spoke her name again, this time with much affection.

She lifted her head and they looked at each other as a man and a woman, not as friends and she found herself in a dream-like state as he kissed her. It was her first kiss. He was so gentle and respectful. Now it was her words that couldn't be understood, but Aaron heard his name beseeching him to kiss her again. And again. Sofie didn't remember him walking her down the narrow passageway, but she was certain he kissed her again at her door for all those who might be watching.

Chapter Six

Aaron slept under Simon's stars. He didn't toss and turn, he slept soundly once he fell into his slumber. The climb back up to the roof took a lot of effort. He didn't want the evening to end. He didn't want to leave Sofie. He didn't know what they would say to each other in the morning. Step by step he replayed the short rooftop rendezvous in his mind. It was as if he were directing a play or a puppet show for the village children. *The man was in anguish...he thought he heard the woman crying...the night was young...he paced and paced trying to decide what he should do...the woman had captured his heart...all his senses had come alive...he called out her name in desperation...the woman suddenly appeared.* He would have continued this saga but as he put one foot in front of another, he noticed olives scattered on the steps. How appropriate he said to himself as he reached down thinking he should pick them up. The olives were all over the place just like his thoughts. *Is she sleeping now? Is she thinking of him? Did he go too far?* He stared into the dark sky wondering if he should go home. Nothing would be the same. How could it be? He took advantage. Her brothers would know as soon as they saw the permanent smile on his face. *Finn.* He would know also. What a wretched man I am he said aloud. I have brought confusion to this woman. *Oh, my dear Sofie, what have I done?*

Sofie prepared her bread and took the jar of honey from the shelf. She would make her honey cakes today. It was a special occasion! *She had been kissed!* She found herself almost floating from room to room as the dawn said hello in soft shades of peach. She listened for Aaron. Surely, he wasn't still asleep. She heard him pacing. His feet were heavy, and she was very familiar with the men of her family using the rooftop for their prayers and meditations. *Why was he pacing?* That action was usually reserved for worry and decision making. Her imagination reared its ugly head and she worked herself into a mess before the sun filtered in her window to dispel the dark thoughts. She heard other young women through the years questioning motives and true affection but now it was her turn. *Oh, my Lord! He felt sorry for me! He kissed me out of pity! He knows I never married. He felt guilty ending such a pleasant evening. Why did I go back up there? Fool! He must have felt obligated to show me kindness.* But this was more than kindness. Boy was he dramatic! He poured it on thick! Poor Sofie he must have thought. Let me make her night. He had his way and then escorted me quickly back to my home so he could do as he pleased the rest of the evening. What was the kiss at my door? *So, I won't forget how wonderful he was. How many men would give poor old Sofie something to dream about?* Everyone knew the things said about her. That cake woman just sits and rocks in her chair. No man ever wanted to marry her. Poor, poor Sofie. All she does is make honey cakes for the children. It's all the attention she ever receives. Such a shame.

She was trembling now. She was sad, mad, disappointed, and grieved, and she was at a loss as to what to do. Aaron would be knocking at her door as if nothing happened ready to listen to her dribble on while he wrote *her* letters because poor Sofie couldn't read or write, and no other man took an interest. *Oh, how dare he feel sorry for me!* She was Sofie, daughter of Stone, son of Simon, son of Selah! This village was witness to faith and perseverance! She came from a family of strength and honor! Why if it wasn't for her family, Aaron, and his family, whoever they were or wherever they lived, probably wouldn't have survived! Let him fend off Roman soldiers who deserted their post and roamed the hills. Her family did and they were victorious in ways Aaron had no idea. *Oh, she was getting worked up!* She needed to calm down. She couldn't let him see how upset he made her just thinking about his false affection. She'd have to pretend the kiss meant nothing! She would give him a taste of his own medicine, but she wouldn't give him a taste of her honey cakes. She practically threw the jar back on the shelf thankful it didn't break. She stood perfectly still listening. Perhaps he left in the middle of the night ashamed of his

Chapter Six

behavior toward her. *Did he think she wouldn't figure out his game of deceit?* Now the tears fell. It was *Aaron*. She couldn't believe this about him. He was a good man and his goodness to make her feel special just got out of control. Too much wine. Yes, that's what happened. She would act as if nothing took place on her grandfather's roof. She would dismiss his advances. Her heart ached. She halfway smiled thinking of her father telling her it was another life lesson. Now, she hoped her brother Scout would hurry home so the hill man would have to leave, and she wouldn't be the one to ask him to.

Aaron heard the village wake up. He knew Sofie had been awake for some time. She would be waiting. His empty wineskin mocked him now strewn across the pillows reminding him of his reckless actions. *Why did she return to the roof?* He couldn't ask her. He didn't even give her a chance to tell him. Perhaps she left her head covering or a bracelet slipped off her wrist and she came to retrieve the item, and he had marched right over and took her into his arms and held her hostage. She didn't have a choice! Yet when he buried his face into her perfumed hair, she had responded. *There was no doubt, so why was he tormenting himself in the hot morning sun?* He was slow in his movements preparing for an uncomfortable greeting at Stone's table. He would look into her eyes and know if things were fine, and no words needed to be spoken except for those she desired him to write down. He found another olive on the way to the door which brought the only smile today. The old women were huddled like hens protecting their chicks when he opened the door.

"Shalom," he said and kept his head down. He wouldn't give them the opportunity to read his thoughts. They were still scattered making his head throb! Sofie's door was propped open, and he breathed a sigh of relief. He wouldn't have to knock, and he simply announced himself.

"Aaron, come in," she called to him. She knew the women were watching.

"Good morning." Her back was to him, so he sat at his usual place at the table.

"I made some food," she said. "I thought we could continue today with Benjamin."

She never turned around so he would have to wait to see her eyes. "Yes, of course, that will be fine."

— *Sofie* —

She was purposely taking her time arranging the breakfast plate. She took warm bread and took a deep breath before turning to greet him properly.

"Good morning, I trust you slept well," she didn't give him eye contact.

Finally, she sat across from him. He smiled as he reached for the bread and looked directly at her. He saw indifference. He didn't want to stare but he needed to make sure she hadn't shed more tears this early morning.

"The bread is good, thank you," he said.

"You're welcome," Sofie replied.

She said no more, and he shifted his position. "Did you sleep well?"

"Yes, I'm fine," she answered.

"I didn't ask if you were fine," he was getting irritated.

"Aaron, I slept, I'm fine, nothing is wrong. I just want to finish the letters."

"And pretend nothing happened?" he asked.

"That's an interesting word you use Aaron," she said.

"What did I say?" He didn't like this conversation.

"Pretend," she answered.

"Sofie, can we talk about last night?"

"No, Aaron. I don't wish to discuss it. I don't know what I was thinking. I shouldn't have returned after you said goodnight. I was foolish and it led to both of us now having regret," she said.

"Regret," he repeated.

She tried not to look at him. She found this impossible. His eyes were sincere, warm, and gold, but he was still a stranger in some sense and her guard was up.

"I believe we both regret what happened last night," she said.

"Please Aaron, I'm very uncomfortable speaking about this. We were both at fault. We both had one cup of wine too many perhaps which led to the circumstances."

"Circumstances? That's how you see what transpired on the roof, regret, and circumstance?" He was hurt by her words. He genuinely cared for her and thought the feelings were mutual.

"I'm only saying, well, I'm asking you to please just forget what took place," she answered.

Chapter Six

"That is what you truly desire Sofie, to forget?"

"Yes," she barely whispered.

She wouldn't look at him. She was embarrassed, he thought. She had allowed herself to be unguarded in the middle of the night with no concern about how this might affect their friendship. Now he felt as if he did indeed take advantage of the moon, the slight breeze, and the empty house.

"It's forgotten," he said.

"It will never happen again. Sofie, please look at me." He waited for her to lift her eyes to his.

"I'm sorry Sofie."

Sofie sat at her father's table as composed as she could. *It will never happen again were the only words she heard. Never.* She quickly picked up a piece of bread so no other sounds would escape her mouth, especially when she wanted Aaron to hold her and profess his love and tell her how wonderful she was and wanted her at his side.

"I'm sorry too Aaron," she found herself saying. "I agree, it will never happen again."

The rest of the day was spent with both avoiding as much eye contact as possible, Aaron with his head down writing her words, but today her words were just words. Life seemed to have left them and he never wanted to make her feel this way again. He scolded himself once again under his breath and cleared his throat.

"Perhaps we should take a break," he said.

"Yes, that's a good idea. I want to lie down," she said.

He didn't ask if she was well. She already told him she slept and was fine. "I think I'll do the same," he didn't know what else to say. The roof would be hot, and he didn't want her to hear him pacing and groaning his regret as she referred to it.

"I think I'll go home," he stated.

"Home?" she looked surprised.

"Just to check in with my family and I'll be back before sunset," he told her.

She could only sit there. Her mind was numb and active at the same time. She wanted to shout at him to hurry back and then wondered if he would return. She waited until he entered her brother's house and then ran up the stairs to her roof. She sat on the floor until she heard him open the door. She carefully rose to peek over the wall. He carried no belongings, and she sighed her relief. She didn't understand this conflict. She knew one thing – she didn't like it. Aaron obviously didn't like it either or he wouldn't journey to his hill to avoid more stressful small talk. She didn't even know what she told him today, but his pen was never in such a hurry to write down her memories. She couldn't check because she couldn't read, and this frustration had her pacing like him. She stopped and stared at the exact place where she had received her first real kiss. She touched her lips now with her hand and recalled every sensation. She sank to her knees troubled by her longings.

Lord, I don't know how to handle these emotions. I'm frightened. I want to kiss him again. But You heard him. He said it would never happen again. Just speaking the words out loud brought a fresh set of tears and she continued to pour out her anguish. *Why now Lord? I have been happy alone. Making my cakes. I don't know anything about loving a man. My brothers, my family, that's different. I feel safe when he is here. I've never been afraid Lord, but I have missed the affection of a man. My brothers have always doted on me, but this is not the same. My father and grandfather of course gave me affection, but this is not the same either. Why have You put this passion in my heart? Help me to get over this! He said NEVER.* She cried herself to sleep.

Finn ran to greet his father when he spotted him on the familiar path. Something was wrong. His father's head was hung low, and he seemed deep in concentration. He carried nothing, which made him more anxious to find out why he was making the climb in the heat of the day.

Aaron of course saw his son. The sun glistened off the large knife Finn carried. He had to decide what he would tell him fast as Finn was sliding down the hill sideways.

"Father! I've missed you!" Finn greeted him as he always did, making Aaron smile.

"What's wrong?" He could tell his father was troubled.

Chapter Six

"Nothing is wrong son, I just wanted to see if the family has any needs. Sabbath is in two days and if there are supplies that are needed, I can bring them."

Finn didn't believe him. It was a first. "We can check with everyone, and I will help you, Father."

"How are things going with the cake...with Sofie?" he asked.

"Fine. I have written several parchments," Aaron said.

"Are you almost finished then?" Finn asked him.

Aaron stopped walking. He didn't know. Maybe Sofie couldn't tolerate him any longer at her father's table, her brother's house, or the roof of her beloved grandfather.

"That of course is up to Sofie and how much she would like to tell me," Aaron finally answered.

Finn wasn't buying anything his father was saying. "Will you stay here for the night?"

Aaron took notice of the sun. He had plenty of time. "No son, I told Sofie I would be back before sunset."

"You write at night?" Finn was trying not to grin.

"Yes, sometimes. Just last night she...." Aaron changed the subject. "Her memories are very special, and I'm honored to help her with this task. And we do talk into the night."

Finn saw something just then in his father's eyes. He had seen the same look before and he searched his mind as they continued up the hill trying to place the time he saw the same solemn gaze. It was when he spoke of his mother. A woman he never met, and his father was mindful of this, careful with his words to not make his son feel bad. They walked in silence until they heard others in the distance.

"Is everyone in good spirits?" Aaron asked his son.

"Yes, Father."

"Do you need anything?"

"We are fine Father," Finn said.

Aaron looked back at the village readying itself for the evening. "I need to go son," he told him. "I'll see you at service."

Yes, his father had something on his mind, and Finn knew his father didn't need any more words for the day. He hugged him once more and then sat on a rock watching him make his way back to the cake woman. He smiled and lifted his face for the last of the sun's rays to say goodnight.

Hannah's skin was getting dark. Sitting at the window with the full sun streaming in had brought a healthy glow. Her grandfather thought that was the only part of her that showed life. Her eyes remained dull, and she hardly smiled. He knew James wasn't to blame. She was homesick. Yes, the small community didn't have a lot to offer, but it gave her everything she desired except James, or rather the love of a man who would be as content as her living in the tiny village. Scout knew she missed her Aunt Sofie. They were the closest thing to sisters each other ever had.

This situation they now found themselves in was delicate. Scout had waited patiently through the young woman's tears telling him James had committed himself to her and her father provided the bride price. She had found James unfaithful. She wouldn't give Scout any more details, but the family had so much difficulty with James that they decided to leave Tiberias and settle further up the coast. Scout thanked the family for their honesty and spoke with the girl's father privately. The man warned Scout that James' family's position and success had proved it almost impossible for anyone to truly listen to their side of the story and the man wouldn't take him to court to redeem his money.

"The man didn't give it back?" Scout asked.

"No," the man said. He grabbed Scout's arms, "It wasn't much, but they could have used it in their home for something. James' father certainly didn't need it."

"So, he's not a man of honor," Scout said.

The man was nervous. "Magdala is a busy fishing town, and everyone knows James."

"Everyone?" Scout questioned.

"Those are your words, not mine, yes?" the man said.

"Yes," Scout answered.

He left angry at the family of James. He imagined the young man did indeed know everyone and his *unfaithfulness* was the talk of many conversations around the harbor and inns that the fishermen frequented. The moon shone on the water, but Scout preferred to travel

Chapter Six

on foot. He tucked his tunic in his belt, secured his weapon, and ran all the way back to Tiberias.

Pella could sense her husband's presence. He would be home soon. Hannah had hardly eaten and when James stopped by to say hello and goodbye before a night of fishing, she looked even more miserable. He told her to stay out of the sun, that he didn't want anyone to think she also had to toil, or that he wasn't capable of providing for her. It took everything inside of Pella to not approach him with a big bowl of hot soup she would accidentally spill on him. She did tell Hannah later of this thought and it was the only laughter the room heard all night.

"Your grandfather will return soon. All will be well," Pella reassured the young girl.

"Grandmother, do you think James will be terribly angry?"

"Let us not think about what we don't know. Your uncles will be arriving with their families, and I doubt James and his father will speak unkind words to all of us," Pella said.

"All of us?" Hannah repeated.

"This family is one," Pella told her. "James and his father will meet with all of us."

Hannah tried to picture the scene. *Would her grandfather send a message for James to meet him here? Would he and his brothers march over to James' father's house and demand the bride price be returned? Would James apologize? Or would he stomp off selfishly?* She was so happy her family would be coming to support her. They wouldn't be disappointed if a wedding wasn't taking place. They would be overjoyed she was coming home! *She couldn't wait! Aunt Sofie would be so surprised!* She fell asleep in her chair in front of the window smiling at the thought of the sun waking her up.

"What did she say? Is it true? Was he committed to her?" Pella kept her voice low as she and Scout made their way to their room.

Scout glanced back at Hannah sleeping in her chair and wondered how her neck didn't hurt. "It's true," he said. "When Joshua and Samuel get here, we'll go speak with James and his father."

"Good," Pella replied. "She's anxious."

"About his reaction?" Scout asked.

"Yes, and anxious to go home," Pella said. "She misses your sister and I miss her too and our house," she added.

"We'll be home soon," he said.

Pella watched him wash his face. "Are you hungry?"

"No, only tired," he answered.

"Do you expect trouble?" she wanted to know.

"I hope not," he said. He saw her smile. She still loved a good adventure.

"There will be no trouble," he assured her, even though he wasn't sure what James or his father might do.

"Honestly Pella, I don't think James will care. He has *some* reputation. His family has a lot of influence, and our sweet Hannah has been kept in the dark."

"It's clear she's unhappy and I will speak to James, man to man. Now, we need rest. Hopefully, my brothers will not be delayed, and we can leave in a few days," he told her.

Pella watched her husband fall into deep sleep. Her mind had come alive this late evening! She knew this city like the back of her hand and wondered if Scout would know if she followed him. She wanted to see the expression on James' face. She would know if he truly ever cared for Hannah. She had all her favorite hiding places memorized and she was still fast as lightning in her movements. She held her hand over her mouth to not laugh and wake up her husband. He seemed to be smiling and she wondered if he knew what she was thinking. Probably. He wouldn't stop her. She turned to extinguish the flame of the lamp when he grabbed her and simply said, "I'll walk slow so you don't have to run."

James had a rough night. He and his men drank their fill and stumbled back to their boats. There would be no fishing. It was Sabbath; however, the men took no notice of the other laws the day presented. He made his way home and climbed the stairs to the room prepared for him and Hannah. He couldn't see a thing, so he lay on the floor and fell promptly asleep. His father's home wasn't too far from the docks, and he woke up to the noise of the morning. He then heard the excited voices of his parents. He went to the edge of the roof to look

Chapter Six

down. A crowd of people had assembled at his father's door. *What has happened?* He wiped his face and tried to clear his eyes. *Scout!* The man looked huge standing front and center. He saw him look up and he was discovered.

"Good morning, everyone," he didn't know who these people were.

His father called him down. This wasn't good. He took his time trying to recall what he and his men did last night. *Hannah.* He peeked over one last time to search for her. He realized it was mostly men standing. Waiting. He also noticed his father looked annoyed. Once he reached his father's side, he greeted Scout again.

"Is Hannah alright? Has something happened? Please, come inside," he didn't want their neighbors to listen in this morning. His head was groggy. Hannah's grandfather had the advantage. He looked refreshed, ready for battle. He stood flanked by two men who looked just like him. *His brothers!* He had met them at their village. They were not smiling, happy to see him, and he hoped he didn't do anything stupid last night.

"We will wait outside," Joshua told his brother.

Scout followed father and son into their home. James' mother seemed nervous scurrying around the men offering anything and everything in the room. Pella watched in amusement from a small window on the opposite side of the room. She stood on a bucket and prayed it wouldn't shift on the ground. Scout saw her but his face remained stern, and he concentrated on choosing the right words.

"James," Scout addressed him without affection. "I have recently found out some information that of course I have verified before coming over today. My granddaughter will not be joining you in marriage and the bride price must be returned. My brothers and their families have only just arrived, and we are all devastated and disappointed. We will return to our village in three days so I will expect full compensation made to our family and you will not see or speak with Hannah."

This is the moment Pella waited for. She didn't breathe. She didn't dare try to adjust her footing. James wouldn't look at Scout. He turned to his father to answer Scout's demands and accusations. Pella thought he looked confused, mad, and relieved at the same time. His mother sat between her husband and son, and she wouldn't lift her eyes either to look at Scout. She was also waiting to see what her husband would say to the grandfather of Hannah. James' father inhaled deeply and leaned in and whispered something to his son which Pella thought was rude. James lowered his head in acknowledgment of the truth.

"Scout, you will have your bride price returned," James' father said. "I will make no apologies for my son. He is a man and will speak for himself."

Scout waited for the boy to look at him. He knew this would be difficult. He also wondered how long his wife could hold her breath balancing on the bucket outside. He couldn't think about her now and let James' family see his amusement.

James wasn't even fully awake. He would like to retreat to his roof and start the day over. He felt trapped, especially with Hannah's relatives standing guard outside. One thing he did know is he didn't want to mess with this family. Both Scout and his father Stone had spent considerable time in the city and certain stories about the men and the infamous Wolf man were retold over many long nights at the local inn. He was at a loss for words. He wouldn't be allowed to see Hannah so he thought he shouldn't bring up her name. He wondered which young girl sold him out. There had been more than one and his father was shocked the first time this happened. Now, he only whispered, "Again James?"

Finally, he sat up straight and looked Scout in the eye as he was taught. "I'm truly sorry and I ask your forgiveness. Hannah deserves better," he said.

Scout nodded, stood, looked briefly toward the window to see the top of his wife's head bob down, and then directed his words to James' father. "Three days."

Pella hurried and ran back to the place where they were staying. This boy James could care less. Even from the distance of the window, she could see his puffy eyes and the smirk he wore. He wasn't sincere. This happened often. She stopped suddenly. What would she tell Hannah? Or rather what would Scout say? Hannah didn't know she snuck out. The families of Joshua and Samuel only went to stand with their brother so James and his family could see they agreed with Scout's assessment. They had arrived early this morning and Scout told them everything. The women surrounded Hannah to offer their love, but he didn't allow them to smother the girl and told his brothers to follow him.

Chapter Six

Pella thought Hannah was relieved it would soon be over and seeing her family members had done wonders for her mood. She was ready to go home. The families agreed to a short rest. No one enjoyed Tiberias. They preferred quiet nights with only distant sounds of the surrounding hills. This city was too noisy, and the women were uncomfortable with the activity found commonplace in the coastal town. They celebrated the reunion and Scout made provisions for their stay. Hannah needed privacy for the next few days to sort out her feelings before journeying home with everyone constantly making sure the girl was alright. Scout hugged his brothers and then shut the door to two of the dearest women in his life. Pella and Hannah. His granddaughter hadn't asked him many questions, but her face was alive now with several. They sat at the table and Scout leaned back in his chair.

"Go ahead, ask," he said.

"Was he surprised?" she asked her grandfather.

"I'm not sure," Scout answered honestly.

"Did he seem upset when you told him he wouldn't see me or be able to speak to me?"

Her eyes were filled with sincerity and he didn't want to hurt her with unnecessary words. Pella couldn't help herself. "Of course, he was upset," she blurted out.

"Grandmother, how do you know?" Hannah asked.

"I saw him through the window!" Pella replied.

"Grandmother!" Hannah laughed.

"Listen to me," Scout looked at both of them. "This is sensitive and even though we have been here all this time, we don't know the family well. James, his father, and their men are never home and are always working. We need to mind our own business. I have given them three days to return our money and then we will go home. Hannah, I don't want you to leave this house until then. Please, no more questions tonight. You will sleep properly, not sitting up in a chair. Our families will rest and prepare for our travel back. Once again, we don't know James' family," he said.

"Grandfather, you're scaring me," Hannah said.

"I'm sorry, I don't mean to worry you. I don't want you to run into James or his hired men because I don't know how he's feeling or what he's thinking. I woke him up. It appeared he had a late night. Now, let's all get a good night's rest." Scout stood so both women would know he was finished talking.

"Thank you, Grandfather, you too Grandmother," Hannah kissed them before going to a separate room.

Scout and Pella waited until she closed the door. Pella examined the rooms that would be filled tomorrow with the family and hoped they wouldn't ask too many questions. Everyone assumed what they wanted. Most times they were wrong. James chose a naïve, young girl from a quiet village that he probably hoped would stay in the shadows and never question anything he did or said. That was his first mistake, Pella thought.

"Did you squander the money?" James' father was in no mood for half-truths.

"I prepared the room," James said while motioning with his head upstairs.

"Son, I won't ask you a third time. "Did you spend all that money?"

"It's gone," James said dryly.

"How dare that man come to our house with a small crowd to embarrass us! What must our neighbors think? Our friends? Our associates? I will not give him my money," he said.

"You will. I promised and gave an oath," his father stated.

"Well, perhaps you should have thought this through," James was smiling now.

His father had enough, "Get out of my house!"

James didn't move.

"Now!" his father said, rising from his chair.

James looked for his mother and his father grew angrier. "Out! Now! Whatever you have to do James, you will pay the man's bride price. You have two days to figure it out." His father moved towards the door.

"You're serious?" James asked. He looked for his mother again hoping she would intervene.

Chapter Six

"Be a man James. Do the right thing, the honorable thing. Two days. Now, please, leave this house before I say anymore."

"Father, wait a minute," James started but when he saw his father's hands almost in fists at his sides, he knew this time his father wouldn't be swayed by his son. "I'll go."

His father followed him out the door blocking his way to go upstairs.

"My things!" James protested.

"You'll get them in two days, son. Now go."

Scout, Joshua, and Samuel sat on top of the hill watching the harbor. Their father had brought them to this exact spot a few times telling his sons this is where he truly learned to be still. They sat in silence as the clouds drifted by and greeted the sea.

"How is Sofie?" Scout asked his brothers. Joshua and Samuel looked at each other waiting for the other to speak. This alarmed Scout. "What is it? Is she well?"

"Oh, she's more than well," Samuel offered.

"Samuel!" Joshua said. "You make it sound as if she...."

"As if she what?" Samuel prodded his brother.

"What are you hiding?" Scout asked Samuel. "How is our sister?"

"She's fine brother. She's writing letters," Samuel told him.

"What? She doesn't know how to write!" Scout looked at Joshua to make sense of their youngest brother's words.

"She has a friend that's helping her," Samuel said.

"Who is this friend?" Scout wanted to know.

"His name is Aaron," Joshua answered. "He lives in the caves. He's a nice man. I believe he knew our father."

"So, he's an older man?" Scout breathed his relief.

"Yes, he's probably around your age," Samuel laughed. The brothers took turns with their innocent insults.

"He's your houseguest," Samuel couldn't wait for his oldest brother's reaction.

"The man is staying in my house?" Scout looked at each of them.

"It was my idea," Samuel said. "He was coming down to the village two to three times a week and so I offered your house while he's helping Sofie. Besides, I thought we'd be away for a month," Samuel added.

Scout knew his brothers were not telling him everything. He would have to trick them into what he wanted to know.

"Hannah is so anxious to go home, especially to see our sister," Scout said.

"This man Aaron will have to go home once we arrive. Do you think Sofie is almost finished? Who is she writing a letter to? She has never left the village!" Scout exclaimed.

"She has asked this man to write about our family," Joshua said. "You know how curious she's been asking our father and grandfather about Selah and all the others that we have spoken of through the years."

"But who is she preparing these letters for?" Scout didn't think it made any sense.

"The children," Samuel answered.

"Whose children?" Scout wanted to know.

"All of our children and those I suppose that will come after us. She wants them to know about our legacy," Samuel looked serious now.

Scout could recall his baby sister following him around especially when Pella showed up. Bless her heart, she had been so faithful to their parents taking care of them and their home. She had sacrificed much for her family, like the sacrifices their great-grandmother Selah made and others. These were the stories she wanted written so no one would forget it had cost them. They *did* have a legacy. Their grandfather Simon was still mentioned almost daily around the cookfires and cups of wine at night.

"Have you seen these letters?" Scout asked them.

"No, they're Sofie's memories," Joshua said.

The brothers were quiet again, each lost in their thoughts as the sea reminded them of their own stories.

"The man Aaron, does he have family?" Scout asked.

"Do you mean is he married?" Samuel replied.

"Samuel! What are you trying to say?" Scout had enough on his mind.

Samuel didn't want to talk about Sofie, but he had never seen her so happy and carefree. "The man lost his wife, but I don't think Sofie

— Chapter Six —

knows. Aaron needs to tell her what he will." Samuel glanced at Joshua, "Sofie seems different," he said.

"What do you mean?" Scout asked him.

"She seems happy like...."

"Like?" Scout was losing patience.

"I think she likes this man," Samuel said.

Before Scout could respond, Joshua quickly added, "She's spending a lot of time with him, that is all. The people of course know we're here and Aaron is a houseguest. He's an honorable man. His family went to the caves right after our father returned with so many people. Others joined them and they seemed fine living in the hills. We have asked Sofie if she has inquired about his family, and she hasn't."

"Where did she meet him?" Scout knew his sister's habits. She never ventured too far from the house.

"Service," Joshua answered.

"They met at church. He's a believer and I think our sister was pretty courageous to seek him out on her own for this passion she has to record our family's lives." Joshua tried to read the expression on Scout's face.

"It's harmless. They share a meal, Sofie repeats the stories she grew up with and Aaron is kind enough to give his time to help her," Joshua said.

Scout turned to Samuel, "You think there's more?"

"They are spending a lot of time together. Sofie will be surprised at our return, but so happy to see Hannah, you, and Pella. Aaron will return to his home, and I imagine our sister will only see him at the Sabbath service. I've just never seen her so...I don't know the word I'm looking for," Samuel said. "I guess you'll see when we get home."

Scout still wasn't satisfied with Samuel's answers. This made him more anxious to leave Tiberias. He should have demanded the bride price right there on the spot and they could be on their way. But his family needed rest and there were still parts of Tiberias they could enjoy. Hannah had been heard singing from her room this morning and that made his heart glad. His brothers were whispering, and he asked them what they were discussing.

"Tell us one of *your* stories, brother, like when father brought you here the first time," Joshua said.

"Yes!" Samuel agreed.

— *Sofie* —

"When you met your Pella," the brothers laughed.

They became solemn when Scout reminded them of the words their father said often. Scout could feel the grief even now when his father questioned his motives. Joshua and Samuel wanted to go to the cave, but the hour grew late, and Scout wanted to check on Hannah. The rest of the family would be waiting for their midday meal. They wouldn't begin until the men returned.

Chapter Seven

"We will leave tomorrow," Scout announced to the family. "I expect James or his father to call on us before the end of the day." He looked at Hannah. He didn't want James to even get a glimpse of her. He didn't deserve one last look.

"Brothers, let us return to the house of James. Why should we wait for him? You told him three days, any respectful man would have already made the arrangements," Joshua said.

Pella kept her eye on her husband. She could tell what he was thinking by the slight movement of the muscles in his face. Going back to the father's house would embarrass the man, however, James then wouldn't have to come here. And see Hannah.

"Perhaps that would be better. If no one comes soon, we'll go to the docks," Scout said.

"The docks?" Samuel questioned.

"Yes," Scout replied, "Trust me."

The brothers stood in a line, their shoulders touching while Pella examined each one. They were a wall of strength and purpose and she almost felt sorry for James. They all concluded his father told him to leave and not come back under his roof until he sorted things out with Hannah's grandfather, and they assumed the foolish boy had spent all the money.

Scout drew Pella to the side, "You will stay here," he simply said. "Don't follow us. I need to be certain Hannah is in the house and I need you to make sure everyone else remains here."

He could see her eyes dance with mixed emotions. "I expect to collect our money and we'll leave in the morning." He turned one last time, "Stay here," he smiled.

James was right where Scout knew he would be found. He stood by his father's boats ready to launch out for a night of fishing. James couldn't pretend he didn't see the wall of men coming and he didn't have Scout's money. He had ten hired men loading nets, ready to fish. Scout didn't have to say a word; James approached him so the men wouldn't overhear their conversation.

"I need more time," he blurted out.

"No James, your time is up. I gave you adequate notice," Scout told him.

James glanced back at the boats. His men had spears and knives, Scout and his brothers only had their strength. "I can't give you what I don't have," he said.

James seemed to be smiling, which Scout found bothersome. "Well then," Scout replied, "I'll take what you do have. Joshua, Samuel, secure the boats!" Scout commanded.

"You're crazy old man! You will not take my boats!" James laughed now.

Scout grabbed him by the throat and easily lifted him, so his feet didn't touch the ground. The hired men stood on the docks waiting to see what would happen. James was unable to shout any orders at them and everyone knew who Scout was. James' eyes looked like they would pop out of his head at any moment and Joshua and Samuel stepped up on each side of their big brother, their hearts racing at the excitement of this exchange.

"Listen carefully James," Scout began. "I am taking your boats as surety. I will use them to escort my family back home. They traveled expecting a wedding celebration and it cost them a lot as well. When you have what you owe me, you can come and retrieve your vessels." Scout knew the boy was having trouble breathing but at this moment he didn't have any sympathy for him. Who knew what or who he spent the money on, and Scout was convinced he never really loved his granddaughter. She was just convenient.

"Do we have an understanding?" Scout asked him. James tried to nod, and Scout released him from his grip.

Chapter Seven

The brothers walked past him as he fell on his knees trying to breathe. The hired men didn't move. One man asked very politely if he could remove his bundle from one of the boats which made Samuel turn so he wouldn't see him grin. Pella also had to cover her mouth. She had hidden between the rocks in the first place she had known when making her way to the harbor so many years ago. Scout would be upset at her disobedience but there was no way she was going to miss this confrontation. She would outrun him back to the house. The women and children had filled the space, and most wouldn't even realize she had left. She took one last look. Scout and his brothers now each occupied a boat. The children would have an adventure rowing back home. Hannah would be reunited with the land sooner than she thought. James was making his way to the fishermen. She knew her husband's attention would be focused on them, so she slipped out from her rock and walked quickly to the group of people who had gathered at the shoreline.

"Why did you not help me?" James asked them.

The man who was allowed to grab his food spoke. "We don't have anything to do with those men. We don't want any trouble."

"These men have cost you a day's wages," James reminded them.

"We can find work elsewhere," another man said.

They were all in agreement. Scout and his brothers commanded the space. Each man said they had a bad feeling should they decide to go against them. The plain fact was they were right, they told James. They clapped him on the back and told him he would have to get the man his money or they would journey with him to bring the boats back. James didn't know what to do. He couldn't go home. *His father would be furious!* This was his livelihood too. Maybe he would pay what was owed before Hannah's grandfather left the harbor. He would go find out.

Sofie

"What shall we do now brother?" Joshua asked Scout.

"Samuel, go to our rooms and have your sons come to guard the boats," Scout said. "I will stay."

Samuel took off. He wanted to stay and not miss one moment of this exciting time. Joshua thought his older brother was just like their father. He resembled their father the most in looks and stature. He didn't think too many men would attempt to challenge his actions today. There were plenty of witnesses at the docks and some old timers who laughed heartily when James was removed from the worn boards, his feet dangling in despair. Joshua noticed one of these old fishermen start to make his way over and he was thankful they had their knives, and the spears also remained on the boats. The man was smiling and carried nothing.

"You are Scout?" the man asked.

Scout came off the vessel to stand before him. "Yes," he answered.

"Permission to board one of these boats?"

"Of course," Scout answered. "Tell us what we can do for you."

"My name is Phillip. I've fished these waters for a long time. I know all the hired men who work for James and his father. They won't come back for any trouble, but I'll watch over these vessels too and so will my friends," Phillip waved his hands behind him indicating to the brothers there were many who would stand with him.

"Thank you," Scout said. "My nephews will also be here shortly."

"I know who you are," Phillip said. "I used to go to the cafe where your wife Pella worked."

"What do you know of my wife?" Scout became uneasy.

"Scout, I was the one who told her about the man they called Wolf and his last moments."

"You are Phillip? The one who showed my Pella kindness?" Scout now lifted him from his seat and gave him the biggest bear hug his brother Joshua had ever seen.

Chapter Seven

"I can't believe this!" Scout shouted. "Pella is here! She would love to see you! You must come and have fellowship with us! We're leaving in the morning!" Scout couldn't talk fast enough.

Of course, Joshua knew the story about the miracle of the Wolf man. He could see the tears welling up in his brother's eyes even now of the memory. He watched Scout embrace Phillip again to hide his emotion. Samuel was coming back flanked by a dozen young men and shouts were heard up and down the docks for several minutes, especially when Scout introduced Phillip.

The stories his baby sister was telling the man Aaron to write surely would include this man. If it were not for him, he and Pella may never have seen each other again. Scout couldn't wait to see his wife's face. He would gently scold her for coming to the docks and hiding. The harbor held too many memories and he didn't blame her one bit for sneaking out.

James cautiously approached his father's house. He could barely see; his mother hadn't lit many lamps. He had practiced all the way here what he would and wouldn't say. What a mess he made of things. His father would be so disappointed. He couldn't believe he would knock on the only door he freely went in and out of his entire life. His father deserved his respect. He knocked and his mother answered. He could tell she had been crying. She was another innocent party in all of this.

"Mother, it will be fine. Is Father home?"

"Say what you have come to tell me," his father yelled from inside. "Have you paid the man?" he added.

"Father, please, may I come in?" James pleaded with his eyes to his mother who hadn't moved from the door. Both father and son knew she stood as mediator.

"Just answer the question, son. Have you paid back Scout?"

James had no choice but to yell back no, but Scout was satisfied. Now his father came to the door.

"Explain this meaning," he said.

It took everything to look at his father's face and he hoped his voice wouldn't crack.

"Scout and his brothers came to collect the money at the port. I hoped to have a good night of fishing and planned to see him first thing in the morning," James told him. His father only looked up at the sky. James knew this was the time they should already be out casting nets.

"Scout and his brothers have taken our boats," he said dully. The expression now on both his parents' faces was hard to read so he talked fast.

"For surety Father. They will release them as soon as I pay back the forsaken bride price. They are leaving in the morning so if I cannot pay, then I will have to travel to their village once I can pay to bring our boats back." He waited for the outburst, perhaps a slammed door with harsh words but his parents stood offering silence.

"Father, what should I do? I need your help. I have no money," James said.

His father turned and James heard him offering prayers. He came back to the door with his cloak and began walking to the harbor. James followed. Once the men reached their boats, they were surprised that each vessel held several men. Scout jumped onto the dock to greet them. James stood slightly behind his father not wanting to give Hannah's grandfather another opportunity to lay his hands on him.

"Here is your bride price," his father said while handing Scout the pouch of coins. "It's all there. I hope you will pardon this transgression against Hannah and your family."

Scout nodded and James watched his father walk back home. The brothers and their sons left the bobbing vessels ready for a good meal and some rest for the journey home. James had nothing to say. He felt small. He wasn't sure if he would be welcomed back into his father's house. He would never see Hannah again. His hired men had abandoned him, and this giant family stood and stared at him waiting for him to say something.

Scout knew how uncomfortable it must be, but this young man needed to learn you can't treat people in this manner. He would only wait a minute or two for James to acknowledge his wrongdoing.

"I'm sorry for all of this," James finally said. "I hope you can forgive me." He didn't wait for Scout to reply. There were too many family members standing there and he wanted to go sulk in his misery.

Scout wouldn't let him leave without a final word. "Son," he called after him. "Learn from this and be a better man."

Chapter Seven

The docks emptied and Scout threw his arm around Phillip's shoulders making his way to their temporary home. He made everyone stand back and told Phillip to knock on the door knowing it would be Pella who answered.

"May I help you sir?" Pella said.

"Is this the place where the man Scout is staying?" Phillip asked.

Pella grew nervous. Maybe she left the dock too soon and her husband did encounter trouble. "What is this about?" she asked the stranger.

Phillip could hardly contain himself. She had scrunched up her nose and he saw the gray trying to overtake the green of her eyes. "This is about a man who once walked into a cafe and...." He didn't finish.

Pella screamed bringing all the women rushing to the door. "Phillip!" she shouted.

Scout and the rest of the men came out of hiding and joy filled the evening. The children were asleep now and the men discussed the supplies they would need. Phillip was having one of the best days he'd had in a long time visiting with Scout and Pella. Seeing them together and catching up on the years and lives of those they knew had blessed all of their hearts on what could have been a troublesome day.

"So, you're still planning on leaving in the morning?" Phillip asked them.

"Yes, our granddaughter is anxious to get home," Pella told him.

"We have been away for some time," Scout added.

"What were you going to do with the boats?" Phillip asked him.

"I was going to take this brood home," Scout laughed.

"But now you'll walk," Phillip said.

"We are all used to the travel," Scout assured him.

"I will take you," Phillip said. He laughed when Scout gestured with his hands at the amount of people in the rooms.

"Scout, I know every fisherman on each coast. I have plenty of friends and we would be honored to take you home," Phillip said.

Pella ran over to hug him and so did Hannah. They would be home in two days!

Sofie

Sofie had all her hair tucked under her tightest fitting covering. Not one strand of hair escaped. There would be no reason for Aaron to want to get close to her and bury his face in the loose waves of brown and gold. She had prepared lentils because that's all she had. The jar of honey was lonely. It sat on her shelf with no company. She wanted to open the lid and speak to the sweetness that she was sorry she treated it badly, practically throwing it against her wall. Aaron should be arriving. She had slept this afternoon, and she was now refreshed and ready for him to continue writing so she could finish and…and not see him every day. She could feel those unfamiliar feelings again, claiming every part of her. She began busying herself sweeping, straightening, rearranging cups and bowls, anything to take her mind off Aaron. She heard him now. It sounded like he was whistling. *How dare he be so happy to whistle as he approached her home. He should be as miserable as she was.*

He knocked, calling out her name. She could hardly stand his voice, all deep and moody, but also warm and gentle at the same time. She would do all the talking and not give him a chance to speak. She put on her best smile as if she had a wonderful, leisurely day and opened the door. She couldn't see his face as he held up a big bouquet of wildflowers.

"For your table," he said.

"Thank you, Aaron," she replied, and she carried the flowers to find a vase.

"Smells wonderful in here," he called after her. "Is it Selah's lentils?"

He was so kind she couldn't bear it! "Yes, I made a big pot."

She was thankful it wasn't strained between them. Maybe he was trying to forget the intimacy they shared. She, however, wouldn't forget because that's exactly what it was. Intimate. She had spoken to the Lord until she fell asleep asking why this happened and was it her fault. She brought the flowers to the table. They were perfect. The bouquet was so big, it blocked her view of him. He pushed the vase away and said he needed a little more room to write.

"Would you like to eat first?" she asked him.

Chapter Seven

"Oh, well yes, that would be nice. I guessed I worked up an appetite," he laughed.

"Worked?" she repeated.

"Gathering your flowers," he said. "I went to the place I used to go to when I was young and I would bring flowers to my mother."

This was unexpected. He rarely talked about his family. "They're beautiful," she said. "I'm sure your mother always enjoyed them as well."

"She did," he replied. "So, did you want to continue with Benjamin tonight?"

Somehow hearing Benjamin's name brought back the rooftop experience and Sofie couldn't handle it right now. She forced a smile, "I thought we might talk about Marcus. He was a Gentile from Greece who became very close to Benjamin."

She watched him smoothing out his parchments, his eyes scanning the pages for mention of Marcus.

"I was told he was a kind man, and he came to Jerusalem for a party," Sofie laughed.

"A party?" It was the first time he looked directly at her since he walked in the door.

"He was a guest of Herod's. I will have to ask my brothers to remind me of the circumstances of why he found himself in the Holy City. He met a young woman named Avi who became close friends with Selah and Kezi. She was the one who worked in the house of Pilate. Do you remember me telling you?"

Sofie seemed like her old self just now and Aaron prayed the rest of the evening would be like this.

"They ended up getting married and followed my great-grandparents here when they left Jerusalem. Little Benjamin watched over the three women and Simon my grandfather while the men traveled. They told me Marcus was instrumental when they started the church in Antioch as he was a Gentile who married a Jew. The people realized the Good News was indeed for everyone," Sofie took a breath. Aaron's head was down writing as fast as he could.

"They had two girls, Rachael, and Leah. Rachael married Simon. Marcus loved his family. It got to the point where he never wanted to leave this village. He had...." She was trying to remember the word.

Aaron stopped. "He had something?"

The look on his face made Sofie laugh out loud like Marcus had a disease and Aaron just penning those words would somehow infect him.

"He had medicine knowledge. I mean medical knowledge. The men trusted him, and he became a pillar of this community just like my grandfather and Benjamin. He was very wise, and many sought his counsel."

She noticed Aaron's bowl was empty and she brought him another full one and more bread. There were no cups on the table, and she knew it was only right to offer him wine. She would refrain but she poured a large cup for him. Their eyes met again, and neither could deny the affection even though both were doing their best to hide it.

"Marcus sounds like another man I would have liked to get acquainted with," Aaron said quietly.

It was words like this that drew her to him. She could hear his honesty and sincerity. It dripped from his mouth like the honey that fell from the honeycomb. She had to tell herself over and over that this was how it should be. She would never make time for someone who was selfish and uncaring. She saw his kindness the first night she met him. He was approachable.

"Marcus didn't believe right away," she continued.

"Believe?" Aaron asked.

"In Jesus," Sofie answered.

"He returned to Greece but his love for Avi brought him back and then he saw and heard the wonderful things our Lord did. His faith was strong and as I said, both he and Benjamin became elders for this village."

"Did any members of Marcus' family ever come here?" Aaron wanted to know.

"I don't think so," she said. "That's kind of sad when you think about it."

Aaron was trying not to gulp his wine tonight, but the soup was a little salty and he indulged his thirst.

"Aaron," Sofie said.

"Yes, what is it?" he dropped his pen.

"I hope you know how much I appreciate you doing this for me, for your time, well, everything," she said.

Chapter Seven

"It's been my pleasure," Aaron said. *Oh, he wished he would have used another word.*

"It's been an honor," he quickly added.

She took his empty bowl and poured a cup of wine out of habit. Aaron said nothing. They found themselves talking once again late into the evening while Aaron listened to her tales and asked her more and more questions so he would have all the information written down correctly. She wasn't tired. She wanted to go back up to the roof to cool off. Aaron didn't seem tired either. Her flowers were beautiful in the soft light, and she spun the vase around to look at each one.

"These are lovely Aaron. Where did you find them? You said it was a place you used to go to when you were young?"

All their talking had made her mouth dry, and she was on her second cup of wine. Aaron noticed. He was happy she seemed relaxed, and they could try and disregard the tension they felt earlier.

"There's a small hill," he turned now to point to the direction he thought it was from where they sat, "And on the east side there is a field where they grow in abundance." He watched her closely now. She seemed to study every petal and the variations of color. "My mother liked the purple ones the best."

"I think I know the place," she said.

"When I was young, I used to hide from my brothers and run and play all day in that field. Later, I took my niece there for picnics." Sofie thought he looked hot. There were beads of sweat on his forehead.

"Shall I open the door? The room has grown warm, hasn't it?" she said.

"That would be nice, or we could go...." and he stopped speaking.

"Go to the roof?" she asked.

"I love it up there!"

"I'll go for a little while. Sabbath begins tomorrow and I need supplies, so I need to rise early," she told him.

"Of course," Aaron said. "I will help you with whatever you need. We won't stay too long."

They made their way up to her roof. Simon's roof had too many fresh memories. Aaron saw the blanket on the ground where it looked like someone recently slept.

"Were you up here earlier?" he asked her.

"Yes," she said a little shyly. "I also enjoy the rooftop and I fell asleep."

That's all she would tell him. He didn't need to know this was the place where she found it easy to pour out her concerns and distress at this newly discovered passion she felt towards a man. *Him*. She prayed all afternoon that she didn't break any commandments. She did ask for God's grace and for Him to give her answers to all her questions. But she fell asleep and now she and the *man* were on the roof again.

"Another beautiful night," Aaron breathed in the fresh air.

He needed to keep a clear mind tonight and hoped he didn't say anything that would upset her. He was glad he took the time to pick the flowers. He knew Finn and his family wouldn't mind if he didn't visit. He had surprised his son by going home today. They didn't expect to see him. He hoped Finn would come down for service tomorrow. And he prayed Sofie would never hear him refer to her as the cake woman.

They leaned against the wall and looked out in the darkness. Only faint fires could be seen throughout the village. There would be no fire on Simon's hill. The watchmen would hide their flame in one of the caves. Sofie could smell the familiar smoke and talk of her family stirred good memories. Aaron's flowers and his mention of the field also brought cheer to her heart. Aaron didn't speak. He would wait for her to address the night before, or they would make new memories watching the sky together.

"Be still and know," she smiled at him.

"Those are the words I heard repeated every time someone was on this rooftop. Be still," she said.

Aaron didn't want to interrupt the tranquility. There was peace in being still. The sounds of the night carried this peace, and they sipped the last of their wine in silence.

"We'll have a busy day tomorrow. Perhaps we should try and rest," Aaron finally said. "Let me walk you down and wait for you to get settled."

Sofie felt all warm again. She liked the feeling of safety when he was close. He didn't tarry and headed straight to the outside of her door and insisted she lock it in his hearing. He called through the door his goodnight. Sofie smiled. All she heard was *We'll*. She liked *we'll have*, or *we'll go*. It was a sense of belonging. She hurried through her rooms

— Chapter Seven —

so she could lie down and be still and listen to what the Lord would say to her. About Aaron. The man from the hills.

Aaron was back on the roof early. He wanted to watch the sun rise from its slumber and he hoped to see the watchmen changing positions with men climbing and descending. Sofies's stories were coming alive in his spirit as he let his imagination run wild thinking about how Benjamin and Marcus lived, traveling back and forth from one city to the next, meeting the very men who wrote the Holy Scriptures he would listen to later this day. It was almost unbelievable. But it was true. He was falling in love with these truths, with these memories, with this family, with Sofie. He needed to be careful. She was so precious. He brought the flowers hoping another memory might be sparked. He would wait. She had waited a long time. He was glad she approached him that first night and not the other way around. He had planned to sit where she could easily see him. He hoped and prayed they could become friends and the Lord answered his prayers. Last night he thought his actions might end this new union. He would watch his words. He wouldn't bring any more flowers. He hoped the fragrant bouquet on Stone's table would speak quietly of a time when she did indeed freely run and play through the fields and then later that day when she visited the special place her great-grandmother Selah found so many years ago. He wondered if this event would make it in one of her letters.

Sofie took her time this morning. She slept well and felt refreshed. She brushed her hair until her arms grew tired. She wanted to look her best today. She and Aaron would go out within the community together. She sucked in her breath. She couldn't do this. Yes, everyone knew by now Aaron was a houseguest of Scout, but the matrons of the small community would probably follow them around while she gathered items from her brother's homes and went to other neighbors for certain supplies. They were just friends. But people talked and it wasn't common for a man and woman to be together if not married walking and shopping. *Oh no!* She hoped he wouldn't be offended when she told him she didn't think it would be a good idea. She pulled off a purple bloom she would tuck in her hair just behind her ear. *Why did simple things have to be complicated? Lord, we just want to go shopping.*

Sofie

She couldn't be still and wait for an answer. She had too much to prepare for.

Aaron heard her door open, and he rushed downstairs. He wasn't ready! Time got away from him as he said good morning to dawn and pictured himself in a field of flowers with Sofie at his side, smiling carefree as she did as a young girl.

He flew open the door, "Hello, can you give me a few minutes?"

He looked so happy she didn't have the heart to tell him she thought she should go on her own today. "Of course, I'll wait here."

His smile got wider, and she began to look around at who might be watching the activity at the houses of Stone and Scout. The clan of village women were shuffling out their doors. Everyone needed to prepare for Sabbath, perhaps no one would even take notice of her and Aaron walking side by side like they belonged together.

He came out and saw her flower. "Well, look at you," he said. "You look lovely Sofie. The color purple is beautiful on you."

"Thank you, Aaron. Shall we go?" She was nervous now. It's almost as if she felt his energy. She didn't know how else to describe it.

"Let's stop at my brother's house," she told him. "I need more oil." She waited until no one was close to Samuel's house and then removed the key from its hidden place.

"Look! He has plenty!"

Aaron saw this home was much like Scout's. "He seems to have plenty of wineskins too!" Aaron laughed.

"Are we out?" Sofie asked him.

Aaron only heard *we*. "I can get some more later."

"Just grab what we need. Samuel won't mind," she said.

She said we again and Aaron grabbed two. He crisscrossed them on his chest and asked, "What else?"

This made Sofie laugh. "I need to prepare enough food. What would you like for dinner after service? I'll need to prepare it beforehand," she reminded him.

"Whatever you make is fine," he said.

Sofie had decided she would make honey cakes for him. She glanced around Samuel's house one last time. She measured out some flour and filled a small container with more lentils. She would need some fresh vegetables. She and Aaron would be seen on the roads with

Chapter Seven

Aaron's wineskins draped over his chest. *They would be the talk of the town!* Secretly, she kind of liked the idea. Most had commented openly that something must be wrong with her that no man ever offered marriage. Aaron was a strong, confident handsome man, and she didn't think anyone would think he was taking pity on her or insincere in his friendship.

They all knew her brothers. It wouldn't go well for this man Aaron should his motives not be pure toward *"Poor old Sofie".* She never felt that way. She didn't mind being alone. Until now. *My God, did these women hope she sat rocking in her chair for the rest of her days?*

"Where to now?" Aaron asked.

His question startled her. "I need celery and carrots, onions and... actually, I think that's all I need."

"I know a place," he said. "Come, let's walk."

He led her to the outskirts of the village. There were three tiny homes huddled at the gate. Sofie saw the garden from the distance and Aaron saw her eyes light up.

"Who lives here?" she asked.

"How have I never noticed this beautiful garden! Look, Aaron! Why there must be all kinds of vegetables here!"

"There are melons also," he smiled.

"Melons?" she repeated.

"Have you never had a melon?"

"I don't think so," she answered.

"Well then, we'll have to get one!"

Between all the *we's* and *we'll's* of the morning Sofie wanted Aaron to just grab her hand and hold it like they were officially *we*. They walked the rows of this well-maintained surprise garden and Sofie thought she could spend the rest of the day here. Aaron had produced a bag to carry all she wanted. They picked leeks and onions and Sofie kicked off her shoes to let the earth say hello. Aaron did the same and they chatted and laughed with Aaron making funny faces with their vegetables when they came upon the patch where the melons rested. He put two in his bag and couldn't wait for Sofie to try them! They were having a glorious day. The sun was high in the sky and Sofie picked up her pace.

"Aaron, we need to hurry. She reached for his hand as if to pull him along as a small child, not realizing she was doing so. It was so natural. They took no notice of anyone else. They simply walked home.

"What can I do?" He watched her move from room to room.

She had swept. She had cleaned. She had the cookfire ready as they wouldn't be able to do anything once they returned from service.

"Find the largest lamp," she told him. "We'll place it on the table so we can see when we return."

She directed him to the section of the room where larger vessels were kept. She began cutting her vegetables. The bread had been baked early this morning and was wrapped in a bundle alongside the honey cakes she also made. Aaron was whistling again. She hoped this meant he was happy. She noticed he hung the wineskins and had two cups ready for use. The melons had been placed on the table in the largest bowl Sofie had. They were green with lighter striping, and she couldn't wait to taste them.

Aaron saw her staring at them. "Oh, I guess I could cut these now," he said.

"Will they be good when we're ready to eat them?" Sofie asked.

Aaron lifted the smaller one out of the bowl. "Why can't we eat one now?"

His eyes were twinkling. "Come, Sofie, sit at the table."

They passed each other as he went to grab a knife. He whistled, she giggled. He wanted her to experience the entire process, so he came close to where she sat.

"Wait, this will make a mess," he said.

"What do you mean?" she wondered now what was inside.

"Perhaps a little juice," he answered.

Her eyes were fixed on his hands holding the knife just above the fruit. He made a perfect cut right down the middle and then split the melon in two. He heard her gasp.

"It's red! Look at this color! Oh my, I can smell it now!" She rose from her chair and bent low to inhale the foreign substance.

Aaron skimmed a flat layer and held it to her lips. "Go on, taste your first melon."

She looked up at him, "Are you not having any?"

Chapter Seven

"Oh, I'm going to cut us both a big slice, but I just wanted you to have the first bite."

She didn't take it from his hands, instead, she allowed him to feed it to her. Her face told him all he expected.

"It's good, yes?" he asked her while laughing at her childlike delight.

"Sit down Aaron and cut us a really big slice!" she replied.

"There are seeds. Just spit them out," he told her.

She spit them in her hand and made a small pile. "Can we plant these?"

"Yes! Let's do that!" he said.

They ate the whole melon while Sofie's stew simmered for later. She looked at the other melon and Aaron followed her gaze. "We'll eat that one tomorrow," he smiled. "Now, I'll wash up and we'll walk to service."

She could only smile. She was having quite possibly the second best day of her life. She hoped the sun would tarry now, so they could putter around in her house doing more things together. She filled the lamp with her brother's oil. She tied up her hair and removed the flower she had worn all day. There was still life in it and she stuck it back in the vase. She thought a life with Aaron would be this joyful every day! They would be separated during service, but they were creatures of habit, and both knew where the other sat, so she was certain he would be in her view the entire time.

Oh, Lord, forgive me. I should be concentrating on You! What a wonderful day You blessed me with. Thank you, Lord! I have never felt this way. Well, yes, I have. Oh, Jesus! When I first met You or rather when I realized who You are, I loved You with all my being! I can't believe how this love has grown over the years, but that first day when I knew You placed Your Holy Spirit within me, I was delirious! Father, that's how I feel right now. Delirious in love. How can this be? I've only known him for a few short months! Is it the flowers and the melon and the rooftop kiss that has brought on this feeling? No, it can't be, but truly it's part of it. I feel such peace when he's around me, in the same room, close where I can sense his heart wanting to tell me something. Is it my imagination

— Sofie —

Lord? Please, don't let me be foolish! This is all new for me. I have no one here to talk to. I mean I have You...You know what I mean. Help me, Lord. Help me to know.

Aaron called at the door knocking softly, "Are you ready Sofie?"

She pulled her head covering tighter. Aaron began walking and she stayed a few paces behind him. Tradition. She prayed the Lord wouldn't get tired of all her petitions.

Aaron didn't see Finn. He didn't want to be selfish, but he was relieved the boy didn't come down. He wanted to get back to Sofie's where they would share a meal and perhaps they would end such a wonderful day on the roof. Something changed today. Sofie wasn't on edge. She had truly enjoyed each moment of their day. *She had grabbed his hand!* He didn't even know if she realized she had done so even now. She had no bad intentions, no impure motives, and no agenda. She was simply perfect.

Sofie thought every woman in the village showed up for service, which was usually the case, but tonight she felt like she was the center of attention. Some of the older women took their time to their seats, smiling with a gleam in their eyes, nodding as though she had a sign pinned on her tunic that read, *I'm finally in love with a man.*

She couldn't wait to go home and discuss with Aaron what was shared tonight. The reading was from the scroll of Matthew, the genealogy of Jesus. She tried to remember every generation. She thought God was very orderly and Matthew very clever to word it the way he did so she could understand. She heard Abraham and David and that was enough for her. Aaron had stolen many glances at her, and she prayed the watching women couldn't see her returned looks. She was grateful that most everyone was anxious to get to their homes for fellowship and food. Except for the watchmen her brothers had assigned to her care.

Aaron waited to see what Sofie would say. She called him over.

"This is Aaron. He's staying in Scout's house, and he will see me home. Thank you, goodnight," and she started walking before the men could respond. *Boy, was she having a fun day!* She practically skipped back to her house.

Chapter Seven

Aaron's heart was full. They *were* having a great day and he loved seeing her so happy. The house was warm and smelled wonderful. Sofie could still detect the slightest sweet aroma the melon had left for her, and her stew smelled delicious! Aaron filled cups of wine for them. She moved her flowers to the end of the table. She didn't want to block her view of Aaron tonight. She brought two bowls to the table and retrieved the bread. Aaron said prayers and their evening began.

"It was a nice service," he said.

"Yes, I loved the reading from Matthew," Sofie agreed. "It's kind of like my letters," she smiled.

"Yes," Aaron replied. "You're writing how you came about!" he laughed.

"I often wondered about my great-grandmother's parents. Did they live on this land their entire lives, or did they travel from somewhere else?"

"It's interesting to think about," he said.

"And your family Aaron, do you know where they're from?"

"I don't know Sofie. I never asked my father. I guess I thought we were always here."

"Abraham left his own country trusting God. I wonder if Selah's parents left their home to come here. Maybe there was trouble like...."

Aaron wouldn't push her. This happened before when she brought up her great-grandmother and trouble. If she wanted it in the letters, she would tell him when she was ready. He refilled their cups and raised his, "Thank you for this good soup," he said.

"There's more," she began to rise.

"I'm fine Sofie. I'm enjoying your company."

"I enjoy yours too Aaron. I've had a wonderful day!"

He saw her looking at the melon. "Shall I cut it?" he smiled.

"We shouldn't," she answered.

"Why not?" he asked.

She jumped up, "Oh, my honey cakes!"

"Honey cakes?" he repeated. "We're going to have a feast!" he laughed.

Sofie laid the cakes down. "Let's wait until tomorrow for the melon," she said. "If we eat it tonight, I'll want another one and we can't walk to get it."

"You're right," he said.

"Do you want to take our wine and dessert to the roof to enjoy?" he asked her. He was prepared for her to decline.

"Yes, let's do that!"

She rose so quickly Aaron thought the table shifted. "Which roof? he asked, holding both cups.

"Let's use mine tonight to watch the stars," she answered.

Aaron talked to himself the entire time climbing the stairs. *Be careful. Don't get too close. Keep it respectful. We're just friends.* As soon as Sofie reached the edge, she took off her head covering, and Aaron had to turn from her dancing hair. He could smell it again over the wine, the honey cakes, and the melon juice that remained in the bowl. He was thankful she didn't notice that her dancing hair was an obstacle.

"Oh Aaron, what a beautiful sky tonight. This day has been blessed. I'm blessed! Thank you for saying yes to my request to write my memories and for your kindness," she said.

She came to sit with him. "Tomorrow we'll have our melon and then once Sabbath ends, perhaps we could take a walk."

"Where would you like to go?"

"To the field where you picked my flowers," she smiled.

"That's quite a distance, Sofie," he replied. "It may be dark before we return."

"Maybe we could get halfway there and then we'll wait until we can walk again," she suggested.

"To tomorrow then," he raised his honey cake this time which made her giggle like a young girl. Aaron thought her charming! They talked for another hour before Sofie stood to stretch.

"Please, let me walk you down. It's been a long day," he said.

He was doing his best to not sweep her in his arms declaring his fondness. He went straight to her door before he succumbed to her house filled with her presence. "I look forward to tomorrow," he smiled. "Goodnight Sofie."

Sofie left everything on the table. Morning couldn't come soon enough.

Chapter Eight

Phillip counted himself blessed to be able to take Scout and Pella home with their families. The children made his ears hurt! He thought the seasoned fishermen were loud at the inns after a hard night of fishing, but they had nothing on these kids! His men weren't as thrilled, and he would need to do something special for them upon their return. The trip was uneventful, and Scout was anxious to settle everyone down before Sabbath. He knew the large cave would be perfect for the night. They would wait to travel the next day, and he would sleep in his own bed tomorrow night. He was ready! Pella cried saying goodbye to Phillip. Scout looked at both her and Hannah. God had blessed his family, and he was overwhelmed with His love once again standing on this shoreline remembering his small fire and God's voice speaking to his heart.

Hannah had almost jumped in the water wanting to swim along with the boat carrying her home. *She was free!* No one brought up James or his transgression. Scout was thrilled his granddaughter laughed with the children, sang familiar songs, and never looked back once since they left the port. They had a few hours' walk to their resting place. He couldn't wait to see his sister's face with the arrival of Hannah.

Aaron tried to calculate the distance to the field. It was further than they were allowed and he already knew it would be too dark for the walk back. He didn't want to disappoint Sofie. He also didn't know what they would do all day. They weren't supposed to do anything. He wondered why Finn didn't come to service. Maybe he thought he would be nervous with the boy's presence in front of Sofie. He had the craziest grin on his face when he left him anxious to return to the village. He was a young man now and Aaron knew the importance of him finding his way. The boy was smart. He could see the change in his father. Aaron smiled to himself. He didn't think Finn would have a problem should...oh...he couldn't believe he dared to think of him and Sofie married one day. His family would be happy for him. Surely Sofie knew he was attracted to her. How could he not be? He had watched her mature into a beautiful woman.

He heard movement outside. It could be the hens gathering to see which door he would exit this morning. He chuckled to himself. They didn't know him. He would never disrespect Sofie or her family, especially when they were so gracious letting him stay in the house so he wouldn't have to travel. He thought about her youngest brother Samuel. Perhaps his motives were not only for Aaron's convenience but for his little sister to wake up to the possibility of romance and a relationship with him. He jumped up to look out the closest window. He was right. The older women were in their usual place, waiting.

"Shabbat Shalom ladies," Aaron greeted them. He went through Sofie's courtyard and knocked on her door. When she answered, he repeated his greeting to her.

Sofie saw the women. "Peace to you also this morning," she replied. Once inside, they both laughed behind their hands at the curious women.

"I cannot write Sofie, so I'm not sure what we'll do all day," he said.

"Can you teach me?" she asked.

"Teach?" he repeated.

"Is it lawful to speak about the letters of the alphabet, not writing them but just telling me about them?"

"I think that will be fine," he smiled.

They spent the better part of the day talking about the symbols, scribes, scrolls, and the Torah. This was also a requirement practiced

Chapter Eight

from their youth. They ate and then went to the roof to relax. Truly, it was a day of rest. It was a nice day and Aaron pointed out clouds, birds, and the direction of the field.

"It may be too far Sofie," he started. "We could go tomorrow!" he suggested. He saw her disappointment.

"That would be fine. I know it's too far to go today," she said. "Can we stop at the garden on the way?"

"Of course, we can do anything you want," he answered.

"Can you show me how to cut the melon?"

"Now?" he laughed.

"I'm so hungry for it!" she admitted.

"I'll be back," he said.

He brought everything in one trip. When Sofie saw his hands full, she rushed over. She spread her blanket down. They had melon, honey cakes, and more wine. Aaron was sweating. She had to come close to him to examine his knife skills. When she placed her hands on his own as he cut into the sweet fruit, he had to concentrate so he wouldn't accidentally cut their hands. She was once again thrilled at the color and fragrance. He sliced up the whole thing and they ate freely along with the honey cakes and wine. He was getting sleepy. The warm sun didn't help. He tried to force his eyes to stay open but when he saw Sofie was having the same difficulty, he quit fighting. They slept. Sofie woke before him and watched the man of the hills sleep. The sun would set soon. They would be free to move around to light more lamps and prepare something to eat. She would add to her lentils and bring more wine to finish the day in the cooler rooftop sanctuary. Aaron was in a deep sleep. When she returned, he stirred at the sounds she made.

"You should have woken me up to help you carry this," he said.

"You were sleeping so soundly," she told him, "And I like watching you sleep." She lowered her eyes now, not believing she voiced her thoughts.

"I could watch you all day," he said, surprising them both.

Their words were pure, and their hearts had somehow joined together during the past few months and they both knew it was useless to deny it any longer. He prayed before they partook in the simple bowl of soup and somehow kept his composure, the sun now spilling over Sofie in warm tones of amber. He was careful to only sip his wine and not gulp it down.

This was all new for Sofie. She had always heard the man was to pursue the woman so she ate quietly and rehearsed what she might say. It was unusual that they could sit in silence and be comfortable. The temperature dropped and Aaron came closer, pulling the blanket around her shoulders.

"Thank you, Aaron," she smiled.

"Tomorrow we will go to your field and stop at the garden on the way back for more melons," he told her.

"I can't wait." She turned to look at him, "Aaron, I…I'm not certain what to do," she whispered into his face.

"I am," he answered, and he pulled her to him to kiss her again.

The shofar blasts startled them. They were loud and came out of a lovely quiet evening echoing around the small village.

Aaron jumped, "Is it trouble?"

She raised her hand indicating for him not to speak while she listened to the watchmen. "It's my family!" she shouted to him.

"But is it trouble?" he wanted to know.

He reminded her now of the men in her family, ready to take on whatever came their way. "No, Aaron, it's a celebration!" she said.

"I can't believe they have returned!" She was scrambling now, picking up bowls and cups and folding her blanket.

Aaron was looking in every direction. Her family couldn't be seen yet.

"Oh Aaron, if Scout has returned…." She didn't know how to finish her sentence.

"I will go home," he said. He drew her close one last time. "But I can see you tomorrow as planned?"

"I'm not sure. I haven't seen my brother for some time. You're welcome to come and join us. I don't think there's trouble, but something has happened for them to return so soon."

She wanted to kiss him again before he retrieved his things to leave. She led him out of view of the watchmen or anyone else's rooftop position. She reached to place her arms around his neck so he would know her desire. She didn't want him to leave, but Scout was home! He

Chapter Eight

would be here within the hour. The watchmen's shofar blasts were ones she grew up with. They had sounds for every warning and occasion.

Aaron spoke his affection into her hair and neck, and they agreed it would be better for Scout to come into his home without a stranger in it. They made their way downstairs and Sofie helped him with his things. He hadn't spent much time in the house. Scout wouldn't notice but she was certain Samuel told him right away he had a houseguest.

"Oh Aaron, I'm sorry, but it's my family," she said as they hugged before he opened the door.

"Please, you don't need to say anything," he assured her.

"I don't want to leave you," he added. "I'll stop by tomorrow and meet your family."

"Promise?" she asked.

He only hugged her tighter.

Sofie couldn't help watching her hill man until she could no longer see his steady walk. Oh, she could shout her joy to the village from her rooftop! People were coming out of their homes with as much joy as she had waiting to welcome the patriarch of their community. That was her big brother! She could hardly sit or stand still! She ran through his house one more time. Aaron hadn't left anything out of place. Oh, how happy she was! She thought she must be dreaming! The Lord had smiled upon her after all these years and brought so much hope of a future blessed with love. Of course, she was loved by her family and the community, but this was so much better! It caught her off guard. She had resolved she could continue to live her life as she had been, and she was content. At least she thought she had been until Aaron. That first night she saw him had troubled her. There was something familiar, yet she had never seen him or met him. His warm eyes spoke to her spirit and now she was filled with expectations of a life with him. The Lord Himself had given her the desires of her heart and she was convinced He had placed them there in His timing, and she raised her hands in her brother Scout's house still hanging on to Aaron's essence and shouted her praise to the Lord again!

The sounds of the village were celebratory, and she knew her brothers had entered the gate. She wondered if Aaron had passed them on his way home or perhaps went the long way around as Samuel and Joshua would recognize him. She took one last look around and headed out to greet them.

Aaron saw Sofie's family moving closer to the gate, so he walked to his friend's garden and waited until the elders greeted the large group of people. The shofar continued to be heard. Sofie was conflicted. He could see it in her eyes. It was too much for Scout and the rest of the family to explain his presence, and he had no doubt her youngest brother Samuel would see the love in his eyes for his baby sister. Yes, it was best that he left, and he would wait until the later part of the day tomorrow to make an appearance. He was also certain the brothers told Scout that he was helping Sofie and that Scout would question his sister about what she had disclosed to him to write down. *His parchments!* He had left them on the table for all to see. With the sudden excitement, he hoped Sofie would put them up for safekeeping. He would dream about her tonight. He wasn't ready to go home. He knocked on his friend's door.

"Back for more melons already?" Ethan laughed.

Aaron saw him look around for Sofie. "She's not here," he said. "All the excitement you hear is that her brothers have returned."

"Come in." Ethan indeed heard the watchmen signaling the village. The brothers knew him, and they knew he wasn't much for socializing just for the sake of it. Aaron stood waiting for him. "Sit, relax," Ethan told him. "What are you doing?"

"I was going home, however," Aaron started.

"Sofie," is all Ethan said.

"Yes. Her brother's return surprised us, and well, I promised I would stop by tomorrow."

"So, you'll stay here of course," Ethan told him.

"Thank you, my friend," Aaron smiled.

"You know this village," Ethan began, "The women who come to buy from me chit-chat all the while they pick their beans," he laughed.

Aaron got nervous. "Do they speak of me and Sofie?"

"Of course!" Ethan clapped his hands laughing at his friend's expression.

Aaron rose, "Ethan, Sofie, she is so fragile. Please, tell me what they are saying."

Chapter Eight

Ethan missed this time with his friend. He had been in the village almost two weeks and had only seen him when he brought the daughter of Stone to pick melons. He knew Aaron. He loved Sofie. The old women knew it too he thought.

"They say they have never seen Sofie so happy," Ethan said.

"That is all?" Aaron knew it wasn't.

"They are certain she has fallen in love," Ethan smiled. "You have been staying in her brother's house, yes?"

"Yes, Scout's house."

"The women wonder what you're doing," Ethan said. "I wonder too."

"I'm helping her with something," Aaron replied. His friend only raised an eyebrow waiting for him to tell him more.

"She asked me if I would write her memories down, stories about her family and who they were so the people wouldn't forget," he said.

"What people?" Ethan wanted to know.

"The generations that will follow us," Aaron said.

"This village knows the family well," Ethan offered. "Who will read these stories?"

"She wants her nieces and nephews to know…she believes if they're written…."

"They won't be forgotten?" Ethan replied.

"Something like that," Aaron smiled.

"Are you finished?" Ethan asked.

"Finished?" Aaron repeated.

"Are you done writing all these memories for her?" Ethan wanted to know.

"No. I had planned to stay another two weeks and well, I told Sofie I would make myself available to her. There's much she hasn't told me. Now, with Scout's return, he may not want her to tell me certain things."

Ethan, along with most who called this tiny community home were familiar with the legends of the past. It was Simon who captured everyone's heart. He couldn't imagine why Scout wouldn't want his sister to remind the young family members of the life he lived.

"Well, I guess you'll find out tomorrow," Ethan said. Aaron nodded, but Ethan could see his mind wasn't at rest. "The women are right you know," he said.

"What?" Aaron asked.

— *Sofie* —

"The woman Sofie has fallen in love." He waited for Aaron to acknowledge his words spoken between sips of wine in the comfort of friendship.

Aaron looked at him smiling at the thought of Sofie in love with him and that her joy was evident to the older women who gathered at her gate each day.

"I do love her," Aaron told him. "She doesn't know."

"Know?" Ethan was the only friend of Aaron's who could press him until he spoke freely of all that was hidden in his heart.

"I don't think she truly knows how much I admire her and hope to one day have her by my side," he said.

"That is all?" Ethan pressed.

Aaron wasn't ready to talk about everything he had kept from Sofie. "She doesn't know about my wife and family."

"Your wife has been gone many years," Ethan said. "What else?"

"Doesn't that garden of yours need attention?" Aaron laughed. "Shall I help you bring water from the well? It hasn't rained in some time."

"You can help me," Ethan answered.

The men spent the rest of the day walking the land. No more sounds of the watchmen were heard. The village had settled down after the native son's return. Joshua and Samuel had only been gone a little over a week, but Ethan had a sense some things were about to change. Change for Sofie and his friend Aaron. He glanced at him now standing at the far end of the garden where he carefully grew the sweet melons. He was looking toward the field of flowers with his head down. Ethan knew exactly what he was thinking.

"Brother!" Sofie ran into Scout's arms and laughed with joy as he lifted her easily twirling her around.

All the women were shouting as they celebrated the arrival of Scout and Pella. Her brothers Joshua and Samuel stood behind their older brother on purpose. They were hiding Hannah. They all wanted to see Sofie's surprised face when the young girl was revealed. Pella wept when she saw her sister-in-law. Sofie looked radiant! She couldn't wait to ask every question she had about the man Aaron. Samuel had told her everything he knew.

Finally, Scout spoke. "Truly, it's good to be home. You look well sister," he hugged her again.

"I am well, and so happy to see you. You surprised me," she told him. "I didn't expect you for weeks!"

"We were all anxious to return," he said. "Especially," .... he didn't finish.

"Especially?" she smiled.

"Especially me!" Hannah yelled as she burst through the wall of her uncle's and ran into Sofie's arms.

Sofie fell back overwhelmed at seeing her niece. Scout was behind her knowing his baby sister would be shocked. Hannah could only cry. Sofie was speechless. The two women moved toward the house with the village continuing to shout their love to the family. Scout called to his brothers to say he would see them tomorrow. Pella ushered Sofie and Hannah into the house while taking a quick look around. There was no evidence of the man from the hills. She noticed Scout also making a quick assessment. Sofie and Hannah were both crying tears of joy. No words were spoken, they only kept looking at each other knowing many words would be released later in privacy.

"Aunt Sofie, may I stay with you?" Hannah knew she didn't need to ask.

The women said goodnight to Scout and Pella and rushed to Sofie's house. Scout stared after them. Pella laughed at the look on his face.

"We're right next door. Sofie was genuinely surprised. Let them have this time. We need to rest, and you can ask your sister all about the man Aaron tomorrow," she told him.

"Sofie must have asked him to leave hearing the family shofar. He would have been uncomfortable in our house upon our return. He could have stayed however, I wouldn't have minded," Scout said.

"Yes, I'm sure both knew this, but Sofie may have been uneasy with him under your roof," Pella replied.

"Why?" Scout asked. Pella gave him one of her looks. "What?"

"You heard Samuel," she said. "I think Sofie has finally found love."

"This should be celebrated!" he replied.

"It will," Pella said.

"When? Scout wanted to know.

"When they realize it themselves." She gave him another look. It took them awhile to admit to the call of their hearts.

"Let her and Hannah have some time. The family sees each other every day. Time will tell," she said.

"I want to meet this man," he told her.

"I'm sure Sofie wants you to meet him too. Now, let's say goodnight to the sky," and she led the way upstairs.

Sofie couldn't form the words fast enough on her lips. Hannah told her she had missed her more than she thought and that she looked completely different to the young girl.

"Aunt Sofie, I'm so glad to be home," she said. "There's so much to tell you and I can't believe I'm finally here! I've missed you terribly! Look at you!"

"You look wonderful! What has changed? Have I been gone that long?" She chattered on while examining the familiar rooms. Her eyes fell on Aaron's parchments. "What are these?"

Sofie quickly moved to the table to gather the letters. "These belong to a friend," she said.

"A friend?" Hannah never knew her aunt to have too many acquaintances. It was always family.

"Well, they're actually mine," Sofie corrected herself. "A friend is helping me."

"Helping you to do what?" Hannah wanted to know. She had never seen her aunt behave like this.

"Aunt Sofie, are you alright? Shall I call Grandfather?"

"No, of course I'm alright," she replied.

"Sit back down and I'll get us some food. You must be a little hungry. You have to tell me *everything!* You should be enjoying your wedding week!" Sofie didn't turn away from Hannah. She would know if the girl was truly happy this wedding didn't take place. And talking about her took her mind off Aaron, or at least having to discuss him and her letters right this minute.

"Grandfather found out James had a previous commitment he never disclosed to us. We got the bride price back and I guess perhaps one day Grandfather will offer it to another," she barely said.

Chapter Eight

"Did this James tell you he was sorry?" Sofie asked.

Grandfather wouldn't let him see me. And I'm glad Aunt Sofie because I didn't want to see him," she said.

"What was the point? He lied to me! I hardly saw him. He was usually filled with drink, and I don't like Tiberias. This is my home. I belong here. I don't care if I ever get married! You never did and look how wonderful you look! You have all your family around and this house and what else do you need?" Hannah saw her aunt's face with a look she had never seen before. She was looking off in the distance, yet her hands were warm and reassuring. Hannah followed her gaze to the parchments she had moved closer to her room.

"Aunt Sofie, what has happened? Did I make you feel bad? Oh, Aunt Sofie, I'm sorry for my words. It's been a long week. I'm not hungry. Perhaps we both should rest, and we can take a long walk tomorrow and talk until the sun tells us to come home. Just like we used to," she said. "Would that be alright?"

"Yes, of course! We'll have plenty of time to take a lot of walks. You've had a difficult week. Let me help now with your room. It hasn't changed. I swept it out just a couple of days ago preparing for Sabbath. Look around and let me know what you need," Sofie told her.

"Can I stay with you, Aunt Sofie? I like being in this house. I have a lot of memories here too," she smiled.

Sofie gave Hannah another long hug telling her she could stay as long as she wanted to and then lit a small lamp for her. *Aaron*. Hannah's return would change everything. He promised to come tomorrow for *their* walk. She waited until the light was put out in Hannah's room and then quietly went up to her roof. She stood at the top of the stairs not giving the watchmen or anyone else the advantage to see her hidden in the shadows of the moon. Aaron would be subject to Scout, Pella, Hannah, and who knows what other family members would be filling her brother's home tomorrow. She didn't want Aaron to be on display. She knew Scout would want to know everything about him! She didn't know everything and now she felt a heaviness she didn't welcome. She would tell Scout Aaron was a friend helping her with a project and earlier when they heard the shofar welcoming him home, Aaron decided to leave so his house would be free of guests. She was the one that needed him to leave. Her older brother would take one look at the two of them in the same space and know. *Oh Lord, what would he know? That I'm in love for the very first time?* She didn't want to rehearse her previous woes and was chewing on her thumb trying to decide what she would tell her big brother about the man.

"Stop doing that."

The voice from the next roof could only be her brother. *"Scout!* Why do you do that? You gave me a start!"

"Because Father used to do it all the time," he laughed.

"Is Hannah sleeping?" he called over.

"Yes, I only came up here to…."

"May I join you?" he asked.

"Of course," Sofie answered.

She hated it when he jumped from one roof to the other, but all the men in her family had done so until they couldn't. She knew Scout still had several more years of this routine.

"Come, little sister, tell me what's been going on," he said.

They sat on the blanket and Scout immediately discovered her purple flower caught in the folds. He picked it up playfully sticking it in his hair. He could always make her laugh.

"Hold out your hand," he told her. He placed two dried up olives in her palm and then let out a roar when she could only laugh too.

"I found these as I was walking up." He took the flower and the olives from her hand. "Did you have a party?" he teased her.

"Scout!" "No, I only…."

"Aaron," he finished.

"That Samuel can't keep his big mouth shut!" she laughed again.

"You look wonderful Sofie," he said. "We have missed you, and Pella and I are so happy to be home."

Sofie knew he would get to the point in his next remark, so she waited.

"So, the man Aaron you met and asked to write some letters, I want to know all about it."

The next hour Stone's oldest and youngest children shared the moon and talked nonstop. The conversation ended with Hannah and the boy James. Sofie began chewing on her nails again while Scout told her what happened. He took her hand away from her mouth and smiled at his sister's habit.

Chapter Eight

"Aaron will be here tomorrow?" he asked.

Sofie looked away from him. "Yes, we were going to go for a walk but now with Hannah here, I'm not sure we should."

"Why?" he asked her.

"Because this boy James must have upset her and I don't want her to see me happy with Aaron leaving for a leisurely walk," she said.

Scout didn't think his sister even realized what she said so he repeated the words he heard. "You're happy with this man Aaron who has come into your life, yes? Why would Hannah be upset at your happiness? And why would you think any of us think you and this man have the same kind of relationship as Hannah and James?" He watched her eyes grow large at what she had said, and he pulled her close.

"Sister, I'm happy for you. You have met someone who seemingly has become a dear friend, and you enjoy his company. That is all. We trust the Lord knows what He's doing. I'm pleased you have carried in your heart all the blessings and wonderful things God has done in our family and have asked for them to be written down."

"Believe it or not, Hannah can read! Perhaps she will be the one to continue this legacy. She's not going anywhere, and you will have plenty of time for walks with her. Finish your letters and when Aaron is here, Hannah can come to my house to give you privacy. Have you told him about Grandfather and his capture?"

"Not yet," she said.

"What about what happened to Selah and Kezi?" he asked.

"No brother, I'm not sure I will," she answered.

"Our family is strong. We have stood on the unshakable foundation of Jesus. Does Aaron know my story?" he grinned. "Or Father's?"

"Scout, you know the village has repeated our family's history for years. I think he remembers when Father returned with those from Tiberias. That's when his parents went to the caves to live. Aaron loves God and has the same passion for His word as we do," she told him.

Scout was tired. He didn't want to press Sofie to say anymore tonight. She hadn't realized the words from her heart spoke of the love she had for this man Aaron. At least he thought it was clear. She had never loved like this, and she was probably excited and confused by these new feelings. Maybe he should tell Hannah after a few days she needed to stay at his house as before. Sofie would have no privacy to just sit alone with her thoughts. He was anxious to meet the man who captured his sister's heart. He saw Pella now from the corner of his eye standing on their roof smiling at him. He helped his sister to rise and said goodnight, and before either woman could say anything, he jumped back to his roof.

Morning couldn't come early enough for Sofie. Aaron would meet Scout today. The two men were similar. Both were strong, caring men who loved God. That was the attraction she had toward Aaron. He seemed capable and confident. She could sense it in his movements and his patience. She wondered now if he might carry his parchments with him so he could write when they were on their walks. She wasn't sure how freely she would speak in front of Hannah. She didn't want to ask her to leave the house when Aaron was there as Scout suggested.

"Good morning, Aunt Sofie," Hannah walked to hug her. "I slept so well. I'm so glad to be home!"

"Everyone will be happy to see you," Sofie said.

"What can I do to help you?" Hannah asked. "Do we need to make bread? Shall we take some on our walk?"

Aaron. Sofie wanted to walk with him. "We should check with Scout...check with your grandfather and see if he has plans for the family."

Hannah had never seen her aunt hesitate to hurry and make plans for the two of them to go on one of their special picnics. She looked around her house. Something was different. There was new life in the rooms. The flowers were greeting the sun and her Aunt Sofie looked younger today. She was humming now preparing for the day.

"I'm going to go see what Grandfather is doing," Hannah said. "I'll be right back."

Before Sofie could say anything, Hannah was out the door, and she could hear the young girl calling her greeting to her grandparents. She wasn't a young girl; she was a young woman and Sofie knew she would understand now her wanting to spend time with Aaron. She didn't want to disappoint her the first day back. She moved quickly through her morning custom. She wanted to ready herself for Aaron. She would twist Samuel's ear when she saw him later giving him a little punch on his shoulder. It was hard telling what he told Scout about her and Aaron. *Oh, she missed him!* It was *his* face she wanted to see first thing

Chapter Eight

in the morning sun. And then in the moonlight on her roof each night. She tried not to let her mind wander with too many thoughts about the rooftop kiss that awakened her heart. But it was becoming difficult to not imagine holding hands with Aaron as they walked through the field where he might try and steal another kiss. And she would relent.

This new closeness is what she had missed her entire life. But there had been no one she desired before Aaron. This is what made the friendship so special. She had waited on the Lord to bring him. She was certain it was all His doing. She could trust Him and rest knowing He wouldn't bring Aaron into her life if there wasn't reason and purpose. She said a little prayer hoping the reason and purpose met her expectations and fulfilled the dreams she now had almost every night.

Hannah's laughter made her smile. Scout was probably the one making her laugh. He had always had a playful spirit about him. She stopped what she was doing and went to join them.

"Sister!" Scout called to her as she came through the door.

Pella was at her side, bringing her to the table to break bread with them. Scout loved this. His wife, sister, and granddaughter all together.

"So, what's the plan for today?" he asked no one in particular.

"Aunt Sofie and I are going to have a picnic!" Hannah said.

Scout looked at Sofie waiting for her to say something, but he knew she wouldn't. It was Pella who replied.

"Hannah, I could use your help today. Everyone will gather here later and there's much to prepare."

"I'm sorry Aunt Sofie. Can we wait and go another day?" Hannah asked.

"Of course," Sofie told her, but her eyes were on her brother. This is where Samuel got it from. She was certain Hannah was told about her plans with Aaron. Pella was trying not to smile but they were family.

"Yes, Aaron will be here to meet all of you," Sofie said, "And you can continue to talk about us while we're on our walk," she laughed.

She was feeling lighthearted. She knew they could see her joy. They couldn't wait for Aaron to sit at the table later and see them together. Aaron had no idea what he got himself into Sofie thought. *I only asked him to write my stories, now he will be assaulted by my brothers!* When the three of them were together it seemed to give them extra confidence in their actions. It was unity and like-mindedness that was one of their strengths.

"When is he arriving?" Pella wanted to know.

"It will be later in the day," Sofie replied. "He knows the family will want to spend the morning together."

"Where does he live?" Hannah asked her aunt.

Sofie wasn't used to all these questions. Her brother took notice.

"When Aaron gets here, there will be time for all your questions," Scout told them. "Let's eat and as your grandmother said, there's much to prepare today."

Sofie could hardly look at Scout. He knew her thoughts and somehow heard her heart. She wanted to be calm and ready when Aaron came. At least there would be time to give him some warning. She would make introductions and then they would go for their long walk and join the family later for their meal and fellowship. The men would surround him, inviting Aaron to share their fire outside while the women made things ready. *How could she hear then what they were talking about?* She couldn't stand at the window.

Hannah seemed to be able to read her thoughts also as she grabbed her hand under the table and said, "Yes Grandfather, we will have a fun evening and I will personally serve my uncles around your fire tonight.

Hannah. She would overhear the men going back and forth making sure the men had their fill of food and good wine. She had grown up, Sofie thought. It should prove to be an interesting day.

Chapter Nine

Aaron took a walk before the village woke up. He wasn't nervous about meeting Scout or any other family members. He wanted to spend as much time with them as he could without wearing out his welcome. He was grateful for his friend Ethan. He could stay as long as he wanted, he told him. They talked into the evening, and as iron sharpens iron, the men were encouraged by their years of friendship and the truth of its foundation. Ethan was a godly man. His vegetable patch as he referred to it was his ministry. This is the place the people of the village and surrounding hills found to walk the ground and witness life in the desert. They knew Ethan toiled over his garden and they were thankful. Most everyone visited regularly. This is where Ethan gleaned all his information. There was freedom to speak between the rows of cucumbers and leeks. This is where the women would repeat the news of the day. He knew who had a baby, who was getting married, who had a bad cough, and who needed prayer. The women's voices carried laughter and concern across the space, and most were unaware of his presence. He was usually low to the ground examining each plant, but those who had walked to his vegetable patch year after year sought his prayers more than the few items they would carry home in their baskets.

This is where he met Aaron over twenty years ago, and this is where he discovered the rumor of love blossoming between his friend and the daughter of Stone. He saw Aaron now walking back through his gate.

"When will you meet the family?" he asked his friend.

"Later," is all Aaron said.

— Sofie —

The men continued to tend the garden together when they came upon a large container of every fruit and vegetable Ethan grew.

"This is for you to take to the house of Scout," Ethan said. "The family has just arrived, and it will be our gift to them."

"Our?" Aaron asked.

"Yes," Ethan answered. "Your labor is included," he laughed.

"Thank you, Ethan. Sofie will be glad when she sees those melons."

"You can bring the cart back when you return," Ethan told him. "I'm happy you're here and as I said, you're welcome to stay as long as you like."

Aaron wanted to purchase some wine for the men. He suspected after their midday meal they would have a time of continued fellowship, and this would be the time Scout and the rest of the family would ask all their questions and get acquainted with him. He missed Sofie. It hadn't even been a full day. He hurried over to Ethan's cart and found the smallest melon. He had everything else he needed for their walk in the field. The sun wasn't high yet, so he walked at ease towards Sofie's house. He was a little surprised to see her on her roof. She was watching for him. She waved for him to stop. She ran down and went through her courtyard before anyone realized she wasn't in the house. She never walked so fast, but Aaron stood with a big smile on his face and checked the rooftop before joining her. He thought she practically ran into his arms.

"Hello!" He smiled while greeting her warmly but wouldn't give her a full hug. He didn't trust himself in the open area. He caught her looking back.

"Do you think your family is watching us?"

"I don't know," she laughed. She had also carried a bag and was curious as to what Aaron brought along for their walk.

They made their way past Ethan's. Aaron knew he was watching too even though he was out of sight. The field lay over the nearest hills to the village and once they turned around the closest rise, they would be hidden from any rooftop watchers. Aaron could feel his heart beating faster. The field held memories of a lifetime and he smiled at its protection of them. Sofie was quiet. It was too beautiful to speak right now. Colors of purple, red, and yellow shouted their greetings and she found herself running to say hello to them. Aaron waited to let her enjoy this moment on her own. He knew the field recognized her childhood days. She did look like a young girl in the early sun taking her time to recall old friends.

The field seemed smaller now from when she ran to it escaping from her mother's view. She stopped and looked back for Aaron to join her. They laid their bags down and Sofie spread out her blanket.

"Let's walk around the whole field!" she said.

"Take a drink first Sofie," Aaron told her, and he draped the skin of water over his shoulder. His knife was secured in his waist, and he took her hand. It seemed to the clouds the two of them had always walked hand in hand and they moved to partially block the sun from the two visitors.

"My niece has returned," she told him.

"She has asked to stay in my house," she added. "My brother Scout knows we haven't finished with our letters."

Aaron stopped walking and turned to her. "Are you uncomfortable with us while she's staying there?"

"No Aaron, I'm uneasy with her listening to my stories, even though most she has heard, but I like it when it's just me and you."

"Shall we stop for now?" he suggested.

"No!" she said loudly. "Scout has already told me she should stay at his house while you're there."

"Sofie, I do not wish to cause any conflict," he said.

"Hannah was supposed to be celebrating her wedding week. It was a shock to see her yesterday. You're not causing conflict. I'm sure Scout has already told her I need my privacy...my time with you to write the letters," she assured him. "I can't wait for you to meet everyone."

"I'm looking forward to a nice evening with them," Aaron replied.

"Selah, Kezi, and Avi came here often," she said.

"Once the children were grown, they would bring a skin of wine and lay in the grass and name the clouds," she smiled.

"What do you mean?" Aaron asked.

Sofie looked at him surprised. "You have never looked at the clouds to see an animal or a face?"

He let out a hearty laugh at her expression. "Of course, all young children see lions and bears charging after them in the sky."

Sofie

"I still like to do so," she smiled. "See the high place?" She pointed to the ridge in the north.

"Yes," he answered. "Tell me about it."

"That's where Elias would keep an eye on the women. I've been told Kezi would run and spend time with him there, sometimes for the entire night!" She hid her smile behind her free hand.

"Have you ever been up there?" he wanted to know.

Sofie shielded her eyes now while gazing at the place. "Scout took me once; I haven't returned," she said. "It's almost too special to go alone."

Aaron waited for her to say more but she only tugged his hand to walk to the furthest part of the field. He was glad he remembered to bring water. He knew if they climbed the highest hill, they could possibly see the water's edge on this clear day. Sofie stopped several times. Aaron was patient. She had run to this field's embrace often. He hoped for more stories.

"Look Aaron!" she pointed down. Several bees and butterflies were skipping from flower to flower.

Her face lit up! She reached down hoping a butterfly might land on her arm for closer inspection. Aaron glanced around. He knew exactly where they were, and once again prayed for memories to be stirred within Sofie's heart. He loved her joy in the simple pleasures of life. She stood still for several more moments and then turned to the north again. Aaron held his breath.

She only smiled and said, "Shall we go back now?"

They made their way to her blanket. Aaron made her take another sip of water and then uncovered the small melon.

"Aaron! Can we have it now?" she laughed.

"It's why I brought it," he smiled.

Sofie went through her bundle, "I want to save the seeds!" She would wrap them in the cloth covering her bread.

"We ate the whole thing!" Sofie said, wondering if Aaron had another one hidden in his bag.

She surprised him by lying down smiling at the sky. There were not a lot of clouds, but she managed to find one that brought a reaction. "A three-legged dog!" she yelled out.

"I see it!" Aaron laughed. He had relaxed and was lying down too.

Chapter Nine

Both searched the sky for another shape. Aaron grabbed her hand and brought it to his mouth to kiss. "Thank you for another wonderful day," he said.

The sun was full on her face, and she had removed her shoes and head covering letting the heat of the day remind her of home. She drew his hand now to her mouth and kissed his palm.

"Thank you for always making me feel special," she said.

Aaron not only looked for clouds but also any watchmen hidden in the clefts. Even Finn came to this area to hunt small game. They would need to head back soon. He could smell the melon on her hand and knew her breath would taste like the sweet fruit. He couldn't refrain. He turned on his side and framed her face with his hands, brushing the loose strands of her hair away. She smiled up at him inviting him to kiss her in the shadows of the hills. He knew one kiss would lead to many and he would sit with Scout in a couple of hours, so he only kissed her hands and helped her to rise.

"We need to go," he told her.

"Do we have time to pick some flowers? I want to gather several," she said.

"Of course, but let's hurry."

She had enough for three bouquets. They stopped at Ethan's, and he was given the first arrangement.

"Well, don't I feel pretty," he said, which made Sofie burst out laughing.

Aaron grabbed the full cart and Sofie looped her arm through his until they reached the main gate. Aaron was ready. He didn't feel nervous or anxious. He thought the sooner all the family met him and came to know him, the sooner he could openly declare his love for Sofie. He sucked in his breath. *Finn.* His attention had been on Sofie's family, not his own. He had avoided this conversation. Ethan reminded him he would need to tell Sofie all. He told his friend that was his intention, but timing was everything. Ethan had tried to read his thoughts when he and Sofie picked up the cart, but Aaron had only shaken his head no. Ethan understood, and Aaron was grateful his friend wasn't disappointed with his procrastination.

Both Aaron and Sofie could hear the activity surrounding Scout's house. The families had gathered. Sofie hoped Hannah would be the focus today and not Aaron, but as she glanced at the man of the hills, he seemed excited, and she had to pick up her pace to keep up with him. It was Pella who ran through the playing children and opened the gate. Hannah followed and the two women practically fell upon Aaron greeting him with warmth and sincerity.

"This is Aaron," Sofie smiled.

Pella looked at the full cart and before she could say anything, Aaron spoke.

"A gift from my friend Ethan. He knew you had just arrived."

"What a blessing!" she replied. She began lifting and moving the items around smiling at Sofie. "Please, come in." She ushered the couple to the house.

"It's about time you got here!"

Sofie looked up to see Samuel calling down to her from the roof. He wore a big grin on his face and held a cup in his hand. She gave him a familiar look and wondered how much wine had been consumed on Scout's rooftop. She handed Pella and Hannah the remaining bouquets.

"These are lovely, thank you, Sofie," Pella said.

"Shall I leave mine here?" Hannah asked.

"I think those will look nice in your room here," Pella quickly said. "The house has been shut up and these flowers are just what it needs."

Hannah smiled at her aunt and tried not to stare at Aaron. Her grandmother was right, and her grandfather had spoken to her while Sofie was on her walk. She would give her the privacy she needed to write her letters. She immediately liked Aaron. He didn't have to do or say anything. He just fit. And her aunt looked positively radiant in his presence. Her aunt had found love. It was obvious. She wanted to rush into her arms at this moment and bless her with her happiness and well wishes for this unexpected love that came down from the hills. She could see how the man Aaron could fall for her. She was kind and had a quietness within her that you wanted to stop everything you were doing to discover its source. She had always carried this peace as long as Hannah could remember. Her grandmother had it also, but her grandmother also had a side to her that she found amusing. She had cried laughing so hard when told Pella balanced herself on a bucket outside of James' house. There were plenty of entertaining stories and it took all her strength not to peek at Aaron's parchments while her

Chapter Nine

aunt was away this afternoon. She wondered which memories she had shared with Aaron.

The children stayed outside, and Pella introduced Aaron to Joshua and Samuel's wives. The women were all scurrying around in circles placing bowls and platters of food on the table. Aaron looked toward the stairs. The men were there. Sofie followed his gaze. Scout was coming down, his brothers following. The men were loud! They had missed Scout and today was truly a celebration of everyone being home. Scout walked up to Aaron greeting him as customary and Sofie noticed her brother's pleasure at Aaron's ease. The house was filled with love and laughter and the women stood waiting for the men to settle at the table.

Aaron sat across from Scout, the women collected at the other end. Hannah scooted close to her aunt waiting for her grandfather to say the blessing. The door was open to allow the children to move easily in and out with their food and Scout saw the full cart resting in his courtyard.

"A gift from Aaron's friend," Pella told him. "Aaron let him know we had been away for some time."

Scout nodded and smiled at Aaron, "Please tell your friend we appreciate this blessing. He's welcome here and could have joined us."

"Let's eat!" Samuel said, and the next hour was filled with chaos.

Aaron loved it! The children didn't walk, they ran from room to room with mothers calling after them. The wine poured freely while the brothers filled Aaron's heart with tales of their baby sister. Sofie laughed along with them. They told Aaron as the only girl and the baby of the family, Sofie was spoiled rotten.

"I was not!" she shouted from the end of the table.

"Mother just treated me special because I was a girl. "You boys were always loud and dirty from hunting and climbing that she kept me close and inside," Sofie proclaimed.

"Not all the time," Samuel replied.

"Our sister liked to run off," Joshua told Aaron. "Our mother would scream at us to go find her on several occasions."

"I was just walking and didn't realize how far I had gone. I didn't run off!" she laughed.

"Your field of flowers," Scout said quietly.

"Is that where you were today?" he asked. He thought he saw the color rise on her neck. He winked at her while everyone else turned, waiting for her answer.

"Yes, I wanted to pick some flowers and it's a lovely place," she answered.

Aaron was holding his breath. He wondered if the brothers would tell more stories of the young Sofie running off to her field.

"Your friend has truly blessed us today, Aaron. The children are waiting to cut into those melons!" Scout laughed.

Hannah stood, "Grandfather, why don't you finish your wine upstairs? We'll cut the melons for the children, and I'll bring you up a plate."

Now Sofie held her breath. Her brothers would have Aaron all to themselves. Hannah saw her panic and called after the men as they made their way up. "We'll join you shortly."

As soon as the men disappeared from the stairway, the women all ran to Sofie.

"We like him!"

"He's handsome!"

"What a wonderful man!"

"How did you meet?"

"Do you think he likes us?"

"Where does he live?"

"What about his family?"

"Does he have children?"

Sofie sat with her mouth open. The women were making her dizzy with their questions. Hannah broke through the circle of frenzy and bent low, "Aunt Sofie, I'm so very happy for you. Aaron seems like he has always been a part of our family. It's unusual, and I hope I'm not speaking foolish words. You waited. You never complained to anyone all these years about not being married or having children of your own. And now the Lord has brought Aaron into your life when you least expected it. God has smiled on His daughter, and we can all see your heart is happy. I pray I will have the same peace and faith as I wait for the Lord to bring me the right person." She kissed her aunt's cheeks, which were wet with tears.

— *Chapter Nine* —

Sofie's heart *was* happy. She was overwhelmed. Sitting with her entire family as they poured out their love for her brought unspeakable joy. Hannah was right. Her words were not foolish. Aaron belonged here with her, and it did seem like he had always been a part of her life, which was indeed strange. However, she couldn't answer the women's questions.

She realized amid all this joy that she didn't know the answers. She felt selfish just then. He had avoided her questions on the few occasions she asked about his family. These were things she needed to know. She wondered if Scout was asking him even now. *She had let him kiss her!* Her heart began to pound! She didn't know anything about him. The women had begun to clear the dishes and were slicing the melons all the while chatting about how happy they were for her. The words that had been forgotten the last few weeks slowly crept back into her mind. *Poor Sofie. She never married. She only sits and rocks in her chair.* What if Aaron *had* kept something from her? Something that would change her feelings for him or would be unsuitable? Like James. Maybe Aaron had commitments he didn't feel the need to mention. She had no idea where he lived. She didn't know if he had more children.

"Aunt Sofie, are you alright?" Hannah's voice was soft in her ear.

"Yes, I'm fine. It's been a long day and perhaps I spent too much time in the sun," she answered.

The men's laughter rolled down the stairs and Hannah jumped up. "Grandfather sounds like he's enjoying himself. I'll run up and see if they need anything."

"Sit here Aunt Sofie and I'll be right back," and she ran up the stairs!

Aaron was surprised that only Hannah came to see if they needed more wine. The men were lounging on their sides, content under Simon's covering.

"Where's our melon?" Samuel asked her.

"If the children haven't eaten all of it, I'll bring some up," Hannah said.

She hurried back down. She knew where her grandfather's wineskins were kept, and she grabbed one. Joshua and Samuel's sons were also on the roof, so she took another one.

"Aunt Sofie, will you help me carry everything?" she asked.

Pella handed them more cups and Sofie followed with the bowl of sliced melon. The men let out a cheer when the women reached them.

Sofie

"Set that bowl right over here," Samuel directed Sofie. "Aaron was just telling us you already had some today," he laughed.

Sofie looked at Aaron wondering what else he told her brothers. *Did he say they were lying down on her blanket watching the clouds? Did he say their baby sister held his hand while they walked the field? Do they know she removed her sandals and head covering?* Aaron was smiling. He looked innocent, she thought.

"I only told your brothers you had never tasted melon before and now it has become a favorite for you," he said.

Sofie heard the word *only* and relaxed. "Yes, and I'm going to have another piece with you, Samuel!"

"Come little sister, tell us about your day," he said.

"We went for a walk, that is all," she said.

Samuel turned toward Aaron, "Did she take off running through the field?"

"Samuel, she's not a little girl!" Joshua laughed.

"I did run!" Sofie said. "I missed my field."

"She showed me the ridge where the man Elias kept watch," Aaron told them. "I would have liked to have known him."

Scout smiled. He liked Aaron. He could see the nervousness resting behind his sister's eyes even though she looked relaxed with her melon.

"Our fathers made sure we all knew about Elias, and we too would have liked to have met him. We do feel as if we know him."

"Has Sofie told you about his cave?" Scout wanted to know.

"Yes, I would like to go there," Aaron answered.

"I will take you," Scout said. "The cave holds our family's bones. And others."

"Others?" Aaron asked.

Scout looked at Sofie.

"I...we haven't finished the letters," she simply said.

"We'll go soon Aaron," Scout said. The moon wanted to make an appearance and the men were getting sleepy.

"Aaron, you're welcome to stay," Scout said.

"Thank you, but I'm staying with my friend Ethan," he said.

"Ethan," Sofie repeated.

Aaron saw something in her eyes he had never seen before.

"Yes," is all he said. He hadn't told her. He saw distrust and confusion.

— *Chapter Nine* —

Scout saw it too. "Let us call it a night," he told everyone. "Once again, you're welcome to stay here Aaron, and please extend our invitation to your friend Ethan." The men slowly made their way down leaving Aaron and Sofie alone.

"I didn't know you were staying at Ethan's," Sofie said. "Why didn't you tell me?"

"I'm sorry Sofie. On my way home yesterday, I made the decision to stay. I wanted to be close to you and not have to travel so far."

All the women's questions were forming on her lips, but she couldn't bring herself to seek the answers. He looked so happy on Simon's roof and his eyes were sincere. They could hear Scout saying goodnight to the brothers and Aaron brought her close.

"I've had another wonderful day. May I see you tomorrow?"

"I should spend some time with Hannah," she told him. "Perhaps the next day."

"Until then," and he brought both her hands up to kiss them.

They came down to an empty house, everyone still saying their goodbyes in the courtyard. Pella had removed everything from the cart so Aaron could take it back with him. They all hugged him and watched as he made his way toward the gate of their community. Sofie didn't give anyone a chance to say anything or share their comments. She told them she was tired and quickly went home. Scout listened for her door to latch. Hannah stood behind her grandfather.

"Should I go?" she asked.

"No, stay here as we discussed. It's been a long day for her and...."

"And what Grandfather?" Hannah asked.

"This is all new for Sofie. I don't think...well...tonight with all of us meeting Aaron, she may have realized she doesn't know a lot about him and bringing him to our homes maybe has concerned her."

"Enough talk," he added. "You also have had a difficult time. How are you?"

"Grandfather, I'm well. I was sad at first, but now seeing Aunt Sofie so happy, I have hope," she answered.

"In fact, I told Aunt Sofie I believe the Lord brought Aaron to her at the right time of her life and He will do the same for me," she smiled.

Scout kissed the top of her head. This was his prayer for Hannah, and it had been his prayer for Sofie too.

— *Sofie* —

Aaron looked back several times. He hoped Sofie was on her roof to see he was reluctant to leave. Something had troubled her, or maybe she was only tired. He hadn't been forthcoming with her. He already received an earful from Ethan. Perhaps he should go home tomorrow and tell his family he had developed a great fondness for her. He wasn't ready to tell them any more than that. Of course, Finn would question his choice of words. Yes, he would go home. Sofie wanted to spend time with Hannah. He understood. The men had rehearsed their departure from Tiberias with him on the rooftop, the sons of Joshua and Samuel had talked over each other retelling how Scout picked up James from the dock. Scout immediately turned to him to say they were not violent men, but they also were not going to allow anyone to take advantage of their good nature. This statement had the younger men break out in more animated moments of the day.

Story after story was shared and Aaron was more convinced of the reason Sofie wanted these memories written down. She didn't have children. Who knew what family members would sit on rooftops and tell their children about people who lived generations ago? There were lessons intertwined in each memory. He learned today Scout was still someone you didn't want to mess with. It was about justice and doing the right thing even when it was uncomfortable, and others wanted to do nothing. He thought his parents were a little timid retreating to the caves in a time of uncertainty. Sofie's family had stood in spite of it, willing to face anything thrown at them. He felt like a coward keeping things from her. She sensed it tonight. It wasn't just that he didn't tell her he was staying with Ethan. He couldn't help himself and turned one last time to look at the rooftop. The lone figure standing was too large to be Sofie. It was Scout.

A light rain began to fall and Sofie thought it appropriate. She hoped it would wash away her rooftop doubts and clear her mind from questioning Aaron's lack of information. She did hope he reached Ethan's before the rain fell. He had pushed the full cart with vigor and

Chapter Nine

excitement earlier. Now the empty wagon would be filled with water to wash away the joys of the day. She was relieved he was staying at Ethan's and not climbing his hill. Especially at night. In the rain. She was mean to him not properly saying goodnight, asking why he didn't tell her he was staying at the garden home, telling him to stay away tomorrow. She might as well have said that, but she used Hannah as an excuse to not see him. She needed to think. *This was happening so fast! Her family loved him!* She wondered if Scout was offended that he didn't stay. The faces of her sisters-in-law and their daughters came before her, along with Hannah, all of them fluttering around her like the butterflies in the field asking her questions she had no answers to. This was when she felt her heart began to beat outside her chest, and her reaction became defensive. She was certain they didn't notice. She smiled politely and Hannah, bless her heart, came to her rescue asking her to help carry things up to the men.

She didn't know why she thought Aaron purposed to hide the fact he was staying at Ethan's, but that's when her mind began to wonder at what else he might be hiding from her. She was thankful Scout talked to Hannah. She was certain he told her to stay in his house. She felt vulnerable and would most likely spill out her distress if Hannah was under the same roof. That wouldn't be fair to Aaron. If people wouldn't think her mad, she'd grab her shawl and run to Ethan's to tell Aaron she was sorry for her sullenness. It wasn't her intention to end a perfectly beautiful day questioning his arrangements. *Is this love Lord? Are these thoughts normal? Is his affection genuine? Why can't I trust?* The rain had stopped. She was wide awake. The moon was almost full. She could still run to Ethan's and tell Aaron she was sorry. She would tell him she wanted to know everything. She would say she needed answers to all her questions. Her life had been peaceful with no worry. She closed her eyes to imagine earlier when they walked holding hands and she showed him Elias' lookout, and how he looked when she pointed out the three-legged dog-shaped cloud and shared the small melon he surprised her with. He was so patient while she picked her flowers and made him stop when she simply watched the butterflies and saw her great-grandmother's bees. She never mentioned them! She had only been a short run from their hiding place. Now she was wide-eyed chewing on her nails. She had kept this secret from him. It was a family secret and even Joshua protested that she wouldn't share the location in her letters.

She tried to remember. When she reached down hoping for a butterfly to light, Aaron wasn't looking. She had glanced up and he was scanning the horizon. She sat up! He had been looking in the exact direction of the bee's hiding place. Only her brothers knew where to find the sweet honey. They had cleverly disguised the path so no one would come across it. She hadn't been there in months! Perhaps tomorrow would be a good time to take Hannah, or at least tell her about it to see if she had any interest in keeping the tradition. She also hadn't thought about her angel that she saw momentarily the day the bees were angry. If she ever brought it up, her brothers seemed to get upset, especially Scout. He would tell her he was the one who found her and carried her home. But she knew that someone was there before he reached her and had whispered that help was on the way, and she would be fine. The voice was comforting, and it was her mother who always said it was an angel. She couldn't understand why it upset Scout so much. *Oh, she needed to go to sleep!* Her head hurt with so many thoughts for one day. Perhaps she would surprise Aaron tomorrow and take Hannah to see the garden of Ethan.

"Aunt Sofie, are you awake?" Hannah tiptoed into her room. She found the door open so assumed her aunt was already preparing for the day. The parchments were in view, but she wouldn't go near them until her aunt invited her to read the letters. She was curious, however, at what she had shared with Aaron. She wondered now if he would be back today to visit. She heard her now and hurried to sit at the table.

"Good morning," Sofie said. "When did you arrive?"

"A few minutes ago," Hannah told her.

"What are you and Aaron going to do today? Will he be here to write more of your memories?"

Sofie noticed Hannah rubbing the ink stain on the table. "No, I told him I wanted to spend the day with you," she answered.

Chapter Nine

"Really?" Hannah sat up smiling. "Shall we go on our walk?"

"I have a special place I'd like you to see," Sofie told her.

"Aunt Sofie!" Hannah said. "What do you mean?"

Sofie sat next to her niece. "My great-grandmother made honey cakes," she began.

"Like the ones you make," Hannah interrupted.

"Yes, the recipe has been passed down," Sofie smiled.

"I have no children to teach who will continue this tradition, and I thought perhaps you might be interested in the secret of your great-great-grandmother's recipe."

"Yes!" Hannah said. "I would Aunt Sofie!"

"We will go to the place where the secret ingredient lives," Sofie laughed. She could see the excitement in Hannah's eyes.

"First, I want to stop by Ethan's home so I can say hello to Aaron and thank Ethan again for his gift to our family. I have everything we'll need."

"Just get ready for a long day. Oh, and don't put on any oil or fragrance," she added.

"Why?" Hannah asked.

"I'll tell you later. Now go and tell Scout of our plans." Sofie grabbed her jar of honey and an extra container. She had a skin of water and bread. She would also tie up a bundle of any leftovers from yesterday to take along.

The flowers from Aaron were dropping their petals and she looked for her large basket she could drape over her shoulder. She wouldn't carry anything in her hands while greeting the bees. She was anxious to see Aaron. He wouldn't be expecting her. And she wanted to see the garden.

The women greeted neighbors as they made their way to the gate. Sofie didn't need to turn around to see Scout watching his sister and granddaughter; she knew he was there. She thought he may have followed them or hurried to the northern ridge to keep watch.

Hannah carried Sofie's bag and also had a skin of water. "Grandfather insisted," she told her aunt. They had plenty of food. They would be gone the better part of the day on this adventure.

"This is so nice Aunt Sofie," Hannah said. "I love spending time with you!"

It was like old times. Hannah had been gone over a year and Sofie did miss her. She couldn't wait for her to see Ethan's garden. She couldn't wait to see Aaron. She heard her name being called. It was Ethan. He was at the far end of his land. She waved they were coming.

"What a surprise to see you!" Ethan said as he greeted her. "Who is this lovely girl?"

"My niece Hannah," Sofie answered. "We came to see your garden and I wanted to thank you again for all the food. I'm also here to surprise Aaron and say hello," she smiled.

"He's not here," Ethan said. "I believe he went home."

Hannah could see her aunt's disappointment and swore she saw her body tense up.

"Was he expecting you?" Ethan asked.

"No," Sofie replied. She saw the empty cart by the fence and thought of Aaron pushing it in the rain last night.

"I will tell him you stopped by," he told her. "Where are you off to?"

Hannah now spoke, "To the field," she answered.

"Where the flowers grow and...." She almost slipped telling someone she just met she was going to a secret place.

"And we're going to have a picnic and enjoy the day," she finished.

Ethan checked the sky. The rain was unexpected last night, and he wondered if more would fall today. One thing he did know; Sofie's family knew exactly where she would be, and he wouldn't be surprised if he saw Scout in a few minutes or spotted him climbing the nearest hill.

"Do you have everything you need?" he asked them.

"Yes, thank you. Perhaps we'll stop by on our way home to say hello to Aaron if that's alright," Sofie said.

"Of course, but I'm not sure he's returning," Ethan replied.

Sofie's mind began to race again. Hannah could sense the tension within her aunt, and she looped her arm through hers telling Ethan it was nice meeting him and he had a lovely garden. If it wasn't too late, they would stop to see if Aaron did come back.

Ethan watched the women head to the same place Sofie had been the day before. He checked the sky, the hills, and the path that led to the village gate. Scout was nowhere to be seen.

Chapter Ten

"Aunt Sofie, is something troubling you?"

Sofie didn't want to talk about Aaron and her thoughts. Hannah just got home, and she had gone through her own turmoil. *Turmoil. Why did she think of that word?*

"I'm not troubled Hannah," she answered. "Aaron has been away from his home and I'm certain he's checking on things."

Hannah bit her lip. She wanted to ask all the questions everyone else had asked. "What things Aunt Sofie? His family?"

Sofie didn't know and these questions are what kept her awake half the night. "Let's talk about you." She tried to sound cheerful.

"Did you feel sick on the boat? Were you afraid you might tip over? Tell me about the man Phillip."

She knew Hannah was a talker and these questions directed at her would buy her some time to think about Aaron. The plain truth was she didn't know what things he needed to check on. She found herself scanning the hills looking to see if she might catch a glimpse of him coming down. Maybe he saw her and was running to greet them.

"I loved the water, and the boat did rock sometimes, but I never thought I would fall in," Hannah told her.

Sofie heard her niece, but she only nodded hoping Hannah would think she was paying close attention. She was distracted. She tried to concentrate on her words.

"Phillip was very nice to bring us home. Like Aaron, he's a very nice man," Hannah said. Her aunt wasn't listening. She purposed to say Aaron's name and her aunt didn't react.

"I'm not sure I told you Aunt Sofie how relieved I was when Grandfather told James he couldn't see me or that I was in love with his best friend, and we had planned to run off together. I felt so bad with all the money Grandfather spent and I told uh...well, I won't mention his name, but we were now free to go to his country." Hannah rambled on as her aunt was still searching the hills.

"I told him I didn't care where we lived, and I would go with him and raise goats if we had to. Doesn't that sound like fun Aunt Sofie?"

"What? Did you say something, Hannah?"

"Aunt Sofie!"

"I'm sorry Hannah, what were you saying?"

"I was telling you I'm going to run off with James' best friend to his country and become a goat herder!" Hannah couldn't contain herself and burst out laughing at both her aunt's startled face and her folly.

"Aunt Sofie, what's wrong? Did you and Aaron have words? Has something happened between you?"

Sofie felt like taking off running to her field as she did as a child to escape all by herself and not answer any questions or talk to anyone. She didn't like feeling this way and was genuinely concerned.

"I'm sorry Hannah. I *am* distracted today. There's been so much excitement with the family and you coming home. Nothing has happened. Now, let's hurry so we can take advantage of the day," she told her. She concentrated on her niece and kept her eyes from searching for Aaron. They stopped for their picnic.

"Oh, I have missed this field!" Hannah said.

Sofie watched Hannah turn completely around in slow motion taking in every color the field wanted to show her today. The butterflies were in abundance and the flowers solicited their attention. Hannah slipped off her shoes and helped Sofie with the blanket and placement of their things.

"I could just run I'm so happy to be here!" Hannah told her aunt.

"Then run!" Sofie laughed.

Hannah took off laughing at all the startled bugs and birds who were having their own picnic and Sofie almost got up to run alongside her. She would stop looking for Aaron and she wouldn't stop by Ethan's on the way home. If Aaron wasn't there, she was certain she wouldn't sleep tonight. She would rather not know. Plus, she needed

— *Chapter Ten* —

time with Hannah. The young girl ran back full steam and collapsed on the blanket.

"What a beautiful day! The sky is blue, the birds are singing, we have food and wine and most of all, we're together! Aunt Sofie, I missed you more than I realized. Remember when we would come here and watch the clouds roll by...." She saw her aunt had that faraway distant look again in her eyes.

She grabbed her hands. "Aunt Sofie, please tell me what has happened. Is it the man Aaron? Has he hurt your heart? I promise Aunt Sofie, I won't tell Grandfather anything! I don't like seeing you this way. Something is different! Are you conflicted, Aunt Sofie?" Hannah held her breath, but she wouldn't let go of her grip. She also wouldn't let her aunt ignore her questions.

Sofie smiled at her niece. She knew the young girl loved her and cared for her well-being. "Aaron kissed me," she said softly. She didn't want her words to travel across the field. Hannah had let go of her hands to clap them over her own mouth to prevent her from screaming.

"It was wonderful!" Sofie told her. She felt a little shy and awkward now telling a seventeen-year-old she received her first kiss.

"We were on Scout's rooftop," she laughed. "We had too much wine! I said goodnight...it was a strange evening. I was upset and didn't understand the feeling I was having and found myself returning to the roof to perhaps confront him, but before I could say anything, he called out my name and then he was beside me and it was like a dream, Hannah." The heat had risen on her neck and face at the retelling and Hannah fell on her shoulder and cried.

"Oh Hannah, have I upset you now? Please don't cry."

"Aunt Sofie, I'm so happy for you! I feel like running again!"

Sofie told her everything from the day she noticed Aaron in service to being disappointed he wasn't at Ethan's this morning.

"But you will see him tomorrow!" Hannah said confidently. "You'll finish your letters and you both will declare your feelings for one another and all will be well Aunt Sofie! I'm certain of this! We will have a wedding to celebrate after all!" she giggled.

Sofie smiled at Hannah's enthusiasm and joy. She didn't want to damper the afternoon with negative thoughts. She did want to take her to Selah's bees. They had time.

"Leave everything," Sofie told her. "I want to show you something."

They started to walk but Sofie turned back. "Wait, I've forgotten my jar." She flung her skin of water over her shoulder and then caught up with her niece.

Hannah saw the container that sat in the special place on her aunt's shelf and knew instantly she was going to the place where her aunt would break off the honeycomb. She became nervous and excited at this privilege.

Sofie stopped several times and now scanned the hills for any onlookers. Her brother Joshua was the last person who made the trip, and he would have been careful to conceal the worn path.

"Aunt Sofie, where are we going?" Hannah wanted to know. Her aunt had stood for a long time looking in all directions not saying anything.

"Do we need to go somewhere else before we reach great-grand-mother's hideout? What can I do?"

"Follow me," Sofie told her. She stepped around a few large rocks and then rolled away smaller ones hiding the trail.

"Oh, my goodness!" Hannah exclaimed. She saw the path leading to Selah's bees. Her aunt looked around one last time and then carefully rolled the stones back. The climb was easy and not steep. A few bees had already come down to investigate.

"Stand still," Sofie told Hannah. "Let the bees see you're no threat."

Hannah didn't move. For a moment she wasn't certain she wanted to continue this tradition and was happy Aunt Sofie had several more years of gathering the honey.

"Look, Hannah!" Sofie directed her attention to the hive. The steady hum of the bees made Hannah nervous. There were hundreds, and they were moving quickly to and from the hive.

"This is their busy time," Sofie told her. "Let's just stand here for a moment."

Hannah kept her eyes on her aunt. Sofie was comfortable with the bees. They seemed to be expecting her. She could see the treasure! The honeycomb was waiting for her aunt's careful hands to reach out and grab a piece. It's all she needed. Sofie took a small cloth from inside her tunic and approached the hive all the while telling the bees she only needed to make Selah's honey cakes. Hannah watched the bees fly away from her aunt's steady hand enough for her to tear off a piece of the comb

Chapter Ten

and put it in her jar. She continued to stand letting the bees know she was thankful. Hannah noticed a few bees had come closer to them landing only for a quick moment. They seemed to understand this family had been climbing to visit them for generations.

"Slowly turn around," Sofie instructed Hannah.

They went down the small hill without talking. The bees were doing all the conversing, and the women didn't want to interrupt their conversations. Sofie stepped over the smaller stones and reached her hand back to help Hannah. She stood again and glanced around. She bent low to the ground and picked a few flowers.

"If anyone is watching," she smiled.

"They will think we are only looking for flowers," Hannah laughed. "That was exciting Aunt Sofie, and a little scary," she said. "I wish you would have shown me this place when I was younger."

"I should have," Sofie said. "I guess I wanted to keep it to myself, but all my brothers know."

"Yes, Grandfather told me you got stung by the bees."

"Scout told you that story?" Sofie was surprised she knew.

"I thought all the family knew this story. That's why only a few come here to gather the honey. What happened that day Aunt Sofie?"

"The bees were angry that day. I had oil on my skin and in my hair. That's why I told you not to wear any," she said.

"Grandfather said you saw an angel!" Hannah watched her face closely.

"I don't know if he was an angel. My eyes were swollen from the bees that I could barely see, and I think I passed out from the pain." She stopped to look back at the mounded earth where the bees had always lived.

"I saw someone though, and I think they stayed with me until they heard my brothers coming."

"It must have been an angel," Hannah declared, "Or else they would have stayed to make sure you were getting help."

"I never thought about that."

"I won't feel comfortable getting the honey until I watch you do it a lot more times."

They collected their things after first sampling the sweet substance, then began walking home. They took their time stopping often at familiar places for Hannah to enjoy.

"That's where I received my first kiss!" Hannah told her aunt as she pointed to the centuries-old wall that kept the village safe from their enemies.

"Hannah! There? Out in the open? Was it at night?"

"Who was it? Do I know him? It wasn't one of those mean boys who lived by Ethan's garden, was it?"

Hannah laughed at her aunt's questions. It was her first and only kiss. Now, she would have to tell Aunt Sofie her big secret.

"I don't know who it was." She waited for her aunt's reaction.

Hannah had the biggest grin on her face and Sofie stood with her hands on her hips wondering if her niece was pulling her leg.

"Hannah! Tell me the truth!" Sofie demanded, but she was laughing along.

"Truly, Aunt Sofie, I don't know. Father had just died, and Mother wasn't well, so I was staying with Grandfather. We were picking up supplies and while he was visiting with people, I just stood by the wall and waited for him to finish. There were several of us playing and some boys were jumping off of the wall making animal sounds and being funny, when one of them landed right in front of me. He said hello and I smiled at him because he was cute, then, out of nowhere, he leaned in and kissed me!"

"On your cheek?" Sofie asked.

"No! He kissed me right on my lips! I started laughing because I didn't know what else to do." She turned to face Sofie as they walked.

"All these years, I wonder if he knew about my father and saw that I was sad. I never saw him again. Isn't that funny? It's like your bee angel!"

They continued laughing with their arms looped as they entered the village gate. Sofie couldn't help herself and turned one final time to look at the surrounding hills. She was comforted by them. They were like a warm hug for the community at the end of the day. Only the watchmen guarded the secrets of the day. They had kept their eyes on the women since they had left that morning. They also knew where Scout had positioned himself, and they smiled at one another as they watched father and son return to their cave. The man, Aaron, and his son had also watched.

Chapter Ten

Sofie and Hannah made more honey cakes than either woman had seen throughout their life. Half the table held the sweet cakes ready for distribution. The first recipients would be the children who somehow knew old Sofie would be preparing them. It was a small village. Everyone knew Hannah had returned, the women were seen leaving the gate the prior morning and they just knew. Scout's heart was happy. He would indulge in the familiar small cakes later. He had gone to his grandfather's hill to speak to the watchmen. His legs had missed the land. Tiberias wasn't challenging and this was home.

"Did you ever lose sight of them?" Scout asked the men.

They shuffled their feet not wanting to tell the son of Stone they had, but it was only a little while. Scout knew Sofie was clever in her ascent to the bees and would keep their great-grandmother's bees secret as long as she could.

"What about the man Aaron?" Scout asked.

Again, they looked around not wanting to admit to losing sight of him. One man spoke.

"His son hunts around the field and easily hides," he told Scout. "They both are very familiar with the land."

Scout waited for the man to say more.

"They followed the women," the watchman said.

"In a protective way?" Scout wanted to know.

"Yes!" they answered. "It was only when we didn't see your sister for a little time that we also didn't see the men."

"Were the men hunting?" Scout asked.

"No, we don't think so. It seemed they only sat down and waited for the women to reappear."

"And then what?" Scout asked them.

"They only watched them until they reached the gate," they said. "The man Aaron is in the field often," the first watchman told Scout.

"Our fathers know him. They told us his family preferred living in the caves. Aaron came down to pick flowers all the time. As we said, he's very familiar with the land."

"He only picks flowers?" Scout laughed with the men.

More feet shuffled before the oldest spoke. "He takes walks," he said. "With Sofie."

"Often?" Scout smiled so they would know he was only concerned for his sister.

"Both have spent considerable time in the field of flowers alone and together," they told him.

It was enough information for now. He didn't want the men to ask him any questions about his sister and the man Aaron. Before his climb down he turned with one last inquiry.

"How old is the boy?" Scout asked.

"About the same age as your Hannah," they said.

Aaron and Finn hadn't left the area and they watched Scout climb up and down his grandfather's hill like he was going to his rooftop to check the sky. Aaron had tremendous respect for him and the entire family. He was anxious for more stories. He was ready to write all Sofie desired for those who would come to live in this village so they would also know the history of this family and community. His heart skipped a beat when he saw her this morning so carefree, laughing while enjoying Hannah running and waking up the field's inhabitants. When the women began walking toward the secret place, he and Finn stayed low to the ground. Finn had discovered many small hiding places on his hunting trips. Aaron was amazed at Sofie's patience at the base of the hill, allowing the bees to know they had a visitor.

"Are they going up there, Father?" Finn wanted to stand a get a better look, especially a closer look at the young woman.

"Yes, Sofie's jar is almost empty. She comes every few months, sometimes sooner."

"Who is with her?" Finn asked.

Aaron knew his son had to concentrate on not calling Sofie the cake woman. He liked hearing Sofie's name spoken. "Her name is Hannah," Aaron said. "She has just returned from Tiberias and is Sofie's niece."

Chapter Ten

"Look Father, there they go!" Finn announced.

The men watched. Aaron smiled to himself as Sofie stopped several times searching the hills for movement. He knew her next move would be to remove a few stones from the path to the bee's hideaway. He could almost hear them buzzing from across the field. He glanced at the sky. It was a perfect day for her to collect Selah's honey.

"Father, how long are we going to stay here?"

"Long enough," Aaron answered.

"What do you mean?" Finn asked.

"We will wait until they come back down and cross the field to go home," Aaron told him. "The bees know Sofie, but she won't tarry. Look, they are already making their way down."

Just then Aaron saw a flash of light on the northern ridge. He wouldn't direct his attention to the high place. He was certain it was Scout making sure his baby sister and only granddaughter were safe. He was a born leader and guardian of these hills. Aaron remembered the rumors of the young Scout strutting on each summit like he owned the place. All the girls wanted to marry him. Aaron was glad he had already met his bride and didn't have to compete with the son of Stone. He also hoped now that Scout was home, he would tell his own stories around late-night fires or while enjoying Simon's stars.

"I will return to my friend Ethan's this night," Aaron told Finn.

"How long do you plan to stay in the village?"

"That will depend on Sofie," Aaron answered.

Finn wished he could join his father. He could help Ethan and he could go with his father to the cake woman's house to hear the retelling of this family's adventures. He could also get acquainted with the young woman Hannah.

"I will leave you here son," Aaron said. "Come down for service and keep your father company."

"I will," Finn said.

Both men knew it was Hannah who swayed this decision. Aaron only chuckled and hugged his youngest. "Be careful. Go now before the sun hides."

"I will wait until I see you disappear around the hill to Ethan's garden," Finn answered.

His boy was growing up. He had become a good hunter and made sure the family had what they needed. He was like a young Scout Aaron thought, confident in who he was, and the hills had also become his friends and he was comfortable alone with them. The field of flowers was one of his favorite places to wait for small fowl and now with the cake lady's niece here, Aaron imagined Finn would frequent the place more often. He whistled all the way to Ethan's house.

Sofie and Hannah had their honey cakes tied up in bundles for the family. Sofie hoped to walk to Ethan's to give him some and share a small jar of Selah's honey. She also hoped Aaron would be there waiting for her to invite him back to her house to continue the letters. With Hannah at her side yesterday, she was reminded of the close friendships the women in her family had made. It wasn't only Kezi and Avi, but those who had married into the family. It was a circle of love that gathered each day. These afternoons were spent sharing hope and demonstrating faith to the younger women. This is where the secrets of the past were spilled with many tears, but it was the joy of victory that welcomed each soul in the morning. Sofie had kept a close eye on Hannah in the field. She seemed to have inherited a little bit of everyone. Innocence rested behind her smile, but Sofie saw strength in her eyes and heard hope in her laughter. They had drunk wine and searched clouds for loved ones and proclaimed Selah's honey would continue to be a guarded treasure. Hannah was the one. Sofie could trust her. There would be plenty of time to teach the young girl and she would make it clear to her to never visit the bees alone. Not until she knew the bees were certain this was Selah's fourth-generation granddaughter.

Ethan was overjoyed with his honey and told Sofie he expected Aaron would make his way down to his house the next day. Sofie would wait to see if he came on his own today. She told Ethan he was welcome to come and have fellowship with her family. Her life had changed, it seemed in an instant. Her niece was home, she met Ethan who had

Chapter Ten

the most wonderful garden she planned to visit at least two to three times a week, and she had quite simply fallen in love. It was Hannah who confirmed she had done so. The two women laughed and cried for hours talking about first kisses and the dreams that gave them hope for their future.

"Aunt Sofie, you have encouraged me like no other," Hannah told her as the clouds had drifted by. "Not even Grandfather could tell me the things you have, and truly, my heart is happy. I know James wasn't the *one*." She had looked at her aunt for several minutes before she continued.

"I know there were boys who liked you," she smiled. "Grandfather told me he used to scare them off! You never gave notice, he told me. I think deep down you knew they weren't the one. You didn't enter a covenant with someone just for the sake of doing so; you waited. Now, God has honored you by bringing Aaron into your life." She couldn't tell if her aunt agreed with her words, but she smiled and then turned on her side away from the clouds to give her niece her full attention.

"When did you gain so much insight? You're right. I believe God has given me the desires of my heart. At least part of them."

"What do you mean part?" Hannah now sat up.

"The voice I heard when the bees were angry that day; I always thought that boy was real. After all these years, Scout, my mother, and friends all thought it was an angel who came to tell me I would be alright. I had dreams of him for years and they finally stopped. Until recently," she said.

"Right after I met Aaron, I had the dream. It was strange. I had fallen asleep at the table, and it had been years since I had it. The only other dream that I have never told anyone...." Sofie wasn't sure if she should tell Hannah. It seemed so silly, and the battle between her mind and heart was exactly that. A battle. She had asked the Lord through the years what it meant and had come up with several conclusions of her own.

"Tell me, Aunt Sofie! I promise I'll never repeat it!" Hannah assured her.

Sofie laid back down. The sky was empty now, the clouds moving west. She hoped for a glorious sunset to finish the day.

"I'm sitting at a large table," she began. "It's big and sturdy, solid as a rock," she laughed.

"Like the one in the house?" Hannah asked. "Great-grandfather Stone's table?"

"Yes! There are three chairs on each side and I'm sitting at one end, and I know my husband is sitting at the other end, but I never see his face." Sofie noticed Hannah moved closer not wanting to miss one word.

"The chairs are filled with boys. Six boys! I can see myself in the dream sitting at the end of that table smiling at my husband who doesn't have a face and I'm so happy! I know they are my boys somehow. They're not small boys; they're all men but I'm not an old woman in my dreams. My hair isn't gray, and I have never understood. I look like I do now. I thought maybe the men represented my brothers, father, and grandfather."

"But there is still one missing!" Hannah's voice said excitedly.

"I know and it's not my husband because he's at the other end," Sofie said.

"It's silly I know, and I've often wondered if that was the family I was supposed to have and that I should have married when I was young."

"No, Aunt Sofie, I don't think so," Hannah replied. "How long has it been since you had that dream?"

"Many years," Sofie answered. "Come now, we'll go to Ethan's and then tomorrow we'll fill that big table up with Selah's honey cakes!"

Now Sofie counted the bundles. She had prepared one for each brother's household, one for Ethan, one for Aaron, and one to pass out to the children. Hannah was a big help. If the day passed with Aaron not stopping by, she would walk back to Ethan's and find out why. Hannah was cleaning their mess and Sofie released her hair to give it a good brushing before the day got away from her. She went to close her door, having opened it earlier to let the heat escape from the room.

"Good morning Sofie," Aaron stood holding the largest melon she had ever seen.

"Hello! Come in, Aaron. What a wonderful surprise!"

Aaron laid the melon on the table and noticed the tied-up bundles, but he couldn't take his eyes off Sofie. Her hair was wild and free and filled his senses. It was longer than he remembered, and it took all his

Chapter Ten

strength to not grab handfuls of it for a closer examination. Besides, Hannah was in the house.

"Shalom dear Hannah," he called to her.

Hannah walked toward both him and her aunt. She realized Sofie had no idea her hair was the center of attention and that Aaron seemed mesmerized by the loose waves.

"Please sit Aaron and have some fresh honey cakes," Hannah smiled.

"Aunt Sofie, shall I help you with your hair?" She saw Aaron's disappointment and quickly said, "Or just leave it and I'll brush it for you later."

"Yes, leave it," Aaron agreed. "Both of you, sit with me and tell me what your plans are today."

"We were going to walk to Ethan's garden to say hello to you," Sofie answered. "We stopped by yesterday."

"Yes, Ethan told me."

Hannah felt awkward. "I'm going to see what Grandfather is doing," and she was out the door before they could respond.

As soon as Aaron heard her close the neighboring door, he stood and grabbed Sofie's hands to rise from her chair.

"I missed you," he smiled, and now he did take handfuls of her hair and brought her closer. Sofie didn't object but he saw her look over at her open window.

"I don't care who sees us," he laughed and then promptly kissed her.

She could taste her honey cakes and tried not to concentrate on any onlookers who may have decided to linger outside her courtyard as the man of the hills was surely seen with his large melon this morning. This thought made her giggle and Aaron only kissed her again. She couldn't help reacting to his warmth and she found herself kissing him back with more passion than she knew lived within her. This man had stirred deep rivers that were never touched, and she could feel the heat rising on her face.

"I missed you too," she told him. They stood smiling at one another until they heard Hannah coming back through the gate.

"What do you want to do?" he asked her. They sat and waited for Hannah.

She came bursting through the door! "Aaron, Grandfather wants to see you," she said. "He's on the roof."

"Which one?" Aaron asked.

"Aunt Sofie's," she smiled.

"He still jumps from his," Sofie laughed.

Aaron wasted no time in meeting the son of Stone. Scout greeted him warmly and the two men sat on Sofie's rug facing each other.

"We are going on a hunting trip," Scout started. "We would like you to join us."

"I would be honored," Aaron replied. "When?"

"Now!" Scout laughed. "Well, as soon as you're ready."

"I will take you to Benjamin's lookout and the cave of Elias," he told Aaron. He smiled as Aaron crossed his arms on his chest indicating his joy at this invitation.

"Your son," Scout said, "Would he like to join us?"

Now Aaron thought he might cry. He could only nod in reply.

"Please, go and gather your things. We'll be gone for three days. You and your son can meet us at the north gate."

"I will need a little over an hour to prepare," Aaron told him as he stood anxious to leave.

"Just bring your weapons. We have everything else you and your boy will need," Scout said.

Aaron didn't remember knocking on Sofie's door and telling her of this unexpected trip. His short sentences and ramblings made Hannah laugh and she was the one who told Sofie of the hunting trip Scout planned. Sofie didn't move. Hannah was talking a mile a minute. The men would be gone three days. Aaron's son was invited also, and Scout was taking Aaron to two special places she had hoped to share with him. Plus, she missed him! Now she wouldn't see him until Sabbath.

Hannah saw her aunt chewing on her nails. "Aunt Sofie, this is wonderful! Grandfather must really like Aaron to include him on this trip. He will be privy to places only our family knows so he must think of Aaron as family already," she smiled.

Sofie only chewed on her knuckles. Scout would possibly find out more about Aaron and his family than she knew.

"Are all the men going?" Sofie asked her niece.

"Yes," Hannah answered. "What has you troubled?"

"I'm not troubled."

— Chapter Ten —

"You're chewing on your hands like you do when you're worried or upset," Hannah reminded her.

Sofie pulled her hands away from her mouth. "I'm only surprised," she said.

The women could hear the men. Their excited voices filled the courtyard. Sofie didn't have to look outside; she recognized each voice of her brothers and their sons. The watchmen would be steadfast, and she imagined Scout had given them further instruction to also watch over their families. She sat at her table with her bundles of honey cakes miserable. Aaron didn't even say goodbye. She chided herself now. She had never seen so much joy and excitement in his eyes.

Hannah tried to read her aunt's thoughts. She didn't want to cause her any more worry with careless words.

"Aaron is a wonderful man," Hannah said. "Grandfather must think so too. I don't remember him ever inviting anyone to the hidden places our family has gone to over the years." "Don't you agree Aunt Sofie?"

Sofie could see Hannah's lips moving but she wasn't concentrating on her words. "What did you say?"

"Aunt Sofie don't be concerned about anything," Hannah replied. "Grandfather must think of Aaron as family. Do you agree?"

Hannah's words sunk in. She was right. Scout never asked anyone outside of the family to travel or hunt with him. And to her shock, he was taking Aaron to the lookout of Benjamin. She was mad now thinking about Aaron experiencing the hidden place in the rock that the young boy Benjamin discovered so long ago. She was selfish. She wanted to take Aaron to this special place. Now his eyes would see the coveted locations of the village with her brother. She heard the rich laughter of Scout as he joked with his brothers about their hunting skills. She got up to tell them to have a safe journey. The sun was bright, and she shielded her eyes to look at the supplies the men would carry. She hoped Aaron would be prepared and her brothers would find him to be a worthy companion. Not too many men could keep up with the sons of Stone.

Scout came over and hugged her. "Don't worry little sister. I didn't plan this to upset you. We all like Aaron. I thought this would be a great opportunity for him to bond with the family."

Sofie didn't speak. Her feelings for Aaron were too personal to share at this moment in the bright sun with her brothers and their sons gathered to listen.

Scout pulled her off to the side. "Is there something you're not telling me? Have I misread your eyes when you look at him?" He smiled now hoping to put her at ease.

"This trip just caught me off guard, that's all brother." She lowered her eyes to confess to Scout she did indeed have great affection for Aaron, and she had truly felt love for the first time in her life.

"We will all look after him and his son," Scout told her.

"His son?" Sofie repeated.

"Yes, I told him to bring his son," he answered. Scout didn't want her to know the watchmen had filled him in telling him the boy was seen often hunting their favorite grounds.

"Sister! It will be well. We'll see you in three days. Oh, and we're taking our honey cakes!" he laughed.

The men said their farewells to their wives and began walking toward the gate. This is where they told Aaron to meet them. Pella had been quiet. She stood at her door waving goodbye to Scout and keeping a close eye on Sofie. Once Scout was out of view, she called Sofie to come over.

"We could follow them," she grinned.

"No, we can't!" Sofie exclaimed. "I'm fine. I had only hoped to take Aaron myself to the lookout."

"How long has it been since you've made that climb?" Pella asked.

"A long time," Sofie answered. "It's better for Scout and the men to show him."

"Perhaps later Aaron can take you," Pella smiled. "Wouldn't that make it special?"

"I guess so," she said.

"Of course, it will be. You can pack a lunch and Aaron can write your letters from the very place the men began watching over this village," Pella said.

"Come inside out of this heat," Pella told her. "Hannah, grab a skin of your grandfather's wine. Let's talk."

Chapter Eleven

Aaron was sweating! He hadn't run up his hill like this for quite some time. Finn stood at the top fascinated by his father's energy. Aaron began shouting before he reached the top.

"Grab your bow! We're going hunting! Hurry! We're meeting Scout and the others at the gate!" Aaron rushed by him, collected his special knife, and rolled up a few supplies in the blanket off his bed. He tied up his makeshift bundle telling Finn to hurry.

Finn was turning in circles looking for the supplies he took with him while searching the land. He was excited! His father's enthusiasm made him laugh. The cake lady's brother had invited them to join him. It was truly an honor. Finn hoped for more feathers for his arrows. He thought himself a skilled hunter and couldn't wait to demonstrate his marksmanship. Father and son didn't talk as they made their way down the incline. It was only when their feet touched the valley floor that Finn started asking questions.

"Why did Scout ask us today? Where would they be hunting? How long would they be gone? Scout didn't mind that he was coming along? Did the young niece of the cake lady know he was invited?"

"The men must have decided at the last minute to go," Aaron started.

"The men?" Finn asked.

"Scout's brothers and their sons are also going. We will be gone for three days. They are taking us to their favorite hunting grounds and yes, Hannah knows you were invited," Aaron told him.

"Let's hurry!" Finn said.

They saw Scout and the others waiting for them. Finn felt like a man today. He could see pride in his father's eyes. He sized up the sons of Scout's brothers. He had seen them hunting before, but they hadn't discovered his hiding place. He found himself continuing to look up wondering how many watchmen were positioned. He thought several. There would be no sight of the women. The men wouldn't take a chance of having them nearby. Not many had been struck by a wayward arrow, but it had happened. Hannah and Sofie would be discouraged from visiting the field of flowers.

Scout stopped several times and Finn watched him turn in every direction and smell the land. The brothers only stood and waited for their older sibling to proceed. The next time Scout stopped he didn't do his rotations but only looked to the north. Finn saw the watchman wave his greeting out of the corner of his eye. Scout looked right at him and smiled. Yes, he was a man today in the company of the sons of Stone. He knew the location where the wild mountain goats fed and hoped to be the first one to strike. The men could feast tonight if he had his way. They had made good time. The hills were happy today allowing the men liberty to run and crisscross over the ancient paths. Joshua's sons were fast runners, and they took off like lightning once able to speed across open space. They returned to the group saying they didn't see any game where they normally hunted.

Finn spoke up. "I know a place."

Scout smiled again, "Lead the way, Finn."

It wasn't long before the men were all crouched low watching the goats graze. Finn took his best arrow to prepare to shoot. The younger men also raised their bows, but Scout held his hand up indicating for them to let Finn attempt the first try.

Finn looked for a young kid. The meat would be tender.

"Steady," he told himself. He struck with success and the men released their arrows.

The goats had scattered too quickly, and Finn was the recipient of shouts and claps on the back as they approached his prize. They would need to dress the goat if they continued.

"Where do you camp when you hunt this place?" Scout asked him.

Finn turned and pointed, "Back on the northern ridge."

Chapter Eleven

The first skin of wine was shared, and they made their way back to the place they would sleep tonight. Aaron was beaming! He kissed his son congratulating him on his skills. The men *were* bonding, and a few smaller fowl were also collected for the evening fire. The watchmen kept their eyes on the twelve men. They weren't surprised to see the youngest carrying the small goat across his shoulders. They wondered if Scout would leave the group to bring them part of the roasted meat.

The hunting party sat around the fire. Scout's brothers were pouring wine liberally while regaling past hunting trips. The men were relaxed under the open sky, the watchmen signaling all was quiet. Finn was celebrated for his cunning skills and for sharing his secret hunting place with the wild goats. Aaron wondered if Joshua and Samuel's sons would now make regular visits to Finn's exposed feeding place. He hoped that all the young men would become friends with Finn during this time together, especially when he let his mind think about a future with Sofie.

The men had their fill of food and wine, and their voices became more exaggerated as the fire's flame wanted to say goodnight. Aaron kept a close eye on his son. He was keeping up with Joshua and Samuel's sons' consumption. Finn was having a good day and a better night getting to know the family. Scout stood to stretch. Aaron stood also. It was habit. He followed Scout's movements. The man seemed to always be on guard. It was a clear night and Aaron noticed Scout peering into the heights where the stars lived.

"Simon's stars," Aaron said.

Scout smiled, "So, my sister has told you his story?"

"He sounded like a fun, interesting man," Aaron replied. "I have enjoyed all the memories Sofie has shared so far."

"I was a little taken back when my brothers told me she asked you to write her letters," Scout told him.

"Yes, I was too," Aaron laughed. "She waited for several weeks to approach me. We have become good friends."

Scout was still smiling, and Aaron thought he was waiting for him to say more.

"We have grown close," he said.

"Close?" Scout asked.

Aaron was thankful they were not alone up in the hills, and he was careful with his words. "I admire your sister. She is simply amazing," he said. "Your family is her rock. I can understand why she wants her letters written. She's also a wonderful storyteller and as I've told her, I feel like I know every member as if I met each one."

Scout nodded. He wasn't sure what Sofie had told him. "Are you tired?" he asked.

"No, this fresh air is life itself," Aaron answered.

"Grab your knife," Scout said. "Tell your boy we'll be back in a couple of hours."

The moon was full. The men could walk the land without relying on torches. Aaron assumed Scout knew every rock that called this hill home. He followed his steps until they reached the steep incline. Scout whistled and out of nowhere the shofar replied. *The watchmen.* Their faithfulness let Scout know they were fine to make the climb.

Finn heard the call and jumped to his feet. The men told him it was Scout, not to worry.

"Where are they?" Finn asked no one in particular.

"Walking the land," is all Joshua said. "Sit, relax," he told the young boy.

Finn sat, but now he felt anxious. He didn't pay attention to the direction his father and Scout traveled. He concentrated now on the whistle he heard before the shofar responded. The northern ridge. He would keep his eyes fixed on the North Star until his father returned to the fire.

"Is this the ridge of Elias?" Aaron asked Scout.

"Yes, but we're climbing to the other side to Benjamin's lookout," he said.

Aaron felt his hands begin to sweat. He gripped his knife for assurance. He was excited and nervous. He prayed under his breath that his feet would be steady. He also knew Sofie wanted to bring him here. He looked up and wondered if she truly could make this climb. He couldn't imagine any of the women coming here but Sofie had been here. Kezi too, and he wondered if even Selah had found the hidden place as a young girl and just never told anyone. Right now, he was with Simon's grandson under the careful eyes of the watchmen with a beautiful moon to guide him to the infamous lookout of Benjamin.

Chapter Eleven

He tried holding his breath so Scout wouldn't detect his anticipation that waited at the crest.

"Ready?" Scout turned to look at him.

"Yes!" Aaron said a little too enthusiastic in his hearing. He knew Scout slowed his pace for his benefit and Aaron didn't want to rush this privilege.

As they continued their climb, he couldn't imagine Sofie doing so. He felt extremely grateful and special that Scout would bring him to this coveted place. Perhaps he decided to bring him at night thinking he wouldn't remember how to get here again. The watchmen would know if anyone traversed this hill, even one of Finn's wild goats.

"We're almost there," Scout called down. He extended his hand and pulled Aaron up the last step.

"Turn around," Scout told him.

Aaron sucked in his breath. It was magnificent! The moon showed off, and its splendor covered the valley below enabling both men to see not only the northern ridge but also the glow of the fire where the men were still drinking and talking of days gone by. Aaron raised his hands in praise. The Lord had smiled on him this night blessing him with this view.

"Come," Scout said after giving him a few more moments to breathe in God's handiwork.

Before Aaron could adjust his eyes, Scout had a small fire lit. He sucked in his breath again. The coveted place was larger than he expected, and it was obvious there were supplies hidden here for those who needed to escape for an afternoon and simply enjoy the space.

"If these walls could talk," Scout laughed.

"I can only imagine," Aaron replied. "Sofie told me about the boy Benjamin who found this place."

Scout made himself comfortable while Aaron continued to examine the sides of the cut-out rock. He didn't think his sister told him about the time Simon was taken from this very spot and there were other stories he could share.

"My grandfather once discovered a man hidden here. My grandmother ran back to the village to alert the men. There was much celebration when they returned to find my grandfather had kept the man at knifepoint, but it was who the man was that had them shouting their praise," Scout told him.

"Who was this man?" Aaron's eyes were wide expecting another great story.

"Peter. The apostle Peter," Scout smiled. He wasn't disappointed in Aaron's reaction. The man of the hills sat with his mouth wide open now.

"My grandfather, and of course, Selah, were very conflicted at first as Peter was the one who had confronted Malchus the night our Lord was arrested, but Peter was invited down to stay in the village and my grandfather told me he spoke with him half the night. My father was named after him," Scout added.

Aaron could only stare at Scout across the flames. He knew he was counted in the company of only a few who were privy to this information.

"My grandfather was young, and he spent countless hours on this rock. I know my sister hasn't told you every family event and I will let her share the memories she has held in her heart."

"I am blessed by your friendship," Aaron said. "And your trust. I haven't repeated anything Sofie has told me. I do remember when your father came home. There was still persecution of believers spoken about in the privacy of our homes. This was the time my family decided to live in the caves. I was a young boy, and your father and grandfather were legends," he smiled.

"I also remember seeing you on occasion on your grandfather's hill. Did you bring Sofie here?" Aaron asked.

"Only once," Scout answered. "She was young. She wore all of us out wanting to see the place where...well, I'll let her tell you about that time."

Aaron thought he heard movement outside and noticed Scout didn't blink. The sound was above him and he grew nervous. There were times when the rock shifted and even quaked.

"The watchmen," Scout said. "They are always close."

Scout left the fire burning. The watchmen would have a time of rest at this post and a small meal. Others were positioned on Elias' ridge and other points scattered across the hills only Scout and his family knew about the secret locations. Not everything would be shared, and

— *Chapter Eleven* —

he knew even Sofie didn't know about these places to accidentally tell Aaron.

"Let's go," Scout said. "The men will be looking for us."

Aaron took advantage and stood once more letting his eyes take in every curve of the valley below him. His imagination was running wild. *Peter!* He could be standing in the exact place the apostle did searching the expanse for anyone who may have followed him. He never felt more alive just then and couldn't wait to see Sofie and let her know how much he appreciated her brother's kindness.

The watchmen alerted that Scout and Aaron were heading back to their camp. His brothers would calculate his arrival. Aaron wondered if Finn heard the second call of the family's signal. They walked at a fast pace, both thankful for the trained eyes at the lookout and beyond.

"You're welcome to visit the hideaway Aaron anytime you want," Scout told him. "Perhaps you'll bring your son here. I don't want Sofie making the climb. There are other places she can go," he told him. "The watchmen know who you are, you'll have no trouble."

"Thank you," Aaron said.

He had no other words. He was overwhelmed with thoughts of being permanently connected to this family. Oh, he wished Sofie were here right now under the moonlit sky with her hair loose letting the soft breeze have its way. He wanted to shout to Simon's hill that he loved her and was prepared to take care of her and cherish her memories, and make sure her letters were written for those who would come to this same valley generations from now and be filled with the awe and splendor of God's creation and the family who trusted in only Him for everything.

Scout seemed to sense the cries of Aaron's heart and he stopped suddenly.

"Do you love my sister?" he asked.

"Yes, I do," Aaron replied without hesitation.

"Does she know?"

"Know that I have fallen in love with her," Aaron said. Scout only looked at him more intently. Aaron suspected he was asking something else.

The men began calling out to them. Joshua and Samuel led the group ready for the two elders to join them for more wine and hunting stories.

"Tell Sofie soon," Scout said, and then he turned to make his way to his waiting brothers.

The following two days were the same as the first. The men hunted during the day and celebrated at night. Aaron kept his eyes and ears open. The sons of Stone were good men, generous in their time, possessions, and knowledge of the land and resources. There were other fresh springs and wells discussed that Finn hoped he could remember the locations. He couldn't wait to be taken to Benjamin's lookout and hoped his father would plan the trip soon. The men embraced as family at the gate and kind words were spoken by every member to Aaron and Finn. Scout didn't think they were ready to go to their own homes and given an invitation, he was certain both father and son would come home with him. Aaron missed Sofie and Finn had made mention of Hannah to Joshua's sons around the late night fires with his fill of wine. These men were considered family already and Scout knew they also felt this immediate bond.

Aaron and his family had been part of the small village even though they chose to live separated by one hill. Scout smiled to himself at Aaron's recollection of his father and that Aaron had also seen him strut around as a young boy on his grandfather's summit. The village was close-knit, and he had slept soundly knowing both his baby sister and only granddaughter would never leave its protective arms.

It was the Sabbath. Aaron had a choice to make. Finn was on his heels the entire day. They would need to stay in the village. Aaron couldn't wait to see Sofie. He imagined Finn hoped to see Hannah. He would stop at Ethan's and ask to stay, however, he thought they would end up on Simon's roof. Finn wrapped his new feathers carefully and would continue to cure the skin of the goat for a new pouch to carry them. Aaron hid the leather he was braiding, hoping to find the special token he wanted to include. It had to be perfect. He also wanted to work on Sofie's letters. His parchments were left at her house, and he would gather them tomorrow or the next day. He had much

— Chapter Eleven —

to write. He spent the day with his family. Soon, he would tell them about Sofie and his desire to marry her. Aaron suspected they would embrace Sofie, especially when they saw how much love he had for the daughter of Stone.

Father and son arrived at Ethan's door bearing gifts from their recent hunt. Of course, they were welcome to stay as long as they wanted, and they made their way to the house of worship. Scout, his brothers, and their sons were waiting for them. Others turned when the greetings were heard from the men. Aaron and Finn were ushered in, and they sat with the patriarch of the village.

Sofie and Hannah were searching for them from above. Sofie's heart skipped a beat when Aaron walked in at Scout's side. The trip had refreshed him, she thought. His skin had that fresh glow, and his eyes were alert and shining. His face was relaxed, and it was only seconds before he began to look for her. Their eyes met and Sofie could have sworn she saw some type of light between them. Hannah gripped her arm suddenly.

"Who is that?" she asked her aunt.

Sofie looked to where her niece was staring. Finn. He wore the same sun-kissed skin, and his eyes were just as bright. Sofie laughed behind her hand when she realized Finn and Hannah were staring at each other as she and Aaron were. *What was the Lord up to?* Service seemed to drag. It was the first time Sofie had ever thought so, but she knew the reason she felt this way. *Aaron.* She couldn't wait for him to hold her in his arms and wondered where they would find privacy for him to do so. The brothers assembled around Scout afterward and the men waited for the women.

"Everyone, I insist you come to my house for dinner and fellowship," Scout told them. "No need to go home, we have prepared for the family."

"Aaron, Finn, you will join us," Scout added. It was a statement, not a question or invitation. They were included as family.

Aaron walked up to Sofie. "Hello," he smiled. "I don't believe I have ever formally introduced my son Finn."

Finn greeted Sofie but his eyes never left Hannah. Before Aaron could say any more, Finn came close to Hannah and introduced himself. Hannah smiled politely and lowered her eyes. She couldn't look at him in front of her grandfather. He would see right away that she was smitten. Joshua and Samuel's sons couldn't get Finn's attention. They wanted him to walk with them and talk about the next time they would try and find the goats. Both Aaron and Finn had lingered behind to escort the women home. Aaron and Sofie walked as close as they could without raising concern. Aaron did manage to brush her fingers delighting in how the blush of her favor rose on her neck and face. Hannah noticed but she was listening to Finn talk about meeting her family and how much he enjoyed the unexpected trip. At least that's what she thought he was telling her. His teeth were white as goat's milk, and he had one dimple on his left cheek. He was adorable. Handsome really for such a young man. She found ease and comfort with him immediately. She thought it was because he knew the land as her ancestors did and the small village community had always been his home. He was home.

Pella had every door and window open, and laughter filled both courtyards. Sofie and Hannah joined the other women. All had been prepared beforehand and now they waited for the prayers and blessing to be spoken. Scout was happy. He loved all his family gathered in one place. The children sat on the floor and spilled out to the walled fronts of the houses. The men would settle on the roof where more wine would be shared, and where Aaron and Finn would sleep. Scout wouldn't take no for an answer. He continued to keep their cups filled almost to prevent them from attempting to walk to Ethan's.

Aaron watched his consumption. He hoped to sneak over to Sofie's roof later. He also watched his son. He only had eyes for Hannah. He noticed Scout kept his attention on everything and everyone. All the men were talking over each other enjoying their Sabbath rest. Finn walked over to the short wall and breathed in the beauty of the night. Scout rose to join him, but Hannah appeared at the top of the stairs, and he waited to see if she noticed Finn standing alone. She had nothing in her hands, and he smiled to himself. His granddaughter had no reason to come up the narrow steps except to check on the men. One young man anyway he thought. Finn must have sensed his granddaughter near as he turned while she walked toward him. Scout saw the delight in each of their faces.

"Did you get enough to eat Finn?" Hannah asked.

Chapter Eleven

"Yes, thank you," he replied.

Hannah glanced back at both Aaron and her grandfather. She wished her aunt would come up to take some of the attention from them.

"You can see pretty far from here," Finn told her. "I'm surprised."

"I've spent many days on this rooftop. It's everyone's favorite place," she smiled.

He pointed to the small cluster of hills. "We were hunting just beyond there."

Hannah nodded. She wanted him to continue to talk. She liked his voice. It hadn't quite matured to the deep tone she knew he would have in a few more years.

"I love this land," he said.

"Do you have a favorite place?"

"Several," he smiled. "Perhaps we could go...I mean, maybe I could take you to one of the areas I go often."

"I would like that," she answered. "Maybe I can show you some of mine," she smiled.

He wondered if she would take him to the field. He also wondered if she climbed to the secret places of the family. His father told him Scout said he could take him to the lookout. Now he was anxious to go so he could also bring her. He looked toward the hills again. *The watchmen.* They probably could see him right now standing with Hannah, and he was certain no matter where she went, they would keep watch and report to Scout. He would like to take a walk right now with her. It was still early. They could walk around the village. Plenty of people would be in their courtyards visiting family and neighbors. They wouldn't be alone.

"Hannah," Scout called to her.

"Yes Grandfather, do you need something?" She quickly went to his side.

"Why don't you show Finn around? I don't think he gets down here too often," he smiled.

Both Finn and Hannah stared at him like he could read their minds.

"Go on now before it gets too late," he told them.

Aaron was jealous. He wanted to take Sofie from this group and have her all to himself. He would have to wait to surprise her later on her roof. He watched his son escort Hannah to the stairs that led to freedom for the young couple. He wanted to follow them down the stairs, scoop up Sofie, and take her to her house so they could be alone. He looked back at Scout who seemed to be reading his thoughts too.

"Will you and Sofie continue your letter writing?" Scout's question took him by surprise.

"Yes, I hope to write all she wants to say," he said. Aaron thought this was his opportunity.

"In fact, I think I'll go and see when she plans to begin again since I haven't spoken with her for a few days." He turned quickly before any of the men could comment. He found Sofie outside telling Finn and Hannah to be mindful of the time.

"Yes, Aunt Sofie, we will," Hannah said.

Aaron stood beside her watching them walk slowly towards the main gate of the village.

Sofie smiled at Aaron, "I trust you had fun with my brothers, and they behaved themselves," she laughed.

"We had a wonderful time. I would like to tell you about it," he said. "In private."

Sofie glanced back at Scout's door and looked up at his roof. Aaron thought she looked nervous.

"My parchments," he started, "They are in a safe place?" he asked.

"Of course, come, let's sit for a while and talk," she answered.

They went out of one courtyard and entered another. Aaron missed her house, the smell of it, and Stone's sturdy table where Sofie's memories were poured out. As soon as she closed her door, he pulled her close and inhaled all his own memories. He could feel her relax in his affection and he waited for her to turn her face up toward him inviting him to express his devotion. It seemed like hours as they stood by her door tracing each other's faces with their hands, smiling with their eyes of their fondness for one another, and Aaron thought each morning would start like this once they were joined together. Sofie tried to read every flicker of gold as she searched his eyes hoping she saw the same love she held in her heart. It had been almost six months since they began meeting. She noticed when his eyes would hide under a hood of pleasure when he enjoyed Simon's stars and a cup of wine at night. He would shuffle his feet when he was uncertain what to say. He would murmur words she couldn't understand when he buried his face into her hair. She could feel the strength in his hands when they walked through the field of flowers. She trusted him. He was the only man outside of her family that she ever felt this safety. She practically collapsed in his arms now rehearsing all his wonderful traits.

Aaron took advantage of this time alone and Sofie reacted to him. He was careful but couldn't help bringing her closer for one last lingering kiss.

"Sofie, I adore you," he told her while he held her now at arm's length. He knew his limits. "Let's sit and talk."

She wanted to sit next to him but chose the chair across the table. This way she could continue to study every feature she had come to love.

"I went to Benjamin's lookout," he said with excitement. "Just me and Scout."

"Isn't it a marvelous view?" she asked.

"Yes! I couldn't believe how far I could see, especially at night."

"At night? You climbed at night?" She couldn't believe her brother. *This wasn't safe!*

"The moon was full! It was simply stunning!" he answered.

"I wanted to show you this special place," she said.

Aaron smiled. He wasn't sure how to tell her of his uncertainty she could climb up there.

"Of course, I wouldn't go there at night!" she laughed.

"Your brother told me there were other places you could show me," he smiled.

"The cave of Elias," she whispered.

Every young heart who had fallen in love visited the cave. She felt shy suddenly and alarmed. Selah's bees also frequented the cave when they were disoriented from noise or smoke. The hive had called the top of the mounded earth home for generations. She would eventually disclose this information, but Aaron wasn't family. Yet.

He looked around for his supplies. He wanted to make some notes about the lookout for Sofie's letters.

"What do you need Aaron? Are you still hungry?" Sofie asked.

"No, but could you bring me my parchments?"

She had hidden them from Hannah. They were in her sleeping area. She hoped Aaron wouldn't follow her. It was dark, and darkness could bring vulnerability. She quickly retrieved his papers and lit another lamp.

"I want to write more about what I experienced without giving away the location of Benjamin's hiding place," he told her. "If it wasn't so secluded, I think I could live there," he laughed.

This was her opportunity. She took a deep breath hoping Aaron wouldn't notice. "Isn't your home very similar?" she asked.

Aaron laid down his pen. "Yes Sofie, it is."

"I would like to see where you live one day," she told him.

"I will bring you," he said.

"When?" she asked. Just then Finn and Hannah burst through the door.

"Here you are!" Hannah laughed. She saw Aaron's parchments. "Oh, are we interrupting?"

Finn was looking around Sofie's house. He could see how his father would be comfortable here. He sat at the large table like he owned it. The thought occurred to him just then if perhaps his father would live here should he and the cake lady marry. He began shuffling his feet.

Sofie smiled. He looked like Aaron and had the same habits. "Shall we go back to Scout's?"

"Yes, Finn and I will stay there tonight," Aaron said. He rolled up his papers and handed them to Sofie to put away.

"Joshua and Samuel have gone home," Hannah told them. "Grandfather is waiting to have one last cup of wine with you Aaron."

Finn thought he saw disappointment across Sofie's face. He and Hannah *had* interrupted them. He understood. He and Hannah had been interrupted also while they stood at the wall that protected the tiny village. It had grown dark, and the moon didn't make an appearance tonight.

Hannah had been uneasy. She was immediately attracted to Finn and now they were alone at night hidden from view, however, she knew deep down her grandfather could probably see her movements throughout the village. Still, she didn't know anything about him except he was Aaron's son. And there was no doubt of this one truth. Finn looked like Aaron, walked with the same gait, had the same gold flecks in his eyes, and father and son were almost the same height. She figured Finn would pass him in stature by next summer. She chatted

Chapter Eleven

about the small community she called home from the time they left her grandfather's roof. She pointed out Joshua and Samuel's homes and proceeded to tell him about every person who lived there.

Finn didn't hear anything. She smelled good. It was refreshing after spending the last few days with sweaty men from climbing and hunting. He walked as close as he could to try and determine the scent. It was musky yet sweet. Cinnamon, he thought. He couldn't imagine she would use the spice on her skin. Maybe it was in her hair, or it was just the smoke from the cooking fires that had lingered on her garment. He wished the tiny village was larger as they had walked the interior twice. But Hannah didn't run out of words and like her aunt Sofie, had many stories and memories. When they stopped at the gate, she became silent. She seemed to stare at the stone wall for several minutes with both sadness and a smile. He waited for her to tell him another story.

The shofar announced the change of the watchmen. The timing was off Hannah thought. She took it as a personal call to return home. Finn hoped to walk with her again soon where they wouldn't be restricted by gates and walls. He knew the watchmen would always be there. He wasn't sure if they knew of every secret hideaway he discovered through the years, and he wanted to spend more time with her.

Scout was calling down for them to hurry up, that he was tired, and he supposed father and son also needed rest. Sofie and Hannah stayed with Pella as the men joined Scout for his nightcap. Extra pillows and mats had been placed under the covering and several lamps illuminated the space. Finn thought it looked magical. A soft breeze swept across the area and the chimes of shells sang a sweet melody. The men enjoyed the end of the day with simple thanks to God for all He provided. Sofie and Hannah waited to say goodnight to Scout and then Sofie stood to go home.

"Aunt Sofie, would you like me to stay with you tonight?" Hannah hoped she would say yes. She wanted to talk about Finn.

Sofie didn't want to deny her niece, but she hoped somehow Aaron would sneak back over. "It's been a long day. I'm also ready for sleep."

"Goodnight then, I'll see you in the morning," Hannah said.

Pella saw something in both women's eyes. Sofie looked defeated and Hannah seemed anxious with Finn above her. Surely, father and son wouldn't attempt any late-night romantic talks with them. Now she could hear the soft snoring of her husband. She was tired also. She wouldn't leave her granddaughter until she could close her eyes in peace.

"Are you not ready to retire?" Pella asked Hannah. "Did the walk around the village wake you up?" she laughed.

"I only thought Aunt Sofie might want to talk a little while. It's been an interesting day." Hannah lifted her head indicating to her grandmother Aaron and Finn sleeping on their roof.

"Finn seems like a very nice young man," Pella said.

"Yes, Grandmother, he is," Hannah smiled.

"Is he who you wanted to talk to Sofie about this evening?" Pella laughed.

"Maybe," Hannah replied, trying to hide her pleasure. "God is a lot of fun, isn't He? You know I wasn't upset about James, and I thought...."

"You thought?" Pella encouraged her.

"I thought coming back home I may end up like Aunt Sofie, all alone."

Now Hannah's face lit up the room. "But Grandmother! I came back to find her in love with Aaron! It was so unexpected. I have never seen her so happy! And now I have met Finn," she took a breath waiting for her grandmother's reaction.

"I feel very comfortable with him. It's as if he's been waiting for my return. It's peculiar, isn't it Grandmother? That's why I think God is fun!" She giggled now at her words.

"Now both of these men who have brought joy to our family are upstairs sleeping and I feel so excited! That's perhaps why I'm not sleepy," she said.

Pella glanced up wondering if Finn was wide awake feeling just as excited about spending time with Hannah. Yes, the Lord was fun as her granddaughter stated. He had moved on behalf of every family member through the years bringing them to people and places they didn't expect. Sofie didn't expect Aaron and Hannah didn't anticipate meeting someone so soon after James, but Finn seemed perfect, and she had no doubt God's hand was upon this possible union. She stood to join her snoring husband realizing the hour grew late.

"Go and rest granddaughter," Pella said. "I pray you have good dreams," she smiled. She kissed Hannah's cheeks and said goodnight.

Hannah sat with the low light of the lamp thinking about Finn. Her grandfather's snoring had stopped, and the house was still. She

— *Chapter Eleven* —

went to the bottom of the stairs and listened. She heard nothing. No snoring. No talking. No movement. It was dark. There had been no moon to light the passageway and she didn't bring the lamp with her.

Finn sat at the top of the stairs. He heard the subtle sounds of movement. He had plenty of training while hunting. He knew it was Hannah. He wasn't sure if his father slept soundly. He didn't think he was asleep and only pretended to be tired so his son would rest. But Hannah was only a short distance and now he could smell the faint spice that had made his knees weak earlier.

Aaron didn't move. He tried not to laugh while waiting to see what his son might do. Finn's actions would determine his.

"Hannah, can you hear me?" Finn called down in a whisper.

"Yes, *shhh*, my grandparents are sleeping," she said.

Finn glanced back at his father. "Can you meet me halfway?" he asked her.

"Alright, but be quiet," she laughed. She walked up a few steps and stopped for her eyes to adjust.

Finn had the advantage. He could not only smell her position, but the lamp left on the table also cast a hint of light exposing her location on the fifth step. He extended his hand.

"Hello," he said. They sat together with Hannah's hand held firmly in his. "I think my father is asleep. Can we sit here and talk for a while?"

Hannah wasn't nervous about Aaron or her grandparents waking up. It was Finn who made her anxious. He hadn't let go of her hand and she turned her head to the wall so he wouldn't see her smiling.

Aaron laid still. He didn't want to eavesdrop. He wanted to sneak out and see Sofie. He got up.

"Children," he addressed them. "I'm awake also. Hannah, when did Sofie leave?" he asked the startled girl.

"Not long ago Aaron. I'm certain she's still awake. Shall I unlatch the door?"

"No, I will climb over," he told them.

"Climb over? Father, just leave through the door," Finn said.

"I have a better idea," he smiled.

Finn and Hannah went to the top of the stairs and saw Aaron looking over at Sofie's roof. Finn watched him look behind him and before he could say anything, Aaron took a running start and jumped onto Sofie's rooftop.

"Father!" Finn rushed to the side, but his father had his arms raised in victory and also did a little dance which had Hannah doubled over.

"My grandfather does that," she told Finn. "He scares Aunt Sofie all the time."

"Well, I hope she doesn't scream when she sees my father in her house," Finn replied.

They tiptoed across the space and waited, hoping to hear only a slight gasp of surprise from Sofie. They settled on the sleeping mats and carpets strewn on the floor.

"What were you doing?" Finn asked her.

"When?" Hannah looked puzzled.

"When you were standing on the stairs," he smiled.

"Oh, I...well...I was just wondering if everyone had fallen asleep."

"That is all?" he asked.

"Yes," Hannah bit her tongue. It was all. Secretly she may have hoped Aaron was snoring away like her grandfather and she and Finn could spend more time together.

"So, did you like Tiberias?" he asked her.

"No, I was homesick the entire time I was there," she said.

"I'm glad you came back," he told her.

Hannah could hardly see his face, but his words sounded sincere. "Me too," she said. "I was taken aback by my Aunt Sofie's friendship with your father. I've never seen her so happy. It's almost a miracle."

"A miracle?" Finn questioned.

"Aunt Sofie has never been involved with anyone. Ever. I think most people figured she would never marry. It's what I thought, but now, I have hope for her."

"Hope that she will join herself to my father?" Finn asked.

"Of course," Hannah said. "Who else?" she laughed.

"And you, Hannah, do you also have hope for a future with someone special?" he wanted to know.

Now she turned to face him, "Yes, I believe the Lord works everything out for our good. Tiberias wasn't for me. My home, this tiny village, is good for me. I'm certain I will never leave this land and the

Chapter Eleven

Lord knows He will have to bring me someone who loves this place as much as I do."

"Like me and my father," Finn's statement was out of his mouth before he could think about what he was saying. The words were from his heart. He loved his home. Here he felt free to roam the hills and the high places. He didn't want to talk anymore. He was getting sleepy, and he didn't want his deep thoughts and feelings exposed so soon to her.

"You should go back downstairs," he said. "I need to rest and listen for my father. I can't imagine him jumping back over here."

"I'll go unlatch the door," Hannah said. "Let him know before he attempts it!" she laughed.

"Goodnight Hannah."

She walked as quietly as she could back through the house. Finn stood at the top of the stairs waiting for the door to be opened. He would tell his father to come through it and to use wisdom. It was too dark for him to be trying to act like he was a young man. He smiled now thinking his father's strength had been renewed since he began making these trips to the cake lady's house. He needed to stop referring to Sofie as the cake lady. Especially if...." He was certain his father wanted to marry her. It was only a matter of when.

Sofie wasn't startled by Aaron. She was expecting him. She heard the gentle thud on her roof and knew he jumped over. She was waiting for him to make his way downstairs. Aaron found her door slightly open and smiled to himself. She stood on the other side, and they fell into each other's arms. They didn't speak. They stood for a long time embracing the warmth and peace they felt together.

"I could stand here with you until the sun rises," he told her. Sofie only buried herself deeper in his hold.

"I can't stay," he said. "Finn will not sleep until I return," he laughed.

"I don't want you jumping back over!" she admonished him.

"I can't knock on the door," he said.

She followed him to her roof. He was right. Finn was standing, waiting.

"Father, Hannah has unlocked the door! Go through the house." Finn waved at Sofie not wanting to say unnecessary words.

— *Sofie* —

Aaron did as he was told and was back on Scout's roof within minutes. He suspected Hannah was also awake waiting for him to scurry up so she could latch the door.

"Thank you, son. I didn't trust myself jumping back."

"Did you surprise Sofie?" Finn asked his father.

"She seemed to be waiting for me," Aaron smiled. "And you son, was Hannah hoping you would call down to her?"

"It's late Father. We should try and sleep now," Finn laughed.

Chapter Twelve

The next several weeks flew by with father and son spending almost all of their time with Sofie and Hannah. Aaron continued writing Sofie's memories and had a collection of parchments that remained under Sofie's watchful eye. He also instructed his son to be careful with his words to Hannah as he hadn't disclosed everything to Sofie.

"Father, you can't hide your family," Finn said.

"Hannah keeps asking if I grew up with brothers and sisters and I don't want to lie to her," he added. "I managed to change the subject, but I will have to tell her soon."

Aaron nodded. He didn't think Sofie would be troubled by the family; he had led her to believe Finn was his only son. Father and son agreed to not take them to their cave, and they preferred staying in the village. Ethan had provided rooms for each man, and they helped him with his land. Both Sofie and Hannah stopped daily to help plant and carry water to the garden hoping for every fruit and vegetable to yield their harvest. The evenings were carefree, spent walking the small community, both women rehearsing the stories that brought peace to the village. Aaron and Finn had spoken late into the night of Simon, Benjamin, Elias, Stone, and Scout. They had been exposed to the inner circle and privy to Benjamin's lookout and the cave of Elias. Aaron cried when he passed the bones of loved ones secured in their carefully handcrafted boxes. They had become his family. He wanted to honor each soul with Sofie's letters. He prayed for a long time in the dark coolness that the Lord would guide his pen. Finn hunted with the sons of Joshua and Samuel, and he felt closer to them than his own brothers.

— Sofie —

His father understood. His brothers were older and began their families at a young age. Finn practically grew up as an only child. His son had fallen in love with Hannah just as he had surrendered his heart to Sofie. He began to plan his intentions with the special token of his love and revealing his family to her. He would need time to collect his thoughts and prepare his offering. He knew just the place.

Finn rose early. He was anxious to spend the day with Hannah. He was taking her to the lookout. She confessed she had never been and that she was afraid of heights. Finn thought she would need to cling to him the entire way up and down.

"Are you truly not comfortable on top of the hill?" he asked her.

"I don't know Finn. Grandfather would never take me."

"You'll be fine. Once you're up there, I think you'll never want to come down," he smiled.

Hannah looked up at the secret place hidden through the ages, "I don't know," she said.

"We'll go slow, Finn told her. "It's not as high as it seems."

Hannah thought about the trail to the bees. It was a short climb up the small hill. A child could easily run up the worn path. Selah had. Her Aunt Sofie did, and now she had been shown where the bees lived. Today, she would take the hand of Finn while he guided her to another family location most would never see in their lifetime. And she would be taken by someone who wasn't family. It was odd. She was nervous. *What if something happened and she got stuck up there? What if Finn fell? What if...she told herself to stop with these thoughts.* Her grandfather and the watchmen would see them. Nothing was hidden from their sight. She took a deep breath and grabbed the skin of water and the bundle of food she would carry. Finn would be there soon. He wanted to reach the lookout before the sun was high in the sky. She had been staying with her aunt. In the last few weeks, both Aaron and Finn arrived together each day. Her aunt was still sleeping, and she went outside to watch for Finn. She tied her food to the strap of her skin of water letting the bread and dried fruit rest on her side. She needed free hands today. She and Finn had been inseparable, and the family was hopeful to hear of another engagement. They also wondered what was taking Aaron so long to promise Sofie his love. When she asked Finn about

Chapter Twelve

his family, and was there a reason his father was waiting, Finn changed the subject which was becoming his usual answer.

"Please Hannah," he said, "Ask my father. I do not wish to speak for him. It's not something we do."

"It's your family," Hannah declared.

He had met every member of hers. Neither she nor Sofie understood this secrecy. Both had several conversations about it. Sofie was concerned but Scout didn't seem bothered, so they tried their hardest to refrain from asking too many questions, but it wasn't normal.

"There's reason and purpose for all my father does and doesn't do," Finn told her. "Please I beg you, don't ask me anymore."

They took their time walking through the field. Hannah wasn't sure which hill Benjamin's lookout was hidden. She knew she would need to rely on Finn for everything. They passed the entrance to where the bees greeted Selah, and she looked the other way so Finn wouldn't see her staring in their direction. She was happy they were quiet today, the colony busy flying among the flowers, working and collecting for their queen. Soon she would make another trip to retrieve the sought after honey.

Finn turned to her, "Are you ready?"

She let her eyes take in the fullness of the large hill. She swallowed her fear and tried to concentrate on the beauty of the land. She couldn't wait to see it from above, like a bird or one of Finn's mountain goats, but she *was* nervous. She watched him adjust his belt and shift his belongings. He had his bow and arrows, his knife, a skin of water, and a small ram's horn. She never saw him carry it before. She knew it was for safety. Now she shielded her eyes and examined each surrounding hill.

"They're up there," he smiled. "I'm certain your grandfather also watches."

Hannah sighed her relief. Her grandfather wouldn't let Finn take her up here if he wasn't confident in his capability. She had to admit he was a strong man; a skilled hunter and he respected the land. Just then he grabbed the back of his garment from between his legs and brought it to the front where he tucked it securely in his belted waist. She saw strength in his legs and began to relax.

"You should do the same," he told her. "I'll turn around." He knew she didn't realize she was staring at his legs.

— *Sofie* —

"Hannah," he smiled, "It will be easier for you to climb."

The watchmen. What would they tell her grandfather? Or was her grandfather waiting to see what she would do?

"Ok, turn around," she said. She didn't bring her tunic as high and only her knees to her feet were visible.

"We'll go slow," he told her. "You can hold on to my leather band with my bow and arrows. If you need to stop, just tell me."

"I'm ready," she said.

Finn felt her tug a little on his belt. He liked that she had to depend on him. When he couldn't feel her full weight, he stopped. It seemed she was taking mental notes of the gray and brown rock. He caught her several times running her free hand over its surface. Like her Aunt Sofie, he imagined she was remembering all the stories she grew up with, and at one point he thought her eyes were closed, smiling, and getting reacquainted with all those who had climbed before her. The sun grew hotter, and Finn checked the sky.

"Shall we continue?" he called down. He didn't want to interrupt this experience, but they would need to drink water soon and get out of the sun.

When they reached the top, Scout exhaled. "Have someone come to my house when they leave. I don't want them to hear the shofar," he told the watchmen.

He also reminded them Aaron was in the cave of Elias and to keep him posted on his movements. Aaron had carried several bundles. Scout thought he would be there for a few days. He had told Scout he wanted to have some quiet time deep within the cave walls. *"A time of prayer and fasting,"* he told Scout. There was no doubt Aaron was preparing to ask Sofie to marry him. Looking over at the ridge where Finn and his granddaughter now stood, he was certain they would have two weddings to celebrate soon. He took one more look at Hannah standing on the peak where his grandfather Simon was taken and prayed now for the boy Finn to be as watchful as the men who had stood faithfully each day guarding their village.

Hannah was crying. She looked at Finn, "It's too beautiful, my heart can't take it!"

Finn leaned against the solid rock and gave her the time and space each new visitor deserved. She saw everything! Birds were taking flight

— Chapter Twelve —

from another animal disturbing their rest, and Finn's goats were quickly jumping from cleft to cleft on the opposite side. He waited for her next discovery. The crying became soft sobs as she pointed to the sea, the shades of blue greeting another long-awaited ancestor. *Selah's sea.* She turned and fell into Finn's arms blessing him for bringing her this afternoon and telling him she never wanted to leave. He retreated into the open niche and started a small fire. The watchmen would see the trail of smoke escaping the hidden place and it was his signal that all was well. He was certain they stood at their post waiting for the young couple to safely reach the top. He knew they didn't doubt his efforts, but he was climbing with the great-granddaughter of Stone, son of Simon, the son of Selah. He thought the entire village breathed a sigh of relief when Hannah gazed out over the expanse, her joy spilling on the ground and on the young man Finn's shoulders.

Hannah was overwhelmed. She no longer had a fear of being so high from the ground and realized for the first time in her life that she preferred this advantage. *She could see everything!* This was the place where so many of her family's legends were born. She thought of her Aunt Sofie. Oh, she wished she was here standing with her now. She understood why the letters were so important. This is where faith lived. Each family member had stood upon this rock declaring to themselves and their enemies that God was the One true God, He sent His Son Jesus, and no matter the consequences, trials, persecution, and hardship they faced, their faith was unshakable, and they wouldn't be moved! It was a declaration that the hills, valleys, and sea had heard throughout the generations. She looked in the direction of the blue water again. She waved her arms hoping it would also hear her heart and that she too would stand and proclaim this truth.

Finn smiled when he saw Hannah waving. He had done the same. He saluted each hill and tree the first time he came. He shouted his praise to the sky that covered all of them and was thankful for this blessing. He would give Hannah a few more minutes to enjoy the view with her own thoughts, and then they would share a little food.

"I could stay here all day," she told Finn. "Is there a reason we cannot?"

"We can stay the better part of the day," he said. "We need to climb down while it's still light out," he reminded her.

"I bet the stars are magnificent from here," she said.

"Yes, they are," he replied.
"You have been here at night?"
"Yes," he smiled.
"I would like to stay Finn," she smiled.
"We cannot," he answered. "Your grandfather will be waiting and it's not right," he said. "Perhaps...," and he stopped talking.

She knew what he was going to say so she smiled and repeated his word, "Perhaps."

They were comfortable with each other eating their bread and dates. Finn pointed out his hunting locations and stole side glances at her to see if she was bored with his conversation.

"Where do you live Finn?" She watched carefully to see where he might point.

Sofie. He hoped his father would hurry up so both could speak freely. "It's not far," he said.

"The wind is changing," he told her. "We should go."

She helped him gather their bundles and covered the fire. She had no idea how they would get down and she embraced the security of the cleft.

"You'll be right behind me," Finn said. "We'll go slow, and I'll block your fall."

"Fall?" her eyes grew wide.

"I'm only saying if your foot slips, you'll run into me," he smiled. "Come, we'll spend time in the field if we leave now," he laughed.

He had seen her too many times to count strolling through the flowers. One day he saw her sit in the middle of red and yellow and bring single flowers to her face to examine their petals closely. He then watched her methodically pluck each petal, her lips moving and smiling with the results of her private recital. She would then lie down for what seemed an eternity and he dared to get closer one time to make sure she hadn't fallen asleep. That's when he heard her giggling like a young girl trying to reach the cloud that brought her joy that afternoon.

"I'm ready to go down. Thank you, Finn." She saw his surprised look. "Thank you for bringing me here."

The watchmen were ready to act if needed but they had seen Finn almost his entire life navigating these hills. Still, it was Hannah, and they wouldn't move until her feet rested once again on the valley floor.

Chapter Twelve

The wind seemed stronger, and Hannah noticed Finn checked the sky often.

"There's no clouds," she said. "Could this breeze be from the sea?"

"Yes," he replied. "There may be a storm passing through later."

He let her take her time with the field. It was like an old friend. His hunting grounds were the same for him, anxious to see him when weeks had passed with no sighting of the young hunter. They made their way to the gate, Finn thankful the wind had ceased. He knew his father was safe, deep in the cave. Once they passed through the gate, several women stopped to greet Hannah. The sun was setting, and last-minute preparations were being made in the small village. Once again, he gave her privacy. He jumped upon the wall for a last look over the land. He would wait until the women left.

Hannah turned to see him walking on top of the wall's width. The sun was behind him, and she couldn't see the expression he wore. Her palms became sweaty for no reason and her mind was recalling all the moments of the day.

Finn watched her turn in a full circle and then she put her head down. He had no idea what she was thinking about. She moved closer to where he stood and she shielded her eyes to look at his silhouette against the orange sky. He could see her clearly. She was stunning with the warm sun on her cheeks, her eyes still holding the sparkle of the sea she had beheld earlier. He jumped off the wall and took the few steps that separated them. He kissed her with no warning. Hannah gasped.

"It was you!" she shouted.

"What?" Finn asked. "Of course, it's me," he laughed.

"No Finn!" she exclaimed. "I mean it was you, the boy on the wall who jumped down and kissed me when I was young!" She watched his eyes dance with his memory of the day.

"Hannah! It was you?" I can't believe this! You were my first kiss!" he blushed. "My only kiss," he added.

The tears he saw on Benjamin's lookout now flowed again. She began to shake. He quickly led her away to a darkened corner where he could hold her, and they could recall the moment in time that left them both in wonder.

"Hannah, tell me! Tell me what you remember of that day," he held her at arm's length. She was still visibly shaking.

"I was waiting for Grandfather. I was so sad. My father had just died, and my mother wasn't well. I felt so alone and scared. I remember several boys jumping off the wall and playing and then one boy...*you*... jumped down right in front of me and kissed me right on my lips. It shocked me! I looked back several times as me and Grandfather walked back to his house and he...*you*...you were gone. Just now, you doing the same thing...I don't know what else to say, Finn. I'm...."

He didn't let her finish. He pulled her into his arms and kissed her again. "My dear, sweet Hannah," he said. "This is fate!"

"I must go! I want to tell Aunt Sofie! She knows the story! Finn! This is crazy! It's unbelievable!" She was smiling ear to ear.

"No, it's not," Finn laughed. "It's God," he told her.

"Yes, you're right! Oh, Finn, I want to tell my aunt now!"

He kissed her again, climbed back onto his wall, and watched her run back to her Aunt Sofie's house.

Aaron was thankful he brought plenty of oil even though his fire provided enough light for him to write. He was almost finished. He held his gift in his hand pleased with the outcome. It was a promise. He knew Sofie would immediately realize what he meant when he placed it on her wrist. He couldn't wait. There would be many decisions to make. He had prayed over each one. He would speak to his sons. And Scout. His parchments were drying, and he would put them in order with his special letter first. The coolness of the cave invited him to stay. His solitude afforded him time to be still. He checked his supplies and came close to his flame. He started reading. His words were heartfelt as were Sofie's. He prayed he would be able to recite his love and admiration without losing control of his emotions, but he had fallen so deeply in love that he could hardly contain his joy. He smiled now thinking of his youngest boy. Finn knew he had fallen in love with the cake lady before he admitted it to himself. Now there was no question that Finn had fallen for Hannah. He wondered if his son was camped out at the

Chapter Twelve

base of the hill Elias' cave called home. Both of their lives would change before the year's end. He fell asleep smiling.

Finn knew his father had moved deep into Elias' cave. He didn't like moving past the bones to seek his interior sanctuary, so he waited outside for him to make an appearance. He was just as excited to tell him about the second kiss at the wall as Hannah was to tell Sofie. This discovery had left them both in awe of God. There was no doubt in Finn's heart the Lord ordered each of their steps their entire lives and he could hardly sit still. He had stopped at Ethan's before running back through the field making sure his father hadn't come back to their temporary home. He had another skin of water and food for him. He had been in the cave for three days now. He knew his father wanted to pray and finish the letters, but he was too excited! Oh, he didn't want to walk through the space that held the family's remains and he couldn't *run* through the solemn resting place; it would be disrespectful. He took a piece of bread and stared at the opening. He also searched for the watchmen. They were there, and he was comforted that the cave of Elias would always be guarded and that the watchmen may already consider him and his father family. Their bones one day would be carried up this very hill. This thought made him shudder. *Would anyone write letters about him?*

He glanced back up hoping to see his father greet the sun. He had been writing for months about the bones secured in their carved boxes. Each life had a story. Sofie wanted to make sure her family would be remembered and honored. They were. At least in this community and he was certain in Tiberias also. He would ask Hannah about her time in the coastal town to confirm that the memories also lived there. He got a lump in his throat now thinking about his father. Perhaps he would ask Hannah to write a letter about him. She had shocked him when she told him she could read and write. If his father didn't come out soon, he would go inside. He finished his bread and waited for some time. He wondered what the watchmen were thinking about the young hunter who would marry the granddaughter of Scout. He squared his shoulders and began the short climb. He stood at the entrance longer than he thought he would. There was a holy hush, the bones deserved respect. He let his eyes adjust to the cave's essence. Beautiful, carved boxes sat in the niches of the cave's wall hoping for visitors. He got gooseflesh from his neck down. He wanted to count the members but somehow, he felt this would be a dishonor. There were many. Most had writing etched in stone or wood and he recognized a few of the markings. He willed his legs to move but the bones held him captive. Now he was curious. He wanted to know where each family member had been placed with love and care.

Selah. Simon. Benjamin. Stone. Another lump in his throat formed and he found himself on his knees asking the Lord to forgive him for his past indifference to those who had gone before him. Now he thought of a mother he never knew, and he began to weep.

Aaron recognized his son's cries, and he hurried through the dark chambers. He saw his son on his knees, his hands supporting his face while he released years of sorrow. He backed up; Finn hadn't seen him. This was the first and only time he witnessed the Spirit of God ministering to his son. He went back to his fire and waited for Finn to find him.

"Father," Finn called out to empty caverns as he made his way deeper into the rock.

"I am here son," Aaron answered.

Finn followed his father's voice. Just like God the Father, his father was there, only waiting for him to call out first. He began to cry again.

"Son, what is it?" Aaron embraced him as a fresh set of tears fell on his shoulder.

Finn halfway composed himself to look at his father. "I'm so happy," he laughed through his sobs.

Aaron pulled him closer and whispered his love to his son until both men sat to make themselves comfortable. Aaron saw peace in Finn's eyes and maturity rested on his face. He had grown to be a man, ready for a family and the joy that would follow.

Finn took a sip of water to clear his throat before speaking. He couldn't remember a time in his life when he was so emotional. It drained him of his strength, and he felt vulnerable under his father's steady gaze.

"The family," Finn started.

"Our family?" Aaron asked.

Finn shook his head no. He could feel the love of God again begin to rise in his being.

— Chapter Twelve —

Aaron nodded and smiled at his son. "The Lord has visited you this day," he said. "The family of Selah still speaks, and their faithfulness has endured for all these generations."

"He has told you this day that you will also be a part of this blessed legacy and it has overwhelmed you," he smiled.

"Father, you too will join this legacy, and one day, future generations will include our names," Finn told him.

"I felt burdened with this responsibility," he added, "But I immediately knew it was part of God's plan and purpose. You're not going to believe this!"

Aaron leaned forward as Finn reenacted his first kiss to Hannah and then the second. It wasn't unbelievable. He praised God in a loud voice that Finn thought even the bones heard. The men celebrated the goodness of the Lord and talked into the evening.

"How long did you plan to stay here Father?" Finn looked at the stacked parchments and a small leather pouch resting on top of them.

"I only want to finish the letters and I also had one to write. We'll return to Ethan's tomorrow."

"Are you going to ask her tomorrow?" Finn smiled.

"I'm going to tell her," Aaron laughed.

Sofie sat at her father's table stunned as Hannah rambled on about Finn and how he was so patient taking her to Benjamin's lookout, and that she cried when she reached the top and saw the land spread out below.

"It was as if it was waiting for me," she told her aunt.

"I can't explain it. And then I saw the sea! Selah's sea!" she exclaimed. "I wasn't afraid being up so high and I told Finn I never wanted to leave!"

Sofie felt the same way. And she couldn't put it in words either. It was something you experienced. Hannah was energetic in her retelling and Sofie made her repeat everything she remembered.

"I wept on Finn's shoulder," Hannah said.

"He's so strong, yet gentle in his ways that he makes me feel special and like I'm the only one, or rather that I've always been the only one," she smiled.

Sofie understood this too. That's how Aaron made her feel. She had responded to his strength and tenderness on several occasions. She was so happy for Hannah, especially after James.

"Did you see Aaron yesterday?" Sofie asked.

"No Aunt Sofie. I'm not sure where he was." Hannah continued like she hadn't been interrupted by her aunt's inquiry.

"We climbed down early so I would have time in our field," Hannah smiled.

"It was a beautiful day! But Aunt Sofie, wait until I tell you what happened next!" Hannah knew her eyes were twinkling, and she laughed when she saw her aunt scoot her chair closer.

"When we reached the gate, several women came to greet me. Finn disappeared so I was left alone to talk. When the women finished with their farewells, I turned to look for him. He was standing on the wall. I had to shield my eyes from the setting sun, and I couldn't see him clearly, but I knew he could see me. Aunt Sofie, he jumped off that wall and walked straight for me and kissed me right on the lips! In front of God and anyone who might be looking. And that's when I knew," she said.

"Knew what?" Sofie asked.

"It was Finn," Hannah said. She saw the confused look on her aunt's face.

"Aunt Sofie, Finn was the boy who came off that wall when I was a young girl and gave me my first kiss."

"What? Wait. What are you saying?" Sofie grabbed Hanah's hands as if holding them would help her understand what she was telling her.

"The story I told you when I received my first and only kiss. It was Finn!" she shouted joyfully.

"Hannah! Are you certain?" She was sure her niece knew, but this was almost a miracle!

"Aunt Sofie, it was Finn. He remembered also. It was strange. When I saw him standing on that wall, something happened inside, and I got all warm and my hands began to sweat."

— Chapter Twelve —

"That day when I was standing there waiting for Grandfather, I instantly recalled the moment, and I couldn't understand what was happening. When Finn jumped off that wall, I could almost see him in my mind as a boy that day. It was the way he jumped, the way he took charge and walked right up to me, and the kiss was the same," she blushed now.

"Oh Hannah, this is amazing!" Sofie said. "Oh, I wish Aaron were here so we could celebrate this story together."

Her aunt's joy didn't seem to last long. Hannah noticed worry lines on her forehead and around her mouth. "What's the matter, Aunt Sofie?"

"Aaron. I haven't seen him for several days. I don't understand why he hasn't come around. I won't go looking for him again. He knows where to find me. Why would he stay away? I confess I'm a little concerned. He still avoids my questions and I have told him *everything*! All my memories and personal stories he has written and look at all those parchments!" Sofie said.

"Where are they, Aunt Sofie? Did you move them?"

Sofie rose abruptly. "My letters!"

They were gone! She ran to her room where she had hidden them before from the prying eyes of her brothers. They weren't there.

"Hannah! Help me look for them! How could they be gone? I haven't touched them. They were right here, stacked at the end of the table!"

Hannah saw her aunt's distress. "Aunt Sofie, perhaps they fell, or you moved them and forgot."

"No! We were almost finished," she said. "I promise Hannah, I didn't move them!"

The two women went from room to room. They were gone. Months and months of memories disappeared. Hannah made her aunt sit down.

"When was Aaron here last?" she asked.

"Oh, I can't think! We were talking about my father and, of course, my brothers and we were pleased at how much we had accomplished. Aaron always left the parchments here."

"Hannah, where could they be?"

"I don't know. Perhaps Aaron took them," she answered.

"Took them? Why would he remove them from my house? They're *my* letters!" Sofie said.

— *Sofie* —

Her aunt seemed angry now and Hannah kept searching. She looked under things and prayed her aunt simply misplaced them.

"Aunt Sofie, sit, let me look. Try and remember the last time you saw them."

Sofie took deep breaths. The letters were gone. She didn't misplace anything. Aaron took them. She didn't understand why he would do this. They were *her* memories, not his. *Scout*. He would know what to do. All her questions and concerns swirled around the room as she sat replaying all the times she asked him about his family. He never answered. He changed the subject each time. *Who was his family?* Finn was the only person they could rely on to know he was who he said he was. *Did he need someone else's memories to cover up his own life? What would he do with her letters?* Nothing made sense. She had lived a quiet life taking care of her parents and minding her own business. She didn't deserve this betrayal. She bit her tongue as the word formed on her lips. Aaron wouldn't do anything to hurt her heart. *Would he?* She didn't know anything about him! *What happened to his wife? Did he compromise the woman who gave birth to Finn? Where did he live?* He wouldn't even point in that direction! *Is he traveling with her stories to show someone her personal memories?* She was becoming distraught! She took more breaths as Hannah continued shuffling through baskets. *Why did she seek him out that day?* She should have waited for a family member to write for her. She knew she didn't like feeling this way, all anxious and upset. She was used to a peaceful life. She walked her field, collected her honey, and watched sunsets from her courtyard. Aaron disrupted everything! Now, he had disappeared.

She began biting her nails, trying to remember how many days it had been since she last saw him. Finn and Hannah would leave them in the house and give them time to go over every person to make sure Aaron had written all she desired others to know. *It was so personal!* She felt violated. He took her very soul. She fought the tears that tried to escape. It was her fault. She initiated that first conversation. She chided herself for being so forward. She prayed the Lord wasn't angry with her. She only wanted to tell others that they could rely on Him and trust Him as did Selah. And Simon. Even her father Stone, who ran to another city, found mercy and grace and came home. God was faithful. That's all she wanted to say. No matter what you faced in life,

Chapter Twelve

He was there. He comforted Selah when her husband didn't return. He sustained her when trouble found her in a weakened state. He brought love to her when she least expected it. And she extended the same grace to everyone. *Everyone.* Even the Roman soldiers who carried her away one stormy night.

Hannah stood behind her aunt watching her chew on her hands. The letters *were* gone. She had no answers to give her. Now her mind seemed cloudy with several thoughts all at once. *Finn.* He didn't stop by either. Especially after....she couldn't think about him right now. Her Aunt Sofie had been her refuge, her rock, stable and steady her whole life, and now her shoulders were hunched over in distress. *Ethan.* Maybe he would know where father and son were. They could be sitting there right now sharing a cup of wine and all this misunderstanding would be cleared up. She hated seeing her aunt this way. There had to be a logical explanation.

"Aunt Sofie, can I get you anything?" Hannah asked. "Would you like to take a walk?"

Sofie stood. "No, I'm alright. I'll wait for Aaron. If he doesn't arrive soon, well, I'm not sure," she tried to smile.

"Should I go get Grandfather?" Hannah asked her.

"No!" Sofie didn't mean to sound harsh. "I'm sorry Hannah. Let's wait. Are you expecting Finn today?"

Hannah didn't want her to see her concern and she smiled back, "I'm not sure. We didn't make any plans. When...when he kissed me again, I told him I needed to leave at that moment. I wanted to run here and tell you."

The two women just stood by the door hoping Aaron and Finn were on the other side when they opened it. Sofie needed fresh air and light to penetrate the darkness that tried to cover her.

"Aunt Sofie, why don't you rest?" Hannah suggested. "I'm going to see what Grandfather is doing." Hannah saw more concern in her aunt's eyes.

"I won't say a word to him," she promised. "I'll tell him I expect to see Finn if he asks. Please, don't worry Aunt Sofie. I'm certain there's a reason for...." Hannah didn't know how to finish her statement.

"I'll see you later," Hannah kissed both her cheeks. She didn't want to expose herself to her grandfather's questions and now she was

Sofie

wondering where the men could be and why Aaron stayed away so long. Finn practically forbid her to ask about his family. *What's the mystery? Why were both men so secretive, especially when they had opened the doors to their hearts and family?* Both men were considered a part of the family already. It *didn't* make sense. *Why would Aaron treat her aunt this way?*

She heard the door close and hoped her aunt wasn't watching from her window. She would walk to Ethan's. She wouldn't stop; she would only see if the men were outside helping Ethan with his garden. She hadn't groomed herself yet this morning and quickly ran to her room before her grandparents could ask what her plans were. She brushed her hair and ran her fingers through it. She took a little oil from the lamp and smoothed her hair down. She wiped the rest on her arms and hands. Finn may want to hold hands and take a walk or stroll through Ethan's garden. She slipped off her sandals and massaged her feet. The climb to the lookout had made her shoes slide around, chafing her skin. She dabbed a little scented oil behind her ears just in case Finn wanted to steal another kiss. She hurried through the door. She walked slowly. She didn't want to exert herself and be sweaty when she arrived.

She knew her aunt missed Aaron and his absence was almost cruel. The garden was empty. She slowed her pace in case the men were inside. She wouldn't approach the house. Once past the boundary of the fenced property, she kept walking as if that was her original intention. She would walk to her field, pick some flowers, and come right back. No one was on the road today. She tried her hardest to not look around like she was desperate. But she was. She wanted to see both Aaron and Finn so she could return home with good news for her aunt. She kept speaking to herself with positive words, not only for her sake but for her aunts. She hoped the flowers would cheer her up and not cause sadness in her heart that Aaron wasn't bringing them.

The garden remained silent. If Ethan or the men were there, she'd tell them she came by to get a melon for Sofie and hoped they were having a nice day. She tried to remember where the well was located. Perhaps the men were carrying water. It hadn't rained for some time. She looked for Ethan's cart. It was gone. That's it, she told herself. Aaron and Finn were most likely helping Ethan pull a heavy cart loaded with

Chapter Twelve

jars of water. She felt better. She would bring her aunt flowers and wait for the men to show up.

Scout watched his granddaughter walk the familiar road home, flowers in hand. She had gathered them for Sofie. He knew his sister was upset. He had seen her on her roof searching the land for Aaron, offering her prayers. He wanted to call out to her many times to have faith and all would be well. He knew she knew this, but everyone needed to be encouraged and reminded God was still in charge. He thought of their father telling them this truth over and over again no matter what circumstances life brought them. Hannah was the reminder for himself. She had Selah's blood running through her veins and had also been told her entire life God neither slumbers nor sleeps, and she could call on Him every waking moment. Both she and his baby sister were making their requests known. Aaron and Finn. He knew where they were. The watchmen told him they remained in the cave of Elias. He smiled when he heard they hadn't left. He wasn't surprised when the watchmen informed him. This is the place where men felt like men; in the deep chambers where there were no distractions, and they could sense the very Spirit of God instruct them in the way they should go. All the warriors before them were witnesses to the Lord's favor and goodness. This was the place where a man's faith was tested. Sofie and Hannah experienced this testing differently. It was in the waiting. The valley and hills had waited for generations for the men to return. These are the stories his sister wanted Aaron to pen. He knew his sister was strong in her faith. And this past week she had been tested. Even through doubts and tears, the women would not be shaken. Now he prayed father and son would petition the Lord for all they had sought to know so they could return to the waiting women.

Chapter Thirteen

Sofie cleaned her entire house. The letters were indeed gone. She was restless. She wanted to escape to a quiet place to fill it with her voice and pour out her heart with no older brother on the adjoining roof or a young niece in the next room staying silent not knowing what to say. She stood in the middle of her father's house and began to proclaim who she was in Christ. She strapped her knife on her leg, grabbed a skin of water, tightened her sandals, and began to walk to a place she hadn't visited in years. She recited one of her favorite scriptures the entire way. I can do all things through Christ who strengthens me. I *can* do all things. I can do *all* things. I *can* climb. I can scale that mountain because *Christ* strengthens me. I've never been on my own. He is all I need. He strengthens my weakness. He strengthens my spirit. He strengthens my mind. He strengthens my heart! She picked up her pace, confident she *could* do all things. It had always been Christ. She smiled for the first time today from her heart remembering when Pella came to the village. She was four years old. They were almost the same size. She was just happy there was another girl in the house. She had laid on her mat while Scout and Pella told her father about the man they called Wolf. That's when her brother realized it was all about Jesus. The story of Wolf opened his eyes to the only story that mattered. God's story. He sent His son Jesus to die so they could live. Wolf had died so her brother and Pella could live another day. But that was one day. Jesus died so they could live forever. *Thank you, Lord, for everything!*

She didn't run through the field. Instead, she kept close to the hills preparing her legs for her destination. She wouldn't look up. She didn't need to. *She could do all things.* Halfway up she began to sweat. The sun beckoned her to hurry and retreat into the shade she would find. She took a deep breath and continued. Pulling herself up on the flatness of the rock was the hardest part of her journey but she stood and celebrated God's promises. Benjamin's lookout welcomed her back. She thought of the young boy bringing her grandfather Simon up here for the first time. She shouted her greetings to the valley below. The clouds danced away so she could see Selah's favorite view. It had been years since her father brought her here. Like Hannah, she wasn't afraid anymore of the high place. Even though she hugged the hills on her way, she knew one of the watchmen already ran to alert Scout she was there. And she knew they would run and tell him when she began her descent. This is the legacy that her letters were meant to convey. The family of Christ took care of each other. Yes, she had brothers, but no matter where she traveled or ended up, she had brothers she had never met.

Aaron was a brother. Perhaps that's all he wanted to be. Her hopes and dreams had only surfaced after spending time with him. She never expected to fall in love. She had questioned and analyzed her feelings until she was exhausted. It was love. She would turn thirty-four soon. She looked at her hands. They weren't as weathered as some women she knew. Aaron told her she was beautiful. She had waited all her life for a man to tell her so. She wasn't sure how old Selah was when God brought her love again, but it had given her a glimpse of hope. She thought about her dreams. Two reoccurring visions. Hannah was the only person she had told. A phantom boy who might have been an angel and a faceless man at a large table. It struck her funny just then and she laughed until she cried. She wondered how many tears had been shed in this cleft. God kept a record. She gave Him more to put in His book. Small clouds were forming over Selah's water, and she prayed for the Lord to keep her foot from slipping. She relocated her knife to her waist for easy reach. She had emptied herself of every concern. She felt refreshed. She could trust God. That was enough for her. She began to climb down.

── *Chapter Thirteen* ──

Hannah entered an empty house. She went to the roof. Maybe her aunt was taking a nap up there. The rooftop was vacant. She looked over at her grandfather's roof. No one was there either. Maybe everyone went to Samuel's house to share a meal. She went back down and sat at the table. The house had been swept and cleaned and there was no evidence of the letters. Perhaps her aunt found them and hid them so no one would ever find them until she was ready for them to be read. She sat for over an hour, maybe two, and her aunt hadn't returned. She found her grandfather's house empty and decided to walk to Samuel's. No one was there. *Where is everyone today?* She searched her mind. There were no special occasions to celebrate. She thought about going to Ethan's again, but her aunt was so troubled, she wanted to be there for her when she returned. She tried to find something to occupy her hands while she sat waiting.

It was early afternoon and still no sign of anyone. She began to worry. She got up and checked the area where her aunt kept her supplies. She noticed one skin was missing from where it hung on the wall. She looked at her jar of honey. It was low. That's it! Her aunt went to gather honey. *She would surprise her!* The bees knew who she was now. She didn't grab anything. Her aunt would be prepared. She still took her time not wanting to perspire in case Finn happened to be at Ethan's this time she passed by. She saw him!

He ran towards her with the biggest smile, "Hello!"

"Where are you going?" he asked.

"Were you coming here to see me?" he laughed. He kissed her cheeks. He smelled the light scent of cinnamon behind her ears and smiled again.

"Is your father here?"

"Yes, he's inside with Ethan." Finn saw her eyes shift to look over at the house.

"Hannah, is something wrong? I've missed you," he said.

"No, I'm just going to meet Aunt Sofie," she told him.

"I'll walk with you," he grabbed her hand.

"Thank you, Finn, but I need to go alone." *No one who wasn't family was allowed at Selah's beehive.*

"I'll wait for you here. How long will you be?"

"Not long," she answered.

— *Sofie* —

"I've missed you too," she smiled. "And Aunt Sofie has missed...." and she stopped talking.

Finn only nodded, "I'll see you soon. Hurry back!"

The sun was warm on Sofie's back as she took the long way home. She purposed not to pass by her field or Ethan's garden. The peace that had been stolen for a few days had found its way back and she found herself humming. She would tell Hannah she was fine, and all the Lord reminded her of today. She would be shocked when she told her she went to Benjamin's lookout by herself and now the two of them could make the climb when they wanted. They didn't need to depend on men. *They could do all things.* Her house was dark. The sun hadn't set but usually Hannah would light a small lamp. She busied herself and prepared some soup. She had two small loaves of bread from earlier that she didn't eat. She couldn't wait for her niece to see she was no longer upset at the missing letters. The stories were embedded deep in her heart and Hannah could rewrite them if necessary. Maybe Aaron had misplaced them and couldn't face her with his carelessness. She just didn't know, but she had cast her cares upon the Lord. He would work out all things for her good. She sat and waited in anticipation.

Scout was positioned on the northern ridge watching the events of the day play out. His sister was safely home. Aaron and Finn had left the cave of Elias, and his granddaughter headed back to the field of flowers probably to gather more bouquets of purple and red. He saw her stop at Ethan's and knew Finn also knew where she was headed. He couldn't believe his baby sister! She needed to have this day. He could tell by her walk she was no longer burdened. He was anxious to speak with her and also to chastise her a little for climbing alone.

Aaron was almost ready. He had Sofie's letters and his prelude he had composed in a neat, wrapped bundle protecting the history of faith, honor, and integrity. He asked Ethan to pray with him that he would have the right words to say to his family and of course to Sofie. Finn was excited! As soon as his father declared his commitment, he

Chapter Thirteen

was ready to proclaim his to Hannah. He searched the hills constantly hoping the women's voices would echo for his hearing. It would be dark soon! Maybe the watchmen didn't see them coming into the field. He went inside.

"Father, I'm going to go look for Hannah," he said. "The sun is ready for sleep and she and Sofie haven't returned."

"Sofie?" Aaron repeated. Now he was concerned, and asked, "She is in the field also?"

"Yes, Hannah was going to meet her."

"No, Finn," Ethan said. "I saw Sofie before I came home."

The men looked at each other. "Are you certain Ethan?" Aaron asked his friend.

"Yes, I took my cart to the village, and I saw her," Ethan replied.

"Son, perhaps Hannah went home also when she realized Sofie wasn't there," Aaron said.

"Well, I'm going to find out!" Finn was out the door in a fast run to Sofie's.

"Let the boy find out," Ethan told Aaron. "You need to keep calm. It's going to be a big night for you," he winked.

"In fact, let's toast now to your future with Sofie!" Ethan told him.

The two men relaxed. Aaron suspected Ethan was right. Sofie was home and Hannah got distracted and would see Finn a little later.

The wild knocking startled Sofie. Hannah wouldn't knock. She rushed to the door to find Finn out of breath. When he saw her, he grabbed his heart in relief.

"You're home," he smiled. "I was worried."

"Please, come in Finn. Let me get you a drink."

"Is Hannah in her room?"

"Hannah isn't here. I've been waiting for her. She must be with Scout. The whole family is gone," Sofie laughed.

"No, Sofie, Hannah went to the field to join you," he said.

"What? I've been home for some time. Where did you see her?"

"Sofie! I need to go! Please, don't leave. I'll go find her!"

"Find her?" Sofie repeated. "Finn, wait! I'm sure she's with my family."

Finn didn't think so, but he didn't want to alarm her. "I'll be back. I'll check each house. I'm asking you to stay home. It's almost dark Sofie."

Sofie had enough excitement for the day. She told Finn she would stay. She was certain Scout and the rest of the family would be home soon. She lit another lamp.

Hannah had run through the field excited to join her aunt in the special place the women had shared with the bees. Aunt Sofie would be so proud of her! She removed the stones and brush and carefully placed them back as she saw her aunt do. She made her way up the path trying to keep her breathing steady. The buzzing seemed extra loud today. The bees were probably happy to see Sofie. She hoped given time she would receive the same reception.

"Aunt Sofie," she called out before the last few steps.

She didn't want to frighten her or the bees. Her aunt wasn't there. She couldn't tell if any honeycomb had been removed. Her aunt must have been here and left and taken another way home.

"Well bees, I'll see you next time."

Several of them were flying around her head and she stood still as her aunt had instructed. She thought they just wanted to make sure she belonged here. One bee was on her cheek now and she brushed it away as gently as she could. It didn't like her rebuff and landed this time with determination, and she felt the first sting. She turned as slowly as she could as there were several swarming around her head. She kept her mouth closed until one found her nostril and she screamed. It was a full-on battle now, Selah's bees angry at the perfumed intruder. She was in pain with multiple stings as she tried to slide down the path to the open field. She never made it.

Finn had no time to stop back at Ethan's to inform his father Hannah was gone and Sofie was home. He ran through the field calling Hannah's name over and over. He stopped to listen. Maybe she fell or sprained her ankle. He moved slowly now hoping for her voice to call to him. It was dark and in his haste, he didn't grab a torch. He continued to step carefully. The animals came out at night.

"God, please let her be home."

Chapter Thirteen

He heard the bees. They usually were quiet at this time unless someone or something disturbed them. He began walking faster. All he had was his knife. He didn't want to fight any animals. The buzzing was intense. He held his knife firmly. If an animal destroyed the hive, maybe he could scare it away so the bees wouldn't relocate. His foot hit something and he sucked in his breath. Whatever it was, it wasn't moving. He moved his foot to jostle the sleeping animal. It was big! It didn't budge. He bent low to feel with his hands the fur or skin to determine what it was. The cinnamon scent invaded his senses. *"Hannah!"*

"Hannah, I'm here. Don't worry. I'm taking you home. You're going to be fine. I'm going to lift you now. Hannah, if you can hear me, wrap your hands around my neck."

He slid with her dead weight down the rest of the path. He clenched his jaw in agony at her condition. She was breathing, however, very shallow, and he was grateful he found her. He wanted to curse and bless the bees. If they hadn't been disturbed, he wouldn't have heard their annoyance and gone to investigate what had troubled them this early evening. He walked as fast as he could. Sofie would know what to do. He was thankful he had carried his fair share of young goats and was accustomed to the extra weight. He would walk past Ethan's and shout to his father. He couldn't stop. He would tell him what he knew on the way. The fires from the village began to come into focus and he held back his tears. Hannah hadn't moved. Her whole body was swollen. He could smell Ethan's garden. He began yelling.

"Father! Ethan! Hurry! Father!"

Aaron jumped. He heard the panic in his son's voice. The men ran out. Aaron almost collapsed when he saw Hannah's limp body in Finn's arms. He took one look at her and immediately knew what had happened. He knew Finn wouldn't release the girl until he reached Sofie's. He thought it might be better if Finn went alone. It was time to face the music. Sofie would be overwhelmed. This wasn't the way this night was supposed to turn out. This was chaos and confusion that would greet Sofie, far from love and a proposal. He knocked on her door and then stepped back in the shadows, Low light escaped from the open door, and he heard Sofie scream at her niece's unconscious body, Finn standing with a wet face not truly knowing what the outcome would be.

Time seemed to stand still Sofie thought. Finn was standing there with obvious concern at the eyes that were swollen shut, Hannah not aware of her rescue. Suddenly Aaron appeared behind Finn and Sofie thought she saw a ghost! She fell to her knees calling for Scout. The chaos came as Aaron expected. Pella was crying as she and Sofie ministered to Hannah. Scout had directed Finn to carry her to her room. He didn't want to leave but there was nothing he could do, and Scout said he would send word or come himself should there be any change in his granddaughter's condition. Aaron practically carried his son back to Ethan's, the boy a complete mess.

"Father, will she be alright? Please, be honest with me," Finn said.

"She'll be fine, son. Come, let's sit. I need to tell you another story."

Hannah's body was cooling down from her vinegar baths and Sofie rocked in a chair at her side until Scout thought she would wear a hole into the floor.

"She got a lot more stings than you did," Scout said to his sister.

Sofie just cried. She knew the excruciating pain she must have suffered. It seemed it wouldn't end until you simply closed your eyes and let the bees have their way.

"She's strong like you Sofie, don't worry," Scout said.

"How did Finn know where to find her?" he asked his sister.

Sofie stopped rocking. She had no idea. She had pushed everything out of her mind when she saw Hannah lying in Finn's arms. She thought for a brief moment she had met her end. She glanced over just then to see the steady rise of her chest and exhaled her relief.

"I didn't speak with him," she mumbled. The entire night had been a blur of panic and emotion, fear and faith tested on her doorstep.

Scout stood, "Will you be alright alone with her?"

"Where are you going?" Sofie grabbed his arm.

"Home. We both need rest."

"But when she wakes up, I don't want her to be alone," Sofie said.

Chapter Thirteen

"Finn is probably outside your door," he told her. "He can sleep on the floor, and you can rest."

She was tired. The entire day was overwhelming. She took the vinegar-soaked sponge and wiped Hannah's body down again. The smell of the house was witness again to Selah's bees and their insistence that if anyone wanted honey, they needed to follow the rules. Sofie smelled the scented oil in Hannah's hair when she was first laid down on the bed.

Scout opened the door to find both Aaron and Finn in the courtyard around a small fire. "Why didn't you let us know you were here?" he asked them.

"We didn't want to intrude," Aaron replied.

Finn was beside himself and only stared into the flame.

"Finn, why don't you go inside? You can stay with Hannah," Scout told him. "My sister needs a break." Finn was through the door before Scout finished his sentence.

"Is she alright?" Aaron asked.

"Hannah or Sofie?" Scout asked.

"Both," Aaron answered.

Scout joined him at the fire, the years of life evident on their faces. Aaron waited for him to speak. Sofie had screamed when she saw him earlier. He suspected the reason and thought she still wasn't sure why she did. It wasn't because they hadn't seen each other for several days. He thought perhaps when he came to stand behind his son, it was confirmation Hannah was indeed gone and he was there to support the family.

"Have you told her yet?" Scout asked.

"Told her?" Aaron repeated. "You mean asked her?" he smiled.

"No," Scout said.

"I know you want to marry my sister, and I know you haven't made your declaration to her yet. I'm talking about the other day," he said.

Aaron was confused. *The other day?* He had been sitting in Elias' cave for the past four.

"It's an odd thing, isn't it?" Scout asked him. "All those years ago Sofie found herself at the same place our sweet Hannah has now discovered recently, and both women found themselves in the same predicament."

Now Scout waited so Aaron would have his full attention. He smiled at the wonder of the Lord's ways. "And what is so curious is that the same two men who have fallen in love with Sofie and Hannah are the same two men who found them after the attack of the bees."

Aaron's eyes grew wide. He really shouldn't be surprised. *It was Scout.*

"How long have you known?" He felt nervous. He had left Sofie when he saw the three brothers charging up the hill.

"Scout, I...." Aaron stopped when Scout put his hand up.

"I know you were young and scared, and it took me awhile to figure it out. Sofie always spoke of the boy who came to her that day and told her she would be fine, and that help was on the way. My family, the watchmen, well, we see everything," he smiled.

"I knew both you and Finn knew where the bees lived. Everyone stays clear of the place. We have always let the women collect the honey. It's tradition," Scout reminded him.

"You saw Hannah go into the field?" Aaron asked him.

"Yes," Scout answered, "But I didn't know she was searching for Sofie. I thought she was meeting Finn. I saw you and him leaving Elias' cave."

"Sofie," Aaron whispered.

"You need to tell her everything," Scout said. "Let her sleep. You can stay in my home of course."

"Thank you, Scout, for understanding why I've waited," Aaron said.

"I never said I understood," Scout laughed.

Pella met the two men at the door. "Shall I go over?"

"Finn is there. I'm certain the boy will not sleep," Scout told her.

"I prefer the roof if that's alright," Aaron said.

"Let us know if you need anything," Pella said.

Aaron stared out at the blackness of night trying to collect his thoughts. Most everyone in the tiny village had a normal day. He couldn't shake Sofie's reaction when she saw him earlier. He thought she would run into his arms for support, happy he was there to comfort her in this unfortunate turn of events for Hannah. *What happened today? Where was she all the time Hannah was looking for her? Did Ethan have his facts right? If Scout knew everything, why didn't he tell him?* He scolded himself now that he hadn't told Sofie he was the one who had found her. Honestly, he didn't know why he didn't. He continued to stare thinking about why he kept this from her.

Finn prayed on his knees next to Hannah's bed. She was almost unrecognizable, and he couldn't control his sobs when he was able to see her in the soft light.

"She will get through this," Sofie told him. "I did and she will too. Please, come and get me when she wakes up."

Finn nodded, not taking his eyes off Hannah. Her hands had been wrapped to avoid her scratching. He looked at her arms. The stingers had been removed. He hoped the women were able to get all of them. She was covered with welts from head to foot. He wanted to scoop her up and hold her close professing his love and whispering his concern. He was sure she knew he was there. Her eyelids fluttered when he first entered the room. The house was quiet. Sofie looked exhausted. They were all grieving this happened. Again. His father shocked him earlier by telling him of the day Sofie had made the bees angry. He probably would have been scared too seeing Scout coming up the path. *Thank you, Lord, for leading me to Hannah,* he prayed. The thought of her out there at night, alone, in pain, made him burst out in fresh sobs.

Sofie heard the young boy. Bless his heart. She would rise early to bake bread so he could eat and rest while she looked after her niece. The swelling would go down in a few days. She and Pella would need to inspect her body again in the daylight for any stingers they may have missed. She wouldn't close her eyes until Finn stopped crying. He would settle down. It was overwhelming. She didn't know what happened. *Why did Hannah go there so late in the day? Scout.* He said nothing! *Aaron. Where was he? Why didn't he come with Finn to check on the girl? And check on her?* He had disappeared again. She had such a lovely day. Scout hadn't mentioned her climb either. She was certain he knew where she was all day. *Why is everyone so silent? They knew her whereabouts, why not speak?* She was sure he knew where Hannah was also. He didn't seem too surprised when he ran over and saw her swollen, limp body in Finn's arms. He was so calm telling everyone what to do, that Hannah would be fine, and had ushered the men back out of the house. He only came back in once Hannah was stripped of her clothes and her first vinegar bath was completed.

She lay there trying to recall every moment from the time she got home. Hannah wasn't there and she began to cook waiting for her. She now remembered the flowers that had been placed on the table. She thought Hannah and Finn were together and stopped by to see what she was doing and maybe Aaron was with them and discovered she wasn't home. It seemed like hours she sat at the table waiting, and the day was ending. She jumped at the loud knocking of Finn. When she opened the door and saw him with her niece in his arms, she almost fainted. She saw the welts on her dangling arms and legs. The night brought shadows and played tricks on her. She brought the lamp closer to make sure Hannah was breathing. That's when Aaron came into view and for a moment, she thought she was dreaming. Finn looked exactly like the young boy that spoke to her when the bees first met her. *Why was it so familiar?* Her mind was shrouded with the phantom of that day so many years ago. When Aaron stepped into the light and she saw the younger version of him in his son, she let out a scream. *Aaron! The phantom was Aaron!* She sat up in her bed! Oh, my Lord in heaven! *It was Aaron!* All these years she questioned herself. *Was it real? Was it truly an angel? Was she losing her mind? Did her family believe her?* All these months he never told her! *Why?* He never said a word! *Why would he hide this from her?* She was gritting her teeth now angry and confused. *Did her brother know? Was this some cruel joke? Why Lord?*

How could she rest now? Hannah needed her. *Was Finn in on this? How did he know about the bees?* This was Selah's secret place! She wanted to throw something she was so mad! Mad at Aaron! Mad at Scout and mad at herself for being a fool! Aaron played her for a fool! And her brother Scout allowed it! *What else had they kept from her? Her letters! Who had them? Why would they disrespect her this way?* Now her sobs matched Finn's and she brought her pillow to her mouth so he wouldn't hear her or Hannah either if she happened to be awake. *God, I don't understand. Why wouldn't he tell me it was him who told me help was on the way? Why would he leave?* This thought only brought more anguish. He saw her condition and left! Yes, her brothers were coming, but he couldn't stay and wait until they arrived. *What kind of man does that?*

He wasn't a man Sofie. He was a young boy.

She heard the answer immediately. "But Lord, even so, you don't leave someone in pain."
Ask him why.
This statement made her cry out again. "Ask him?"
"He should have told me. I don't want to see him! I don't think I can trust him. You know he hasn't told me anything. I don't even know where he lives! This is ridiculous! I've been a fool! What else is he hiding? Where is he hiding now? Oh Father, my letters." She cried herself to sleep.

Scout greeted Aaron as soon as the sun did. "Finn is resting. Hannah woke up long enough to see him at her side and she is sleeping again."
"And Sofie?" Aaron asked.
"She's upset, not only at you, but me as well," Scout said.
"I think it would be better if you return to Ethan's," he added. "Finn is waiting downstairs and Sofie is fine with him coming later to see Hannah."
"But not me," Aaron replied.
"Not today." Scout felt bad for Aaron.
Sofie would cool down and sort out her feelings. He would try and speak with her later, probably tomorrow. Taking care of Hannah would take her mind off things. At least he hoped it would. Aaron looked defeated. Every man he knew went through this stage at one point in his life. Everyone needed time. He offered his prayers as father and son slowly made their way back to the edge of the village.
"Sofie is upset at Aaron," Pella told her husband.
"Yes, me too," Scout replied.
"Was it truly Aaron who found her that day?"
"Yes," he answered.
"What about the letters?" she asked him.
"The letters?" Scout questioned.
"Yes, her letters. They're missing!" Pella said. "That's what first upset her."

"Hmmm," is all Scout said.

"Scout, you need to fix this!"

"Me?" he replied.

"Yes. Go to the man Ethan's house and ask Aaron what he did with Sofie's letters."

"Are you sure he has them?" Scout wasn't going to accuse Aaron of taking them.

"Well, she doesn't have them, and she and Hannah tore up the house looking for them," Pella said.

Scout thought it might do him some good to get away from the women. He would walk to Ethan's and walk back with Finn. Several people stopped him on his way offering their prayers for Hannah and the family. He thanked each one for their thoughtfulness. All the men were outside when he approached. Finn ran to him asking if Hannah was better.

"She's sleeping, but the swelling is starting to go down," he told the boy. "Have you slept?"

"A little," Finn said.

"Why don't you try and sleep and us old men will enjoy a cup of wine. You'll come back with me when I leave as I imagine you'll have another long night," Scout told him.

Finn recognized this wasn't a suggestion and he waved at his father he was going inside.

Scout walked the garden with Aaron and Ethan making small talk as they went from one end to the other. Ethan, like him, probably knew everything so Scout felt free to speak in front of him.

"How's your granddaughter? I hope she's not suffering too much. Look around; if there's anything you need, grab it," Ethan told Scout.

"Do you have any melons left?" Scout asked.

"Take two," Ethan said. "I know Sofie is fond of them also."

The mention of Sofie's name made all the men uncomfortable. Aaron shuffled his feet not knowing what to say. Ethan excused himself.

"Let me grab those melons and I'll bring us some wine."

Scout waited until Ethan was a good distance away. "Do you have Sofie's letters?"

"Yes! They are here bundled up with my gift for her," he said.

Chapter Thirteen

Scout was relieved the letters were not lost. "I think she thinks you took them for another purpose."

"What other purpose?" Aaron was bewildered.

"I don't know," Scout said. "She's been upset now almost a week!"

"Because of the letters?" Aaron asked. He never thought that taking them to put them in order would trouble her.

"She hasn't seen you. I've been careful of my words. As we spoke last night, you need to tell her about that day," Scout said.

"I was planning to," Aaron told him. "Now, she doesn't even want to see me. What should I do?"

Scout saw Ethan leaving the house with a skin of wine and cups. "Give her a few days. Hannah's swelling should be all gone by then. Let's pray and let the Lord minister to her. His timing is perfect. We need to wait," he said.

Finn and Scout each carried a melon as they headed to Sofie's. Scout was swaying the tiniest bit as the men drank two skins. He hadn't eaten and that's why it affected him this way today. Finn slept and asked his father if he wanted him to say anything to Sofie.

"No, son, she needs to only hear my words," Aaron answered.

His father was hurting as much as Sofie was. He promised himself he would always tell Hannah everything. It wasn't good to keep secrets. He sort of understood why his father kept silent and didn't tell Sofie the identity of her *angel*. His father had his reasons. He hoped Sofie would allow him to tell her.

Pella was feeding Hannah soup when the men arrived. Hannah heard Finn's voice.

"Grandmother! Hurry! Close the door! I don't want Finn to see me like this. I must look awful," she cried.

"Hannah, Finn is the one who found you, so he has seen you already, and he was here at your side almost the entire night," Pella said.

"He was?" Hannah was sitting halfway up and saw her grandfather coming toward her. He bent low to kiss her.

"Grandfather! You smell like old grapes!" she laughed.

"And you smell like they've gone bad," he laughed with her. "I'm glad you're awake and eating. Finn is here. Sofie has already made him sit down to eat."

Sofie

He examined the room, but Pella knew he wanted to make sure their granddaughter was covered. Only her arms and feet poked out of the blanket. "The swelling has gone down quite a bit," he said.

"Yes Grandfather, but I'm still itchy," she complained.

"Ethan has sent a melon for you. Perhaps it will take your mind off scratching," he laughed.

"How many cups have you had husband?" Pella smiled.

"Enough," Scout told her, "And I'm starving. Let's go home."

Hannah smiled. She saw the shared glances of love between her grandparents. She hoped she would feel the same way with Finn in their later years. She asked her grandmother to brush her hair lightly before Finn came in. Pella was afraid she would only make her itch more. Hannah's hands would remain wrapped. She ran her fingers through, careful not to touch her neck. Her face was still full, the venom hadn't been released completely.

"One more day," she told Hannah, "And we can unwrap your hands. I'll see you in the morning."

"Goodnight, Grandmother, I love you," Hannah said.

Sofie said goodnight to Scout and that was about it. He would take it. He kissed her and she smelled the wine also. Pella would have her hands full this evening. This thought made her happy and sad. She was alone. Finn was with Hannah. Her brothers were all home with their families, and she sat by herself. She missed Aaron. She missed their conversations, also sharing a cup of wine or two under the stars. Finn and Hannah were speaking in low tones. They needed privacy. She wrapped her outer garment around her and went to her roof. There was no moon. She sat on her rugs and rocked. It brought her comfort. *How did everything change so suddenly?* This past year had been glorious! *Was it all her imagination? Had she been dreaming? Was everyone pretending?* Nothing made sense. But it wasn't *everyone*. It was Aaron. He hadn't been forthright. It was as simple as that, and now his son had fallen in love with her niece, and he would be forced to continue to pretend. *And* he had taken her letters for whatever purpose she couldn't imagine. This was her story, not his.

The air was cool tonight and she wanted to shut the door to all her thoughts that wanted to rise and cause her grief. She didn't want to disturb Hannah and Finn so she walked back into the house as quietly

Chapter Thirteen

as she could. The young couple were still talking, and she was thankful Hannah was feeling so much better. She would grow tired of being confined to her room and Sofie thought perhaps the next day or so she could sit on the roof or in the courtyard for some fresh air. She hadn't even told Finn thank you for bringing her niece safely home. She would tell him tomorrow.

Hannah sat at the table waiting for her aunt to wake up. Most of her swollen body had returned to normal and she told Finn to unwrap her hands as she didn't feel the urge to scratch. She told him he saved her life. He told her he wanted to spend the rest of his life with her. She knew he loved her as much as she loved him. She had cried when he told her how beautiful she was when she was certain she looked hideous with her puffy lips, ears, and hands. He had kissed each place disagreeing wholeheartedly. *She was so happy!* Now she wanted her aunt to be just as happy. Finn wouldn't speak for his father, but she had pressed him through the night about his family until he asked her to please be patient.

"Hannah, you're up!" Sofie came near to her for a closer examination.

"I feel fine," Hannah told her. "I may not look it, but truly, I'm well."

Sofie knew her niece's healing was encouraged by love. Her eyes sparkled today! She would let Hannah tell her what her heart suspected.

"Aunt Sofie, where were you the day I went looking in the field?"

"I was here."

"No Aunt Sofie, I came back, and the house had been swept and you were gone. I waited for some time," Hannah said.

"I went to go think," Sofie said.

"Where?" Hannah asked.

"I went to the lookout."

"By yourself?" Hannah couldn't believe it.

"No," Sofie smiled.

"Who went with you, Grandfather?" Hannah wanted to know.

"The Lord went with me," Sofie said. "We had a lovely day."

Hannah just stared at her. She was serious! "Aunt Sofie, please, don't climb alone. I will worry about you," Hannah squeezed her hand.

"Scout had the watchmen keeping an eye on me," she laughed.

"Please Aunt Sofie, I will go with you next time."

"It's a very special place. I couldn't believe what I saw! I cry now thinking of our ancestors standing, waiting for loved ones to appear on the horizon. I understand more than ever how important it is for you to capture our family's history and what this village has meant to so many. I want to know everything! What have you not told me, Aunt Sofie? I want to start with Selah. Wait! Aunt Sofie, why were the bees so mad? Was it the time of day I went? What did I do wrong? Do you think the bees don't like me? Was it because you weren't with me?" Hannah asked.

"What were you wearing?" Sofie asked her.

Hannah looked at her, "My tunic. The one I always have on," she answered.

"Think Hannah of the first time we visited the bees," Sofie said.

Hannah's brows came together as she concentrated. "Oh no! I wore oil! Scented oil! That's it, isn't it?" She clapped her hands thinking that the bees had no choice but to let her know it wasn't welcomed. It wasn't that they didn't recognize Selah's fourth-generation granddaughter, it was cinnamon!

"I will tell them I'm sorry," she smiled at her aunt.

"So, you will keep the tradition?" Sofie asked.

"Yes, Aunt Sofie. This land is everything to me. When I stood as Benjamin did the first time he looked over the valley, his heart must have been overjoyed. I want to know everything everyone remembers hearing about him." Hannah tried to read her aunt's thoughts.

"Aunt Sofie, I want to know. *Everything*. I'm never leaving this land."

"I have written everything," Sofie finally offered, "Only for my letters to be taken."

"Taken? No, Aunt Sofie, they're somewhere. "We just haven't found them yet," Hannah assured her.

"Can I help you with something?" Hannah asked. "If you're fine, I may go back and lie down for a while. Finn and I...." she stopped.

"Finn and you talked through the early morning?" Sofie laughed.

"Yes, I'm a little tired," she said.

Chapter Thirteen

She didn't want to mention the proposal yet. Her aunt looked sad. If Aaron didn't come today, she would walk to Ethan's and plead with him to make his intentions known. She hoped he would consider her swollen feet and perhaps push her back home in Ethan's cart. Her aunt wasn't humming like she usually did when baking her bread. Hannah went to her and picked up the almost empty jar of honey.

"This is why I went to the bees. I figured you were going to get more."

Sofie took the jar and held it up to the light that had just appeared through the window. The color of Aaron's eyes. She swallowed her sorrow so Hannah wouldn't see it.

"Aunt Sofie, do you find it peculiar that Finn found me? How would he know where to look? The field has many places I could have fallen or stumbled over, yet he knew where the bees lived. He told me he heard them, and that's when he began to come up the path. I asked him how he knew where the path was, and he looked away. I kept pressing him because I feared others also had discovered Selah's secret place. He then told me he found it one day while hunting." Her aunt just kept twirling the jar around, so Hannah kept talking.

"The boy that found you, do you think he just happened to come across the place? Or was it truly an angel Aunt Sofie? Is this written in your letters?"

Sofie could barely breathe. "You truly want to know everything?" she asked.

"I'll tell you. It wasn't an angel. All these years my brothers have looked at me as if I was crazy and my dreams began to tell me I should accept that. But it was so real! There was no angel, Hannah."

Hannah had never seen the look her aunt had on her face right now and she backed up a little. She still had the jar of honey in her hand and looked like she was ready to cast it on the ground!

"Perhaps you had a fever from all the stings," Hannah offered. "And it seemed like an angel."

Sofie placed the jar in Hannah's hands. "No fever. No angel. It was Aaron. If you see him later, you can give him this and ask if he would like to refill it."

Hannah couldn't believe her ears. "Aunt Sofie! What? Aaron? Impossible!"

Sofie only stared at the jar in Hannah's hand. "It was Aaron, Hannah."

"But how? I mean, when...wait...you have known all along it was Aaron? No, you couldn't have. Oh, Aunt Sofie! Did Aaron know it was you?" She saw the pain in her aunt's eyes and laid the jar down.

"I don't understand," Hannah said.

"I don't either," Sofie replied.

"Aaron has known this entire time I was the young girl he heard cry out that afternoon. He never told me it was him. Scout knows it was him. They both have kept this from me for reasons either have attempted to tell me and now....." and the tears came.

"Now I wonder what else they have kept hidden from my heart. My own brother! I'm not mad anymore. I'm deeply hurt. It feels like what betrayal must be. No one has ever treated me like this. I still don't understand why Aaron stayed away so long. I needed to go by myself to Benjamin's lookout to clear my head. That day the Lord ministered to me. I recited my favorite scripture all the way there and realized I only need Him."

"That's all. I will live my life as I have. There's no more to say. Now, go as you said and lie down. I'm sorry if I have upset you, but I will never keep anything from you Hannah. I hope you know that and I'm so happy you're well and will continue with Selah's legacy."

Sofie sat down once Hannah retreated to her room. She wondered if Scout had slept off his wine. It was early. She left the house before anyone could notice. She went to her field to lay in the grass and let the sun heal her soul. She had tossed and turned last night and now the warm colors made her sleepy. She felt refreshed from her little nap and continued her long walk. She went by the path to see it exposed. Finn hadn't returned to set the stones back in place. She didn't say hello to the bees; she would wait to come back with Hannah. She stopped several times and looked at every place that had been memorialized in her letters. The northern ridge of Elias. Benjamin's lookout. Simon's summit. The watchmen's post. She turned north and imagined her father returning home, her grandfather running full speed to embrace his son. The hills had covered acts of rebellion and showered many with grace. Hannah would never leave this land. Those words had brought joy this morning. The flowers invited her to stay. They were all stretched out in the late afternoon sun waiting for Selah's bees.

Chapter Thirteen

Sofie found Hannah sitting at the table with several lamps lit throughout the house.

"Hello, Aunt Sofie!" Hannah called out to her.

"Why do you have so many lamps burning? I'm not sure how much oil is left," Sofie blurted out.

"Sit down Aunt Sofie, I want to read you something."

Hannah saw the surprised look on her face. "I told you I learned to read, didn't I?"

"Yes, you did," Sofie smiled. The table held only the lamps and Hannah's hands were empty.

"Please Aunt Sofie, sit there at the end of the table and I shall read you a portion of something I found most interesting and heartwarming."

Sofie couldn't imagine where Hannah might have found something to read. She sat down playfully, "Is this alright?" She felt silly at her table.

Hannah pulled a hidden parchment from her lap. She held it firmly, lowering it so she could see her aunt as she read. She began.

"Selah was grace. She extended grace to everyone she met. Her innocence and wonder were her strengths. She walked in love, and because of her pure heart, she saw God. The young women sought her counsel. They learned to embrace their faith and she taught them through life's most difficult and challenging times, to be still and know. God is faithful, and His ways are right. Selah showed kindness and lived with forgiveness in her smile. Her legacy began with Simon, and it continues.

Kezi was strong. She had no choice. Everyone relied on her strength. Her friendship was coveted, and her generosity spoke volumes. Her love and admiration for Selah and her family was genuine and she can claim this family also as part of her legacy.

Benjamin was a man of honor. The first watchman. He also embraced this family as his own and God blessed him with His favor. He taught others to be men of integrity. Like Kezi, he too was grafted into this family of faith.

Sofie

Elias was a servant. He served this family like no other. He wore his battle scars with admiration for those who stood alongside him. Iron sharpens iron. He was a man's man. He would lay down his life for this family and in many ways he did. He abandoned his position for truth and followed those who were living it.

Simon is a legend. He stood as the hills that surround this village and protected his family. He offered grace to those who never expected it and extended mercy to those who didn't deserve his kindness and love. He was a true follower of Jesus and the bones in the cave of Elias are a witness. He was faithful, his leadership reliable, and he was a tower of strength for the community. The hills sing his accolades. Like a tree planted by the water, he wouldn't be moved. He stood for justice and righteousness. His name will be repeated throughout the ages in love and respect.

Stone was the definition of home. Land. Heritage. Family. He represented the very nature of God in His never-ending mercy and grace. His heart remained open for the Lord to continue to teach and instruct him for the benefit of the village. He left a boy and returned a man after God's own heart.

Scout is a presence who reminds this family and village of the generations that have gone before him and will continue. He is protection, like the sturdy wall surrounding this community and the hills that spread their warm embrace. He continues his watch.

Sofie, you are all of them wrapped up in the most exquisite jewel that I've ever seen. You wear honor, strength, and grace. Truly, you are a faithful servant, and you fill your home and the hearts of your family with joy.

Sofie was gripping her father's table, visibly shaken.

Hannah held her breath and waited for the right moment. She then retrieved her aunt's letters neatly tied with a beautiful turquoise ribbon that shimmered its silver offerings in the brightly lit room.

Sofie began to cry. Hannah stood and carried the letters to the end of the table. "There's one more thing," she said. She opened the door.

Aaron walked in and knelt before the daughter of Stone.

"I cannot find any more words that my heart feels for you and your wonderful family. I'm sorry for keeping things from you. I have loved

Chapter Thirteen

you my entire life from afar, and now if you will allow me, I would like to love you even more and never be apart again."

He laid a small leather pouch in front of her. "May I?" he asked, still on his knees. He loosened the drawstring and pulled out a bracelet, a three-stranded cord of beautiful warm leather.

Sofie wasn't looking at the tightly knit braided wristband. Her fingers grasped the two polished red beads of promise. She could no longer contain her emotions and Aaron stood to bring her into his arms.

"No more secrets," he whispered. "Please, forgive me, my dearest Sofie, and please, sit back down."

She heard the door open behind her and Finn walked in. Aaron directed him to sit in the first chair closest to her. Another man walked in and sat next to Finn. Sofie had never seen him before, but he looked like Finn who was smiling ear to ear. One more man came in and Aaron put his hand up indicating to her more were coming. Three more men marched in and took their seats across the table from the first three. Aaron went to the other end of the table where Hannah had been sitting. He remained standing and addressed Sofie.

"I would like to introduce my son Adam."

The last man that had entered sat closest to Aaron. He stood now, "I am firstborn," he smiled at Sofie.

"Benjamin," Aaron said.

Benjamin stood, "I believe I'll be your favorite," he laughed, "Because of my name."

"Caleb," Aaron said.

Caleb was closest to Sofie's left side. He kissed her hand which made the brothers moan in delight.

"David," Aaron said.

David looked exactly like Aaron and Sofie was overwhelmed with the likeness. "Shalom Sofie," he said.

"Eli," Aaron said.

Eli placed his hand over his heart, bowed, and smiled.

"And of course, my Finn, the youngest of my sons."

Finn scooted back in his chair and pulled Sofie in his arms like his father did.

Aaron sat down with his six sons flanking his sides and Sofie drew in her breath. The faceless man had a face. It was Aaron. Her angel was

Aaron. It had always been Aaron. There was only a pause in their lives for the purposes of God. She wouldn't question His ways. Her heart was full.

The room exploded and Hannah opened the door to Scout, Joshua, Samuel, their wives, and children. The families were all gathered with the young men on the rooftops beginning to celebrate. Sofie thought she floated up to her roof or Aaron carried her. It could have been his sons who placed her on their shoulders, the night was a blur! Ethan once again blessed the family and tents had been pitched around his land for Aaron's families to stay.

Aaron pulled her off to the side in the only private space he could find.

"Are you happy?" he smiled.

The entire village was celebrating this late blooming love of Selah's great-granddaughter.

"You have given me another family to love and cherish. You have kept your promises. I was mistaken concerning your motives," she told him.

She looked around locating Aaron's sons, their names on her lips as she studied each face. She felt she had nothing to offer him to compare to the outpouring of this new life she would be living with him.

"What could I possibly give you that would bless and fill your heart as you have filled mine?" Her eyes were filled with tears of joy.

Aaron noticed she continued to look at his sons and study each feature. He waited until she turned her attention back to him.

"You can give me a little girl," he smiled.

Epilogue

Walking through the Selah Series

Selah. Simon. Stone. Scout. Sofie. Names whispered in love through the ages, each with a story to tell. Their journey is our journey. It's personal. My prayer has been that the reader will experience the emotions and personalities of the characters in each book. The Selah Series represents a season in most believer's lives and I hope the reader will know that they are not alone on this journey of life and that God is faithful. We can trust Him. Selah.

Selah – **Personal**

When you decide for Christ, you become born again. Selah and others were on their ***personal*** journey of faith, and as Jesus said to Nicodemus, "You must be born again". How many of us would have liked to have been the proverbial fly on the wall to witness this conversation between Jesus and the powerful Pharisee? My hope and prayer in writing Selah were for believers to rediscover their first understanding of who Jesus is, and the wonder He brings, and for those who haven't yet made that decision, to ask God to reveal His Son Jesus to you, so that you may also inherit the Kingdom. Selah

SIMON – Persecution

Jesus instructs us to walk in forgiveness and love. This is where faith is tested. Simon, son of Selah, and many followers in the time of Jesus fled Jerusalem when **_persecution_** began. Unfortunately, persecution has survived the ages. Simon is a story that hopefully encourages believers to continue to stand, and not be moved by the world around them and circumstances that challenge their faith. Read the Book (Bible). We have victory!

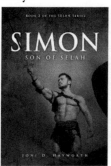

STONE – Prodigal

Believers go through times of desiring worldly things, only to have the Father *woo* them back in His tender mercy and grace. It's either black or white, there are no shades of gray (lukewarm). We are to enter the narrow gate. The road that leads to destruction is broad and many find it appealing. Stone took the road into the city that offered everything he lusted for until the Father spoke to the **_prodigal_** in His still small voice. Whatever road you're currently traveling, know that the Father loves you greatly and hopes to lead you back to the narrow gate.

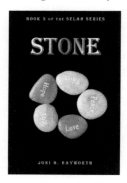

SCOUT – Pride

We get saved, we face trials, and we run away only to find the Father waiting to clothe us in His grace. We think we know it all! Especially for those who grew up in the faith. ***Pride.*** No one wants to recognize this arrogance that creeps in. Scout thrived on his family's heritage. It was his too. Until he realized it wasn't. We all need to acknowledge who is the Lord of our lives. Is it us or God?

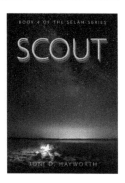

SOFIE – Peace

Finally, after seeking truth, experiencing trials, running away, and demanding answers to justify our actions, we find the ***peace*** that waited patiently for us to understand and claim as our own. The Potter has molded His clay and we rest in Him. Write your letter. Tell others. It has always been about Jesus.

Milton Keynes UK
Ingram Content Group UK Ltd.
UKHW021023290724
446271UK00015B/822